Duck Egg Blue

Duck Egg Blue

A Novel

Derrick Neill

Essex, Connecticut

Prometheus Books
An imprint of The Globe Pequot Publishing Group, Inc.
64 South Main Street
Essex, CT 06426
www.globepequot.com

Library of Congress Cataloging-in-Publication Data

Neill, Derrick.
Duck egg blue : a novel / Derrick Neill.
p. cm.
ISBN 978–1–57392–685–0 (cloth)
I. Title.
PS3564.E298D83 1999
813'.54—dc21 99–10415
CIP

For Martha, my wife, with love

Part 1
July

Chapter 1

"And now, gentlemen, as this board of review prepares to consider young Mr. Wright for Scouting's highest rank, there is one more very important thing we need to ask him. Cameron, tell us, please. Do you believe in God?"

Cameron Wright stiffened in his chair. For the first time during the board's questioning, he felt unsure of himself. With the three men at the table waiting and watching stoically, Cameron glanced up at the walls. To him, the small church conference room suddenly seemed to be shrinking.

"Cameron?" one of them said.

Not knowing what to answer, Cameron looked down at the report in his hands. Its title read: AN EAGLE SCOUT SERVICE PROJECT BY CAMERON WRIGHT. The cover snapshot showed him posed in front of a modest house, and topping it was the Mexican tile roof he built for his project. In the center of the photo, all red hair and dimples, he smiled proudly. He didn't feel like smiling now.

"Cameron?" one of them repeated more loudly.

Startled, Cameron looked up. “I’m sorry. I didn’t mean to ignore you. What was your question again? I mean, well, what do you mean exactly?”

Across the table, the Scout council representative cleared his throat. “It’s a simple question, son. Yes or no. Do you believe in God?”

Cameron pursed his lips. He didn’t consider it a simple question at all. As congenially as he could, he asked, “Uh, *which* God?”

The board member on his left bristled. “Are you trying to be difficult, young man?”

“No, sir,” Cameron answered. “I just want to know what you mean.”

“We mean just that,” the council representative said. “Do you, or do you not, believe in God? Do you believe in a Supreme Being?”

“You mean like someone who actually answers your prayers?” Cameron asked.

“Yes,” he said, “that’s what we mean.”

Exchanging glances, the other two men nodded their agreement.

Cameron regarded them silently for a few moments. He couldn’t help but wonder why they would ask him such a personal question in the first place. After all, it didn’t really seem appropriate. But on the other hand, he couldn’t just sit there all day straining his brain over it, either.

Then it came to him. The first Scout Law said, “A Scout is Trustworthy.” Scouts always tell the truth. He knew what he had to do.

Looking straight at the council representative, he said, “You know, I guess I don’t. Believe in God, that is. I mean, I don’t really know at this point. I’m not totally sure. You see, I’m only fourteen. I guess I haven’t decided yet. It’s kind of a big question. Isn’t it?”

From the looks on their faces, Cameron knew immediately

they didn't approve. Abruptly, the board member to his right asked, "Now, isn't John Wright your father? Isn't he an elder here at Mesquite Lutheran?"

"Yes, sir," Cameron answered. "He's also the committee chairman for our Scout troop. Mesquite Lutheran is the troop's chartered organization."

No response. The man just stared. But seeing his puzzled frown, Cameron guessed what he must be thinking.

"You see, my dad goes to this church, but I don't. I go to my mom's church. I live with her, so I usually go to her church. It's 'cause, well, my mom and dad are divorced."

The board member nodded slowly at him, then gestured at one of the medals pinned to his Scout uniform. "But, isn't that a religious emblem there?"

Cameron glanced down at the badge with the red lamp flame set against the white world globe. Across the top it read: RELIGION IN LIFE. Looking up, he answered, "Yes, it's a religious badge."

"Well, then, I'm confused. I don't know what church you and your mother go to, but how on earth does a Scout who doesn't believe in God get a religious emblem?"

"My mom's church doesn't have that requirement," Cameron said. "It doesn't tell you what to believe, or what not to believe."

Under his breath, the board member on his left remarked, "What kind of a crazy church is that?"

Hearing him, Cameron suddenly felt worse than merely unsure. Much worse. He felt put down, attacked. He did his best to hide it but, the way they looked at him, he could tell they knew.

"All right, gentlemen," the Scout council representative said quickly, defusing the situation. "I think it's obvious this matter warrants discussion by our Eagle review board. Cameron, would you mind waiting outside the room for a little while, please? You can leave your Eagle project report with us. We'll call you back in a few minutes."

"Okay," he said, getting out of his seat.

Stepping into the hallway, he closed the conference room door behind him and breathed a sigh of relief. "Now I know how Galileo must've felt," he said out loud.

"What was that, Cameron?" came a voice from next door. From the Board of Elders chairman's office. The troop committee chairman's office. His father's office.

"Nothing, sir," he called back.

"Come in here, Son."

Uh-oh, he thought. From the frying pan into the fire. Bracing for impact, he stepped through the doorway and stood before the deacon's desk.

Busy at his computer, his father didn't look over at him. Not even a glance. Robotlike, peering at the screen, he asked, "How did it go?"

After his experience with the board, Cameron considered himself lucky not having to look into his father's dark, bulging, piercing eyes. A handsome man with strong features and thick combed-back hair, John Wright could sometimes be severe and intimidating, especially when something displeased him. And this would.

Gingerly, Cameron answered, "They asked me to wait outside while they discuss it."

"Not a good sign, Cameron," his father said, continuing to work. "Not a good sign."

Cameron wanted to change the subject. "Dad, do you know where Ricky is? He needed some help with his taut-line hitch. He's got his Tenderfoot board today, after my Eagle board leaves."

"You mean he has his *third* Tenderfoot board today, don't you, Cameron?" John Wright said, fingers hovering over the keyboard.

Starting to type again, he added, "Look, you mean well, Son, but you're wasting your time. Ricky McGee will never get it. He probably shouldn't even be in Scouts. To use politically correct terminology, he's mentally challenged. The kid's a walking safety hazard."

"Mr. Smith says he's just learning disa—"

His father cut him off. "Your overly permissive Scoutmaster and I disagree on this, Cameron, as we do on so many things. Ricky's a danger to himself and to others."

"Well," Cameron persisted, "I want to help him out anyway. Scouts are supposed to help each other, you know. Do you know where he is?"

Disgusted, his father waved dismissively toward the front of the church. "He's sitting in the vestibule. So, go."

Great, Cameron thought, off the hook. Wasting no time, he said a quick, "Thanks," and turned for the doorway.

"Son."

Turning back around, Cameron froze. No longer trained on the computer screen, his father's eyes riveted him with the intensity of their glare.

"You know, Cameron," John Wright said gravely, slowly stroking his thick lower lip, "if I were you, I wouldn't be so concerned about teaching some borderline retarded kid a knot. As you know full well, you have much bigger problems."

"Sir?"

"And let's get another thing straight before you run off to do your good turn. You, boy, have nothing in common with Galileo. You see, in his trial before the Holy Office, he never told anybody *he didn't believe in God*."

That said, John Wright turned back to his computer and, with renewed vigor it seemed, resumed pounding the keys.

Backing slowly out of the office, Cameron felt stunned. How? How did his father know? Did he put a stethoscope up to the wall, or what?

Barely aware of his surroundings as he walked the short hallway to the church entrance, Cameron kept shaking his head.

"No way. No way," he said to himself. "There's no way he could've known what the Eagle board asked me, unless—"

"Hi, Cam!"

Looking up, he saw Ricky McGee waving at him from the bench by the front doors. Putting his own problems on the back burner, he forced a smile and crossed the vestibule to sit with his friend.

"Hey, Ricky," he said. "Ready for your board, I see. You look good in your uniform."

"Thanks, Cam," Ricky said, grinning behind glasses so thick they magnified his eyes. "You look good, too."

"How are you today?" Cameron asked.

"I'm missing my cartoons."

"What?"

"It's Saturday. I'm missing my cartoons," Ricky repeated. "But, it's okay. Ya know how come?"

"How come?"

"'Cause after I get my Tenderfoot, everybody will stop calling me 'Scrub.' They won't call me 'the Scrub' anymore."

"Everybody doesn't call you that," he said, ruffling Ricky's hair. "I don't."

"You don't. But, everybody else does."

Cameron gestured at the piece of cord in Ricky's hand. "So, show me how your taut-line's coming."

"I don't think I'm gonna be able to tie it right, today," Ricky said doubtfully. "But, I'll try."

Cameron watched closely as the boy struggled for several minutes with little success. Scratching his head, he made a suggestion. "Wait, Ricky," he said. "Do you know what the word *taut,* in *taut*-line, means?"

"What?"

"It means *tight*. It's much easier to tie a taut-line hitch if you make sure the standing part of your line is tight. Here, pretend this is a tent stake." He held up his arm.

"Okay," Ricky said, shrugging. With the tip of his tongue stuck out determinedly, he passed the cord around Cameron's wrist and started over.

It took a while. A long while. So long, in fact, that eventually Cameron's arm felt like it would fall off. But he didn't complain. And Ricky *did* make progress. Slowly. Slowly. Until, finally . . .

"You did it!"

"I did?" Ricky asked. Studying the knot a moment, he got a big grin on his face. "I did! I did it!"

"Just remember, when you do it for the board, tie it around something," Cameron said. "A table leg or something."

Frowning, Ricky asked, "Was I too slow? I'm prob'ly the slowest person in the world."

Cameron shook his head and smiled. "Hey, sometimes slow and steady wins the race. You've heard that old story about the desert tortoise and the jack rabbit, haven't you? The rabbit was way faster but the tortoise still won. He had patience. And persistence."

"Really? You can be slow and still win?"

"Sure," Cameron said. "See, no matter who you are, there's always gonna be somebody, sometime, who's faster. Or smarter. Or better at the things you like to do. And, there are always other people who are slower, not as smart, not as good at stuff. That's just the way the world is. You just gotta be the best Ricky McGee you can be. That's all you can do."

Nodding thoughtfully, Ricky suddenly pointed a finger at Cameron. "Jordan's the best basketball player in the world. Nobody's better than His Airness."

"Oh, yeah," Cameron answered playfully. "How about . . . Sir Charles?"

"Jordan."

"Barkley."

"Jordan!"

"Barkley!"

"Excuse me, Cameron. We're ready for you to come back in now." The Scout council representative stood waiting in the hallway looking very serious.

Slipping the cord off his wrist, Cameron handed it to the boy and then got up. "Cover me, Ricky," he said. "I'm goin' in."

Chuckling, Ricky called after him, "I got your back, Cam!"

After returning to the conference room and taking their seats, Cameron took a deep breath as the council representative addressed the board from across the table. "Well, we'll keep this short. It's summer, it's Saturday, and I'm sure there are lots of places we would all rather be."

Everybody smiled and nodded.

"Reviewing your materials, Cameron," he said, "we are very impressed. These letters of recommendation from your teachers and basketball coaches; from Ralph Smith, your Scoutmaster; and from your minister—a Dr. Dreyfuss-Campbell, is it?"

Glancing over, Cameron thought he noticed the left board member rolling his eyes.

"Well, they're all just glowing," the council representative continued. "It seems everyone thinks very highly of you."

Nodding, Cameron waited for the other shoe to drop.

"And your Eagle project," the man went on. "Planning, developing, and leading this red-tile-roof construction job for Habitat For Humanity. Raising the funds for the materials, drawing the plans, supervising the Scouts doing the work. As I'm sure you know, Cameron, you helped a low-income family's dreams come true."

He knew. Okay, cut to the chase, please.

The man kept going. "And your responses to the board's questions today. All exemplary. The best we've heard. It's obvious you've completed all the requirements for Eagle Scout. All, that is, *except one*."

Uh-oh, Cameron thought, sitting up. Here it comes.

"We're really very sorry, Cameron," the man said, shaking his head. "Considering all your outstanding accomplishments, it is with heavy hearts that, for now at least, our board cannot forward your application to the national office. We do have a suggestion for you, however, that we think will help you become a better Scout."

"Yes, sir?"

"Read your Scout Oath carefully, Cameron, and think about it. Hard. And read your Scout Law. Especially, the *last* Scout Law. Think about that last Scout Law, Cameron, and get back to us when you're ready to try this again."

With that, the three men looked back and forth a few times and then stood up, leaving Cameron sitting there as they filed toward the door.

On the way out, the board member from the seat on his left tapped him on the shoulder. "You know, young man," he said, pausing in the doorway. "There is something else you could do."

"Sir?"

"Pray, son," his voice called back as he disappeared with the others into the hallway. "It couldn't hurt you to pray."

For what seemed a long while, Cameron just sat there, mulling things over. It had been quite a day so far, that's for sure. Finally, shaking his head, he got up, pushed his chair back, and headed into the hall.

Hoping to avoid his father at all costs, he hurried past the open elders' office doorway. As he did, something surprised him. He glimpsed the Scout council representative in there, jawing quietly with his dad. Evidently they knew each other.

Arriving in the vestibule, Cameron made a quick stop to touch base with Ricky. "Well, I got dipped and fried to a crispy, crackly crunch by my Eagle board," he told him, only half joking. "I hope your Tenderfoot board goes easier on you. Who's chairing it, anyway?"

Grinning innocently, Ricky answered, "Your dad."

Cameron just stared. Sometimes the not-so-amusing ironies of the universe amazed him.

Managing a "Great. . . . Good luck," he quickly turned to the front door and pushed it open. He gasped. The hot, dry air hit him like a blast furnace and the loud buzz of cicadas assailed his ears. July in southern Arizona.

Climbing on his bike, he started pedaling out into the church parking lot when something grabbed his attention, stopping him cold.

His father's big Suburban Silverado. More specifically, the old sticker on the bumper of his father's Suburban Silverado. BUCHANAN FOR PRESIDENT it read.

He should've realized it sooner.

His father made Pat Buchanan look like a bleeding heart liberal. His father knew of his uncertainty about God. His father knew he liked his mother's church better than his. And, his father knew the Scout council representative.

And, now, Cameron knew.

He knew exactly how his father had known what the board asked him, and what he'd said.

He knew. He knew.

Chapter 2

"Well now, look what the cat dragged in. If it isn't Deloris Edwards's firstborn son come to visit his little brother's humble hobby shop. To what do I owe this unexpected honor, Mark?"

"Morning, Justin," Mark Edwards said, closing the door behind him. Walking up to the storefront register counter where his brother sat, he answered, "I'm ready to start my next model. I have to make sure that growing collection in my science classroom keeps you in business."

"Haven't you just about covered the entire history of manned spaceflight already?" Justin Edwards asked, reaching into his shirt pocket for a pack of gum. He held it out, offering him a stick.

"Yeah, but now I'm working on space travel of the future," Mark said, taking one. "This time, I want to build a starship."

Using his left hand—his *only* hand—Justin slid a piece out for himself. "Well, you know where my science-fiction section is," he said.

Mark watched as Justin deftly removed the foil wrapper before popping the gum in his mouth. A neat trick for a one-armed man, he thought. But then, even the simple ways his brother had adapted since the accident never ceased to amaze him.

Glancing away to gaze out the window, Mark suddenly did a double take. "Hey, Justin," he said. "What are all those people with signs doing standing out there by the curb?"

"Oh, they're a bunch of Christian Coalition assholes," Justin answered, spinning in his swivel chair to scowl at them through the glass. "They're demonstrating against the Planned Parenthood office a few doors down. I can tell you one thing. They're not doing business in this shopping center any good."

"Well, they're committed, that's for sure. It must be over a hundred degrees out there and it's not even noon."

"If you meant to say they should *be* committed," Justin answered, "then I'm in total agreement with you."

Not wanting to get his brother started on one of his soapboxes, Mark turned toward the science-fiction area. "I better go get my model, Justin. Then, I'll need about ten different colors of enamel and some brushes."

"Let me know if you need any help," Justin told him, as he headed down the aisle.

Mark already knew the kit he wanted and, searching the shelves with his eyes, it didn't take long to spot. Pulling a box from the stack, he slipped it under his arm and then stepped over to the model-paint stand.

As he went about choosing the colors he needed, he heard the shop door open and close. Looking up, he saw a woman and a teenage boy standing at the front of the store. Both had striking strawberry hair.

"Cameron, I'll be browsing in the art supplies, Hon," he heard the woman say. Then he lost her as she disappeared behind one of the craft displays.

Finishing up at the paint stand, Mark took his model and his little jars of enamel and headed back up to the counter. As he did, his brother greeted the red-haired boy. "Hello, young man. What can I help you with today? It's Cameron, right?"

"Yes, sir," the boy answered, nodding. "I need some paint. I'm not sure what color. Blue-green, I think. I'll have to check out your selection."

"Well, the paint center's right behind you there," Justin said, pointing. "Go ahead. Take all the time you like."

"Thanks."

As the boy started looking, Mark handed Justin his model kit and then carefully placed his jars of enamel on the glass countertop. Squinting across at the paintbrush rack, he said, "Justin, will you please hand me two size 5/0 sable spotters and two size 0 sable liners?"

Obliging him, Justin handed over the brushes and then took a look at his model kit. "The fiber optic *Next Generation Enterprise,* eh?" he said, studying the box top. "I hear this is a hard one. With all these tiny light-up windows, it's gonna take you a while."

"Afraid it might crimp my nonexistent social life?" Mark asked.

"Hey, we do stuff," Justin answered. "We socialize with that karate club of ours—even though, most of those people are contentious, overbearing assholes."

"Oh, c'mon, they're not so bad," Mark said. "But, now that you mention it, all the available women there do seem to either want to break your elbows or choke you into unconsciousness."

Justin raised his eyebrows. "And that doesn't turn you on?"

"Excuse me, sir?" Cameron broke in, stepping back up to the counter. "I think I found the color I want, but your bin is empty. I wrote the number down. Do you have any more paint in stock? Like, in the back, or something?"

"Sorry, kid, I don't," Justin answered. "I can order it, though. Take a couple weeks."

He looked disappointed.

"What do you need it for?" Mark asked.

"I'm making a papier-mâché cross section of the Grand Canyon for my geology merit badge," Cameron answered. "I wanted the paint for the Colorado River water."

"A Scout, huh? My brother, Justin, and I were Scouts when we were your age."

"Yeah. Even though most of our leaders were militant, power-tripping assholes," Justin said, mumbling to himself.

Sometimes Mark couldn't believe his brother. "C'mon, Bro. Behave yourself." He turned to Cameron. "Don't pay any attention to that man behind the counter. He has a . . . bowel condition. Makes him cranky."

Justin ignored Mark's chiding. "So, kid. Do you want me to place an order for you, or not?"

Before the boy could answer, Mark got an idea. "Wait. Wait a sec. Just before you came in, Cameron, I cleaned out one or two of those bins myself. Maybe, I have a jar of the paint you need, right here. What's that number, anyway?"

"Oh. No, sir. I couldn't—"

"Please. I want to," Mark told him. "It'll be my good turn for the day. Scout to Scout."

"Well . . . okay." Reaching into his shorts pocket, Cameron produced a tiny, folded-up scrap of paper. Opening it, he asked, "Are you ready? Here it is."

"Shoot."

"It's FS 35622."

Repeating the number to himself, Mark scanned the little labels and smiled. The fourth jar matched. "Here you go," he said, handing it to the boy.

"Thanks." Turning to Justin, Cameron asked, "Would it be possible for me to see a dried sample before I buy it? I mean, it might not be what I want after all."

"Not a problem," Justin said, reaching for the jar.

But, there was a slight problem. As Mark and Cameron watched, Justin struggled to twist the lid open using one hand. He couldn't do it.

The boy frowned. "Sir, let me help you with that."

"It's okay, Cameron," Mark said, winking. "He could get that lid off with one arm tied behind his back."

"Kid," Justin said, glancing over at Mark, "if my smart alec big brother there is making fun of my unfortunate appendage shortage, you can tell him, for me, at least I have hair."

"Cameron," Mark said, glancing back at Justin, "if my smart alec little brother there is referring to my follicly challenged scalp, you can tell him, for me, that I'm losing my hair worrying about him only having one arm."

Noticing that Cameron seemed a bit flustered, Justin grinned at the boy. "I think our lively, familial repartee is scaring him, Mark. Watch this, kid."

Holding the little paint jar, Justin reached behind the counter for only an instant. When his hand reappeared, the lid twisted right off.

"How did you do that?" Cameron asked.

"I have a nifty ratchet gismo installed back here for just such situations," Justin answered, brushing a sample of the paint onto a white index card. Blowing on it, he handed it to Cameron. "What do you think?"

"Looks fine," Cameron answered, nodding at the card. "I think I'll take it."

Waiting for the two of them to complete their transaction, Mark picked up his model kit and started reading the information on the box.

Glancing over, Cameron asked, "Is that for your son?"

"No. No kids. Not even married. It's for me."

"Oh . . ."

"Here's your change," Justin said, dropping several coins in the boy's palm. "Hope the paint works out for you."

"Thanks," Cameron answered. "I think it will."

Glancing up from his model specs, Mark suddenly noticed Justin and Cameron staring at him. No, not *at* him. *Past* him. He felt someone put a hand on his shoulder. He turned around.

The redheaded woman. The *beautiful* redheaded woman. He'd forgotten completely about her.

"I wanted to be sure and thank you," she said, looking up at him. "Letting my son have that last jar of paint was a very kind thing to do."

As she spoke, she slowly slid her hand down and, for a moment, allowed it to rest on his bare forearm. The gesture caught him completely off guard.

"Oh, well, uh . . ."

"Okay, Cameron, let's go. Bye, now."

Kicking himself for his lack of suave, Mark watched speechlessly as they turned away and headed for the door. Vaguely aware of his brother saying, "Smooth, Mark. Real smooth," he started to at least say good-bye when the woman spun around, catching him totally off guard *again*.

"You know," she said, a small smile forming on her lips, "you really do learn something new every day."

"What's that?" Mark managed to ask.

"Well . . . it's just that I really had no idea putting together spaceship models was something grown men like you actually did."

He couldn't be sure, but he thought he heard her giggle as she turned away and led her son out of the store.

"Boy, she is good," Justin said, hardly able to contain himself. "First she pumps you up, then she flattens you. And practically in the same breath."

Mark just stared.

"I know one thing, big brother," he continued. "If *that* woman ever put her hand on any one of my body parts—intact *or* missing—I'd lose it right there."

"Has it really been that long?" Mark asked, glancing over.

Sticking his lip out in a pout, Justin nodded at him. "You?"

"It's been a while," he answered.

"Bro, did you happen to notice those luminous, sea-foam-green eyes of hers?"

"Yes, Justin."

"That freckled, ivory skin?"

"Yes."

"That full, sensual mouth?"

"Yes, yes."

"Those nice, big—"

"*Yes, Justin,*" Mark said, cutting him off. "Those, too. They were kind of hard to miss. But, I don't want to think about it." Tapping his model-kit box, he added, "I get the feeling she wasn't too impressed with my macho pastimes."

"Get outta here," Justin said. "She was just flirting with you, busting your balls. Hell, she was checking you out the whole time she was in here. Didn't you even notice?"

"No. I didn't."

"Come to think of it," Justin went on, "how come women always seem to like you best? I'm the one with hair."

"Well, if that's true—and I'm not saying it is—do you think maybe it could have anything to do with your attitude? I mean, how many different societal groups did you call 'assholes' today, anyway? I lost count."

His brother shrugged. "So, I'm not a people person."

"Put it this way, Justin. Is there anybody in this entire world you *don't* think is an asshole?"

"Well . . . there's you, I guess. You're not an asshole. At least, not all the time."

Mark laughed. "Thanks, little brother. Thanks for the overwhelming display of sibling affection. Now, put this stuff in a sack for me, please. You can add it to my tab."

"You got it, Bro."

Suddenly, thunder boomed in the distance, rattling the glass in the storefront windows.

Glancing up in response, Mark noticed something new happening out by the curb. "Hey, Justin. Now, there's some guy out there screaming at those picketers through a megaphone. Any idea who it could be?"

"He's the one in charge of the damn thing," Justin answered. "The head ass—"

Mark shot him a look.

"—hole. Sorry."

Again, thunder rumbled above them. Closer this time.

"Well," Mark said, taking his bag of merchandise, "either we're just about to get one of our afternoon thunderstorms or those religious protesters are invoking the wrath of God in your parking lot. Either way, I'm outta here. Catch you later, Bro."

"Take care, Mark."

Pausing just inside the store's glass entrance, Mark turned, frowning. "Man, this guy's really going at it out here, Justin. Do you have any idea what his name is?"

"Let's see. Somebody told me once. It's Wright, I think. Yeah, that's it. Wright. John Wright. Ring any bells with you?"

Mark shook his head at his brother and headed out the door. "Nope. Sorry. Never heard of him."

But, hearing the man rant and rave through that damn megaphone on the way out to his pickup, Mark Edwards discovered he did know something about this John Wright, after all.

He knew he didn't like the guy.

Chapter 3

"Hi, Mr. Smith. I'm so sorry to bother you. I hope I didn't call at a bad time."

"Heavens, no. Please, come in, Ms. Anderson. Scout parents are always welcome here."

"Thanks. And, Mr. Smith, Cameron's been in Troop 424 over three years now. Please, call me Harmony."

Harmony Anderson made the same suggestion whenever she saw Ralph Smith. By this time, she knew the gray-haired man probably wouldn't ever take her up on it. But, she thought, it never hurt to keep trying.

"Please, come and sit down," Mr. Smith said, ushering her into the den. "You can have a seat there by the desk. When I hung up the phone after our conversation a few minutes ago, I put on some coffee. Would you like some?"

"That sounds nice."

Turning to the mug rack that covered most of one wall, Mr.

Smith rubbed his chin. “So many mugs, so many memories. I always have trouble making up my mind.”

“Would it help if I picked?” Harmony asked, smiling.

“Would you?”

Getting up, she stepped over to the rack and pointed out the first two mugs that caught her eye.

“Trees,” he said, lifting them off.

“What?”

“It’s interesting. Both mugs you selected have trees on them. Crossed palms on this one, and some kind of large, broadleaf tree, here. If memory serves, you run your own plant nursery, don’t you?”

“Why, yes, I do,” she answered, delighted by his observation.

“I’ll be right back with our coffee.”

Sitting back down, Harmony gazed around the room. Surrounding her, a fascinating collection of memorabilia—ribbons and plaques, photos and certificates, plates and mugs—filled the room’s many shelves and decorated its walls. Each piece, she knew, represented its own special moment from a lifetime of Scouting.

As Mr. Smith came back in carrying a coffee tray, Harmony asked him, “How many years, Mr. Smith? As Scoutmaster, I mean.”

“Over thirty,” he answered, handing her one of the mugs. Taking his seat behind the desk, he added, “I started the troop in my thirties, back when my own boys were Scouts. And now, well . . .” With a shrug, he blew on his coffee and took a sip.

“Tell me more about these mugs I picked,” Harmony said.

“Well, yours there, with that broadleaf tree, that’s from the 1973 National Scout Jamboree in Farragut State Park, Idaho. The theme was, ‘Growing Together,’ hence the tree. I met Bob Hope at that one.”

“Really? And yours?”

“This one is from Pimaree VII, an international camporee

between Scouts from southern Arizona and Sonora, Mexico. It was held in Guaymas that year and we were all camped in a palm grove near where that movie *Catch-22* was filmed. Anyway, one night, it rained the whole time. The next morning, we were caught in a flash flood. It was a real mess."

Shaking her head at his story, Harmony sipped her coffee.

"So," Mr. Smith said, looking over his glasses at her, "what can I do for you today, Ms. Anderson?"

"Well, it's about Cameron, Mr. Smith," Harmony answered, putting her coffee mug down. "He's been kind of depressed lately and I'm worried about him. He told me he didn't pass his Eagle board, but he wouldn't tell me why. Will you?"

Mr. Smith took a breath and let it out slow. Then he shook his head. "You know, Ms. Anderson, of all the Scouts I never thought would fail a review board, Cameron topped the list. No Scout has ever more fully demonstrated true Scout spirit, by living the Oath and Law, than your son."

"So, why did he fail?" Harmony asked, puzzled.

Mr. Smith sat up in his chair. "Ms. Anderson, the Eagle review board asked Cameron if he believed in God."

"Yes. So?"

"Well," Mr. Smith answered, frowning, "he said that he didn't."

A bit bewildered, Harmony cocked her head. "I still don't see the problem, Mr. Smith. I mean, I know it's a question he's been struggling with for a while now. Since John and I divorced, actually. The important thing is that he answered honestly, isn't it? I mean, 'A Scout is Trustworthy,' and all that. Why in the world should that be keeping him from getting a badge he's worked so hard for?"

"Ms. Anderson, a Scout is also supposed to be reverent toward God. To do his duty to God."

Harmony bit her lip. Measuring her words, she said, "Well, Mr. Smith, I have a few problems with that. First, whose definition of God is Cameron supposed to consider, your Eagle board's? Cameron knows from the teachings in his own church that people around the world, Eastern religions for example, see God very differently."

Mr. Smith nodded amiably.

"And," she went on, "isn't Scouts a public organization? Doesn't it receive funds from places like United Way and meet in public-school buildings? How can 'duty to God' be a realistic requirement in such a case?"

"Both excellent questions, Ms. Anderson," Mr. Smith answered, still nodding. "And, you might be surprised to hear that I agree with you on both counts. However, the unfortunate fact remains that, back in December of '93, the Supreme Court let stand a lower court ruling permitting the Scouts to withhold advancement—or even refuse membership—to any youngster who doesn't swear to 'do my duty to God.' Now you and I may not like it, but there it is."

Shocked, Harmony slowly shook her head.

"You know, Ms. Anderson," Mr. Smith said, smiling ironically, "Scouts has a tradition of teaching religious tolerance and I think it should practice what it preaches. Any organization which inspires love of nature and respect for character needs to be as open as the great outdoors. And I suspect most Scout troops across the country do welcome any faith, from Methodism to Zen.

"But our troop is sponsored by Mesquite Evangelical Lutheran. *My* church, I'm afraid. And, even though I don't necessarily agree with their stand on this, it seems they are within their rights."

"So, that's that?" Harmony asked.

"I'm afraid so," Mr. Smith said. "I'm sorry. I truly am."

It helped some knowing Mr. Smith sympathized with her. But not enough. Feeling suddenly overwhelmed, Harmony got out of her chair. "I'm sorry, Mr. Smith. Finding all this out has really upset me, I'm afraid. I think I should go."

"Of course."

On the way out to her Volkswagen bug, one question still nagged at Harmony. Turning to the Scoutmaster, she asked, "Mr. Smith, there's something I still don't understand. If it's true you agree with me on this, why in the world did you ask Cameron if he believed in God in the first place?"

"Oh, *I* didn't ask him, Ms. Anderson," he answered, opening the car door for her. "You see, I wasn't on Cameron's Eagle board. It's the Scout council that sets those up. In fact, I wasn't even at the church last Saturday when his board was held."

"Oh . . . ," she said, getting in.

Still confused, she frowned at him as he closed the door and headed back up the walkway toward the house. "Well then, I still don't get why they would ask him that, Mr. Smith," she called, shaking her head. "Who *was* there from Troop 424, anyway?"

Clearing his throat, Ralph Smith called back. "Didn't Cameron tell you, Ms. Anderson? John was there. Your ex-husband was at the church that day."

Harmony Anderson's jaw dropped. Staring blankly as the Scoutmaster waved good-bye and went back in his house, her mind started to race.

Could it be possible? Could he actually sink so low?

Slowly, she nodded to herself as the realization sunk in. Of course. Of course, he could. After all, all the earmarks were right there.

No, no doubt about it, she thought. This whole repugnant scenario was vintage John Wright.

Part 2
August

Chapter 4

"Hey, I know you. Cameron, isn't it? How's that Grand Canyon model coming?"

Surrounded by elbow-to-elbow students, Cameron Wright stood at the edge of the crowded sidewalk and checked his new class schedule against the numbers posted above the classroom doors. Looking over at the sound of the voice, he had to think a moment before recognizing the man standing in the near doorway.

"Now, I remember," he said, grinning. "The hobby shop, right? A couple of weeks ago. Are you a *teacher*?"

"Guilty as charged," the man answered. "And not just any teacher, *your* teacher. If you're in the right place, that is. Freshman Earth Science, Room 320, Mr. Edwards?"

Double-checking his schedule, Cameron closed his binder and headed up the sidewalk toward the door. "I am. I'm in the right place."

"Well, then, greetings and felicitations," Mr. Edwards told

him. "C'mon in and sit down, it doesn't matter where. I've already arranged a random chart. As soon as everyone arrives, we'll assign your permanent spots."

"Random?" Cameron asked. "You mean, we can't just sit where we want? We can't sit with our friends?"

"Sure you can," Mr. Edwards answered. "For about ten minutes. Then, like I said, I'm putting you where *I* want you. Besides, my way, you might just meet some new friends."

"If you say so," Cameron said, shrugging. But, he didn't really buy it.

Finding himself a temporary seat, he started to check out the science room while the rest of the class filed in the door. Right away, he discovered the models.

They were everywhere, hanging down from the ceiling. Air and space vehicles of every size and description. From the Wright brothers' first plane all the way up to the space shuttle.

Gazing at them, Cameron grew more and more astounded. If he'd ever seen anything cooler, he certainly didn't remember when.

The bell rang.

Pulling the door closed, Mr. Edwards walked to the front of the room and turned to face the class. "Well, good morning, everybody," he said, smiling affably. "Welcome to Mesquite High. I trust that, after an enjoyable summer break, you've all returned refreshed and rejuvenated and eager to learn."

Cameron looked down from the models a moment to glance around at the other students. A few looked refreshed, but the rest of them looked like they were in a dentist's office waiting for a filling.

Mr. Edwards continued. "Now, in your registration booklets, this class is called 'Earth Science.' But since we're going to be studying about much more than just planet Earth, I like to call it by a different name. I like to call this class 'The History of Life, the Universe, and Everything.' "

Life, the universe, and everything? Cameron thought. That sounded like a lot of material. He wondered what a test on *everything* could possibly be like.

"We'll begin at the beginning," Mr. Edwards went on, stepping over to the first of a series of posters he had on the wall. "Here, at the very start of it all. The birth of the universe. The Big Bang explosion."

Moving down the line, he lingered at each picture just long enough to mention its significance.

"After studying the Big Bang," he said, "we'll then learn how the galaxies formed, including our own Milky Way . . . how new stars and new solar systems are born out of clouds of gas and dust . . . how our own star, the Sun, and its nine planets came to be . . . and how planet Earth, our home, began.

"We'll study about the Earth's formation and its geologic history . . . about the oceans and the atmosphere and how they're really one . . . about matter and energy and how they're related . . . and, most miraculous of all, about the evolution of life."

Arriving at the last poster, a depiction of a shuttle launch, Mr. Edwards pointed to it. "And, finally," he told the class, "we'll learn about human and cultural evolution, winding up our school year with a unit on the manned space program. *That* will bring us full circle. Because, you see, born ultimately of the stars, human beings are just now beginning their long voyage home."

Born of the stars, Cameron thought. Yeah, he liked that. He liked that a lot.

"So, as you can see," Mr. Edwards said, walking back to the front of the room, "earth science is a very broad field of study. And, it involves a large number of more-specific sciences. Can anybody name one for me?"

Without hesitation, a black girl sitting in the front raised her hand. "Umm, would life science, or biology, be one?"

"You bet," Mr. Edwards nodded. "Great answer. Anyone else?"

"How 'bout astronomy?" a boy in the back said.

"Good."

"Oceanography?" somebody asked.

"That's right."

"Chemistry."

"Right again."

Oh, what the heck, Cameron thought. He raised his hand.

"Yes?"

"Geology," he answered. "The study of rocks and minerals."

Mr. Edwards winked at him. "Another good one. Thank you, Cameron. Anyone else?"

Cameron looked around. No more hands. It seemed the supply of the bravest students had already been depleted. He smiled to himself. He knew, if he wanted to, he could name a few more. Like physics and meteorology and paleontology . . .

But he also knew showing off, especially on the first day, would be a fatal freshman faux pas. No, he'd bide his time. He'd have plenty of other opportunities to prove himself.

"How about physics . . . meteorology . . . paleontology?" the black girl in front suddenly asked.

Cameron almost choked. She took the words right out of his brain. *And how brazen*. She didn't even raise her hand.

Surprisingly, Mr. Edwards didn't seem to mind. Looking very impressed with the girl, he said, "Excellent! What's your name, miss?"

"Mandy Ross."

"Well, Mandy Ross, nice job. In fact, nice job, everybody! Unless I'm mistaken, I think you guys nailed all the most important ones. But, there are more . . ."

Patting a stack of papers he had on his desk, he said, "In a moment, I'm going to hand out crossword puzzles listing over *fifty* fields of science we'll be learning about this year. Before I do, however, we need to get you into your permanent seats so I can take roll and start learning your names."

Uh-oh, here it comes, Cameron thought. The *random* seating chart.

Mr. Edwards asked everyone to gather up their things and move to the back of the room. Then, one by one, he called out their names, assigning them seats at the room's eight rectangular tables. Because *his* last name began with the letter W, Cameron had to stand to the very end.

"And last, but certainly not least," Mr. Edwards finally called, "Mr. Cameron Wright."

Crossing the classroom to his seat, Cameron felt the eyes of the entire class watching him. Looking around nervously as he sat down, he glanced to his right. Then, he did a double take. Mandy Ross smiled at him from the chair next to his.

For the first time, he saw her face.

And when he saw it, all prior thoughts of her brazenness simply melted from his mind.

It was heart-shaped with dimpled lips, an upturned nose, and gentle almond eyes. And, framed by a halo of luxurious brown ringlets, it seemed to be glowing.

"Earth to Cameron . . . Earth to Cameron . . ."

"What?"

"Snap out of it, boy," Mandy Ross told him. "You look like a zombie or something."

"Oh . . . sorry," he said, trying to stop his staring. But it wasn't easy. He'd never seen anything like Mandy Ross before.

"I like your T-shirt."

"What?"

"Your T-shirt," she repeated.

At that particular moment, Cameron had absolutely no idea what shirt he had on. So, he looked.

Ah, yes . . . the Arizona Wildcats 1997 NCAA National Championship shirt, official locker-room version. Yeah, cool tee, all right. Not only did this girl have brains *and* looks, she had good taste, too.

"I got mine at Penney's," she said.

Looking up, Cameron couldn't believe his eyes. Mandy Ross had on the exact same shirt. It seemed she liked basketball, *too*. Would wonders never cease?

"Okay, everybody," Mr. Edwards announced, holding up the stack of puzzles, "the next thing I want you all to do is pair up with the person sitting next to you."

Pair up? Did he say, *pair up*? Cameron glanced at Mandy. Yeah, he could do that. No problem at all.

Handing out the crosswords, the teacher said, "Here's the plan. I'm giving you these puzzles facedown. Please don't turn them over till I tell you. Your two-person teams are going to be competing against each other for the first bonus points of the year, and I want to make sure you all start at the same time."

Bonus points on the first day? Cameron thought. Cool.

"After I tell you to start," Mr. Edwards continued, "please work as quietly as possible so you don't accidentally give answers to other teams. Remember, this *is* a competition. As soon as both you and your partner are finished, raise your hands and I'll check your work. Are there any questions?" He glanced around the room. "Okay, begin."

" 'Across' or 'down'?" Mandy whispered.

"What?"

"It'll be more efficient if we split up the workload," Mandy explained, whispering in his ear. "Do you want 'across,' or 'down'?"

Discovering he liked the way her breath felt on his cheek, Cameron had to fight to concentrate. " 'Down,' " he said.

"Well then, get started, boy," Mandy told him, smiling. "I want to win this thing."

Nodding, he did the best he could to focus on the puzzle. It didn't look too hard. A box in the lower-right corner of the worksheet gave them all the sciences they needed, but jumbled up.

Working fast, he started reading the clues, locating the correct answers and filling them in. Seismology, check . . . mineralogy, check . . . botany, check . . . anthropology, check . . . nephology, ch—

Nephology?

Cameron racked his brains. He had absolutely no idea whatsoever about what nephology meant and his expression must have shown it.

"Which one?" Mandy asked.

He pointed to it with his pencil.

"The study of clouds," she told him, not missing a beat. "Now, go. *Go*. We're almost done."

Working as fast as he could, Cameron soon found himself with only one answer left. And *what* an answer: Sexology—the study of human sexual behavior. Feeling mischievous, he quickly filled it in and then showed the word to Mandy.

At first she acted shocked by it, letting out a little gasp and biting her lip. But she was only teasing. Smiling a brilliant smile, she winked. No kidding, *she winked at him*. He felt warm all over.

"Now, get your hand up, boy," she said excitedly, thrusting hers in the air as she glanced anxiously around the room. "I think we're the first ones done!"

It seemed like it took forever while they waited for Mr. Edwards to check their work. But finally, the teacher looked up and said, "Looks like we have a couple of winners here. Nice job, you guys. You two make a good team."

Defeated, the rest of the class groaned in response and started to get noisy. But Cameron barely heard them. Watching Mandy, he couldn't believe how impossibly bright her eyes looked exulting over their win.

Mr. Edwards checked his watch. "Well, we're almost out of time and there's one more thing we need to do before you go—so listen, please. Later in the year, as part of our unit on evolution, we'll be studying human *sexual* reproduction."

That's all it took. Once again, the class was his.

Stepping over to his desk, he picked up another stack of papers. "As part of that unit," he continued, "we'll be seeing a video showing a live human birth and a signed parental permission slip will be required. Please, take these home and have them signed and returned as soon as possible. Also, tell your folks I encourage them to come in and preview the film if they have any concerns about it." He started passing them out.

"Mr. Edwards?"

Cameron glanced over. A blonde girl at the table next to theirs had her hand up.

Checking his seating chart, the teacher answered, "Yes, Miss . . . Kelly Brown."

"What do we do if our parents won't let us watch it?" the girl asked. " 'Cause I already know mine won't. You might as well not even give me one of those permission thingies."

"Well, yes, I am going to give you one of these permission *thingies,* Miss Brown," he said. "And I'd appreciate it if you'd take it home. If your parents decide they don't want you to view the video, then we'll send you to the library with an alternative research assignment. *But* the assignment will cover the same subject matter."

"Well, my parents don't think the schools should be teaching us how to have sex," the girl declared, frowning.

Mr. Edwards smiled slightly. "That's *not* what the schools are doing, Kelly. And for your information, we're mandated by the state to teach sex education. But don't get me wrong. It's a good mandate. One I heartily agree with."

The girl smirked back at him as the class looked on. A very awkward moment.

Then the bell rang.

"Whew," Mandy said, rolling her eyes as she stood up from her seat. "Saved by the proverbial bell, once again." Leaning close, she asked, "What do you think, Cameron? Do you think there's just a bit of friction there?"

"Just a tad," he answered, nodding, as they joined the rest of their classmates filing out the door.

Outside at the busy sidewalk intersection, much to his chagrin, Mandy Ross turned one way just as he turned the other. Watching her go, he quickly called out to her. "Bye, Mandy."

"Bye, Cameron," she called back with a wave. Then, flashing that brilliant wide smile of hers, she added, "Mr. Edwards was right, you know. We *do* make a good team."

Yes, they did, he thought, heading to his next class. And Mr. Edwards had been right about another thing, too.

Despite what Cameron first thought about it, the teacher's sit-randomly-and-make-new-friends plan was one heck of an idea!

Chapter 5

Following her bliss, Harmony Anderson flitted from room to room through her Spanish Mission–style home, faithfully tending her ever-growing jungle of beloved household plants. And while she did, she hummed softly to them, accompanied by the classical music wafting from the old portable cassette stereo in the family room.

The tape she'd picked out—a sampler of Impressionist selections from Monet's nineteenth-century France—was a favorite of hers. *And* of the plants. Listening to Ravel's *Sonatine,* she just started to water the big ficus in the corner of the living room when the kitchen phone rang.

"Oh, it never fails," she said to herself, feeling her bliss start to slip away. Glancing down, she frowned at the moisture meter in one hand and watering can in the other. "Cameron," she called. "Would you get that, please? It is Scout night. It's probably for you."

To her relief, the ringing stopped.

Several minutes later, as she climbed up on a chair to reach a hanging spider plant, Cameron appeared in the archway leading to the dining room. He looked disappointed.

"Who was it, Hon?" she asked.

"Ricky McGee."

"What did he want?"

Cameron shrugged. "He told me he failed his *fourth* Tenderfoot board last Saturday. He wants me to help him with his knots again tonight."

"Oh, I'm sorry to hear that, Cameron."

"I just don't understand it, Mom," he said, shaking his head. "He *knows* how to tie 'em. He's just slower than most of the other kids, that's all."

"He's slower than all the other kids, Hon," she said, stepping down off the chair.

"Okay, *all* the other kids," Cameron admitted, rolling his eyes. "But, I'm tellin' ya, he *does* know those knots. I just don't think his board's giving him enough time."

Harmony crossed the room and kissed her son on the forehead. "Well, then keep working with him, Cam. The more he practices, the faster he'll get."

Nodding at her, Cameron shrugged again and glanced into the family room. "What's this you're listening to, Mom?"

Harmony closed her eyes and swayed with the music. "This lovely piece happens to be Claude Debussy's *Snowflakes Are Dancing*."

"Snowflakes? In August?" he said, wrinkling his freckled nose.

"Hey, smart guy, what better way to beat the heat?"

"You know, you really oughtta get us a CD player, Mom. Then I bet *I'd* even learn to appreciate this classical stuff."

Turning away, Harmony stepped over to the Boston fern and resumed her watering. "Nice try, young man. But as you know, we're on a budget."

"Oh, well. Just thought I'd give it another shot." She watched him head for the front door. "Well, I'm gonna go shoot some hoops in the driveway until Dad comes to pick me up. Do you know where Barkley is?"

Unconsciously, Harmony tried to put her hands on her hips the way she usually did when she scolded him for something—but her hands were full. "Cameron, you're *not* planning to play basketball in your Scout uniform, are you?"

"No, I'm not gonna *play* any basketball, Mom," he answered. "I'm just gonna shoot a few hoops. I have a bunch of stuff on my mind and it helps me think. I promise, I won't mess up my uniform. Now . . . about Barkley?"

No use to argue. Her son's constellation of dimples and periwinkle eyes always turned her into a real sucker. Shaking her head, she said, "In the guest room, sacked out on the bed."

He whistled.

Down the hall, their large German shepherd came out of the nearest bedroom, stretched a big stretch, and then trotted toward them wagging his tail.

"I always shoot better with an audience," Cameron told her, grinning. Then he hurried away, out the door and through the entry courtyard, the dog at his heels.

Watching him go, Harmony smiled to herself and then slowly shook her head. She knew that, even though her plants were essential to the nurturing of her soul, it was that beautiful boy of hers who was her *true* bliss.

Oh, well. Back to the watering, she thought.

Refilling the watering can in the kitchen, Harmony added a few drops of liquid plant food and returned to the living room. Gliding from plant to plant in time to Satie's *Gymnopedie,* she gave the philodendron a drink, the dracaena a drink, the begonia a drink, and the—

"Come check it out, Dad. It's really comin' along. I have it set up over here, in the corner of the courtyard patio."

John had arrived.

And now Cameron wanted to show him the Grand Canyon project he'd been working on.

Considering how well she knew her ex-husband, Harmony decided she'd better witness this. Setting the moisture meter and watering can on the fireplace hearth, she took a seat in her rocking chair and quietly watched through the patio doors as Cameron led his father over to the card table where his papier-mâché model was taking shape.

"See, Dad," she heard him say excitedly through the screen, "I have every rock layer marked. From the Kaibab Limestone at the top here, which is about 250 million years old, all the way down to the Vishnu Group at the bottom. It's the most ancient at 1.7 *billion* years. The whole model represents about one-third of the life of planet Earth. So . . . what do ya think?"

Silence.

Then John Wright shook his head at Cameron. "It's all wrong."

Uh-oh, Harmony thought, grimacing. She feared this would happen.

"What do ya mean, Dad?" Cameron asked timidly.

She watched as John started pulling the little labels off the boy's model. "Well, the main problem with it is the Earth is only five to ten *thousand* years old, Son," he answered. "So, all of these tags here will have to be changed."

"But, Dad, none of the geology books I have say that."

"I don't care what your science books tell you, Cameron. As you know—or *should* know—there's only one truly accurate record of Earth's ancient history and that's the book of Genesis in the Old Testament of the Holy Bible. If you read Genesis, you'll find it was the Great Flood that carved out the Grand Canyon here, and it happened in a matter of weeks or months, not millions of years."

"But, there's no real evidence of a worldwide flood, Dad,"

Cameron said. "And even if there was, there's no way the Grand Canyon could've been formed that fast."

"Look at something like Mount St. Helens, Cameron," his father answered. "That happened very fast."

"Yeah, but Dad, from what I've read, there's no evidence of any volcanic activity *at* the Grand Canyon. And what about the fossil record? And radioactive dating? Scientists say the Earth is at least four *billion* years old.

"And *really,* Dad," Cameron persisted, "the story of Noah's ark? C'mon. Cramming two each of forty *million* species onto *one* wooden boat and then feeding and cleaning up after 'em for a whole year? An aircraft carrier wouldn't have been big enough. And how come the dinosaurs didn't get to go? What's *that* all about?"

"Son," John Wright said, anger creeping into his voice, "just this kind of *nonsense* is exactly the reason you don't have your Eagle badge yet. When are you going to learn, boy?"

Cameron didn't answer. He just shook his head.

"And another thing," his father said, turning back to the model, "the color of your river water is all wrong. The Colorado is muddy brown, not—" He scratched his head. "What color is this, anyway, blue-green?"

"Well, I made some of the rocks brown," Cameron answered, almost too quietly for Harmony to hear. "So, I thought this color would make the water show up better."

"Well, anyway, it's wrong," his father repeated.

Harmony couldn't just sit there and listen any longer. Getting up, she went to the front door and opened it. "Cameron, come in and get your book bag with your Scout things in it, dear. It's almost time to go. You don't want to be late."

"Okay, Mom," he said, shuffling past her into the house. She waited till he was gone to turn to her ex-husband.

"How can you do this, John?" she asked finally, shaking her head. "How can you use his Eagle badge this way? He's been working hard on it for three years. How can you use it to *black-mail* him? He's your *own son*."

"I don't know what you're talking about," the man answered.

"Don't give me that garbage," Harmony told him, frowning. "You're not fooling anyone. I know exactly what you're up to. And what's worse, Cameron knows it, too."

Tossing the handful of model labels back on the card table, he turned to her. "I'm simply trying to give the boy some spiritual direction."

Harmony laughed at him, but she wasn't amused. "Yeah, you're giving him direction, all right. You're pushing him *directly* away from you."

Glancing over, she suddenly noticed Barkley watching them from his favorite shady spot between the courtyard fishpond and the big honey mesquite tree. Silly or not, she no more liked to argue in front of the poor dog than she did in front of her son. So, turning away, she went back into the house.

John followed her, through the living and dining rooms and on into the kitchen. Once there, he asked, "What's wrong with me wanting my son to develop spiritually, Harmony?"

Spinning around, she shook her head at him again. "John, don't you see these tricks you're always pulling have exactly the opposite effect from that? And, anyway, Cameron *is* getting spiritual direction—from me."

"Yeah, with whose help, that so-called church of yours?" He sneered. "C'mon, Harmony. It's a haven for people who can't make up their minds, for wishy-washy, creedless heathens walking the line between confusion and indecision. They pray 'to whom it may concern,' for crying out loud. Hey, down south, they don't burn crosses on *your* church's lawns, they burn question marks."

"Your semi-quick wit doesn't do it for me anymore," Harmony told him. "And that reminds me . . ."

Stepping over to the cork bulletin board hanging above the kitchen desk, she pointed to one of the slips of paper tacked to it.

"These little beauties, John. I'd really appreciate it if you'd stop already with the cute messages on the memo lines of your child support checks. What's this one say? Oh yes, 'for the cross I have to bear.' Last month it said, 'for the stake through my heart.' C'mon, John, give it a rest."

"Dad? Mom?"

Turning, Harmony saw Cameron standing by the pantry. "Yes, dear?"

"I'm ready to go now, Dad. But first, there's something I've been forgetting to give you, Mom. I got it last week. Here." He handed her a folded-up piece of paper. "It's a film permission slip from my science teacher. You remember, the cool teacher I told you about, the man from the hobby shop? Anyway, it's on sexual reproduction. Mr. Edwards says you can come in and preview it if you want."

"Sexual reproduction?" John asked, frowning.

"Oh no, John," Harmony said, shoving the slip in her pocket. "Don't *even* start thinking I'm going to discuss this one with you now."

"But, I have a right—"

"*No, John,*" she said, cutting him off. "Now, both of you, get going. I need some peace and quiet."

"What're you gonna do tonight all by yourself, Mom?" Cameron asked, kissing her good-bye.

"Oh, I rented an old Tracy and Hepburn video this afternoon, Hon," she answered, straightening his neckerchief. "I'll pop some corn later and then I'll cuddle up on the floor with Barkley and we'll watch it together. Don't worry about us, Son. We'll be fine. See you later."

"Bye."

Watching as the boy left the kitchen, she suddenly flinched when John Wright put his hand on her shoulder. Glaring at her with his dark, piercing eyes, he said, "This sex education thing isn't over, Harmony."

"I mean it, John," she told him flatly, pulling away. "Just go, *please*."

Much to her relief, he did. This time.

Finally, Harmony Anderson had the house to herself. Hurrying to finish up the watering chores, she made some microwave popcorn just like she said she would, then headed into the family room to watch her video. Popping it in the VCR, she grabbed the remote and took a seat on the sofa, ready to go.

But before pushing PLAY, she decided to look at the information on the cassette box. WITHOUT LOVE it read, the story of a marriage of convenience that later turns to love between a widow, Hepburn, and a scientist, Tracy, who—

A scientist.

Harmony smiled.

Pulling out Cameron's science film permission slip, she carefully unfolded the creases and held it in her lap. Searching for the line labeled TEACHER NAME, she read what it said.

"Mark . . . Mark Edwards . . . nice name. Tell me, Mark Edwards, is there any chance you like quiet evenings at home, eating popcorn and watching old movies as much as I do?"

Slowly tracing his name with her fingertips, she suddenly wondered what her son might think of her. "Well . . . ," she said out loud. "For the first time in a long, long while, Cameron, Mommy has a secret. And you know what? It feels nice."

Gently placing the form on the coffee table in front of her, she looked up and pressed the remote.

The phone rang.

"Oh, man," she said, quickly pushing PAUSE. "Here we go again."

Stepping into the kitchen, she picked up the receiver. "Yes, hello?"

"Hi. Is this Cameron's mom?" *A girl's voice*.

"Yes, it is," Harmony answered, surprised. "And who is this?"

"I'm Mandy Ross, Ms. Anderson. Is Cameron there?"

"No, I'm sorry, he's at Scouts tonight. Can I take a message?"

"Oh . . . well, it's no biggie. Just tell him I called to remind him about his parental permission slip. He forgot it a few times, so . . ."

Now Harmony was more surprised than ever. "Actually, Mandy," she told the girl, "I was just looking that over this very minute. Isn't that something? But, thank you, anyway. It was very thoughtful of you to call."

"Okay, Ms. Anderson. Nice talking to you. Bye."

"Oh, but wait—"

Too late. She hung up.

Hanging up herself, Harmony returned to the family room sofa and, without further interruption, started her movie, at last. Ironically, the opening credits went by without her even knowing it.

Lost in thought, she stared blankly at the television screen as she nibbled a piece of popcorn. "Mandy Ross, eh?" the woman asked herself. "Why, Cameron, you little rascal."

Then Harmony smiled.

"It seems Mommy isn't the only one around here who has a secret," she said.

Chapter 6

At the rate of five freshman science classes a year during his fifteen-year-long career, Mark Edwards estimated he'd seen the program his students called the "sex video" over seventy-five times by now. And, in all those showings with his ninth graders, not once had he been the least bit aroused by it. Until today.

But today *was* different. This afternoon he had a special visitor to his sixth-hour preparation period. A beautiful visitor. A very sexy visitor. Cameron Wright's mother.

"Thank you very much for coming in, Ms. Anderson," he said when she arrived. "As you might imagine, my principal and I get quite a few concerned phone calls when I show this program, but very few parents actually take the time to come in and preview it. You must care very much for your son."

"I do," she answered simply.

From the very moment she stepped in his room—and not unlike that day in his brother's hobby shop—he found her beauty disarming. So much so that, right from the get-go, he'd been more than a little nervous.

After starting the program for her, he switched the lights off in the room. But then he switched them right back on. "I'm sorry, Ms. Anderson," he said. "When my classes watch science videos, we watch them in the dark, but if you'd be more comfortable with the lights on . . ."

"Don't be silly," she told him. "Off is fine."

She called him silly. Or did she? Maybe that's not what she meant. At that point, he didn't really know. He wasn't thinking straight. Anyway, he ended up turning them back off.

While she watched in the subdued light, he tried to get some papers graded using the lamp at his desk. And for the first part of the period at least, he actually did get a little work done.

Oh, he halfway listened as the film's female narrator explained in a monotone voice about the miracle of life beginning in the shallow primordial seas, the significance of DNA, and the female and the male reproductive systems. But none of that was terribly provocative. After all, he'd heard it over and over again.

He even had the composure to joke with her once, to try and make her feel more comfortable. When the part about testicular sperm storage came up, he remarked, "Hey, 'epididymis.' I tell my students to try and say *that* three times fast."

Then, to his surprise, she did it. And with very little effort, it seemed.

No, it wasn't until the program started talking about the "complex rituals of mating," "attraction and desire," and the "need and drive to reproduce" that things started getting a little dicey for Mark Edwards.

Again, in an effort to lighten things up, he tried to joke about it. When a man and a woman performed ballet as a metaphor for "the dance of courtship which may lead to conception," he told her, "I do make it clear to all my students that there's absolutely no requirement to dance around like that beforehand."

Smiling at him, she replied, "Maybe there *should* be. I have a feeling we'd all be getting into a lot less trouble that way."

For some reason—he didn't know exactly why—he found that particular comment extremely exciting. Consequently, all hope of getting any more of his work done went completely out the window. And as the video's narrator started talking about sexual arousal and listing the erogenous zones, Mark couldn't seem to stop looking at Ms. Anderson.

"The eyes," the narrator said.

He tried to catch a glimpse of *hers*.

"The skin."

He found himself staring at the wisps of hair at the nape of *her* neck, the silkiness of *her* arms, *her* crossed legs . . .

"The penis."

Oh no, Mark thought, I don't *believe* what's happening to me.

He recalled that, earlier, the program mentioned the problem of defective sperm production caused by the testicles being held up too close to the body's heat by tight blue jeans. Well *now*—try as he might to prevent it—he started experiencing a kind of involuntary "tight-jeans" problem of his own.

"Is it getting warm in here?" he asked suddenly, getting up to check the cooler control.

Oblivious to his plight, she answered, "I'm fine."

Then matters grew even worse. On the screen before them, a penis went from flaccid to erect as it became engorged with blood. In thermal camera imagery, of course.

In a futile attempt to get his mind off his predicament, he tried feebly to make yet another joke. "I tell the kids that's what happens when the Predator gets lucky," he said.

"What?"

"The thermal photography. You know, in that Schwarzenegger flick. That alien had heat sensors in its eyes."

She shook her head. Either she didn't have a clue or she was toying with him.

"Oh, well. Not a sci-fi fan, I guess," he answered, standing stiffly, his hands in his front pockets. "Never mind."

Noticing the bemused look on her face, he wondered nervously whether or not she was aware of his dilemma—

His dilemma. It grew worse and worse, moment by moment. *Damn his masculinity!*

And then the video reached its climax. From inside the body, actual film footage showed semen being ejaculated, at last, into the woman's vagina.

Looking amazed, Ms. Anderson asked, "How did they get *that* picture?!"

Mark gulped. The photographic process used in the film was the *last* thing he wanted to think about right now, but in an attempt to further conceal his problem, he answered, "Oh, I don't know. A really tiny cameraman in a wetsuit, maybe. . . . Listen, would you excuse me a moment?"

Making a beeline for the hallway restroom, he frantically splashed cold water on his face. Actually, he could have used an ice-cold shower, but under the circumstances, his face had to do.

Gradually—*thankfully*—the tempest started to subside.

Minutes went by.

Looking up finally, he stared at his dripping face in the mirror as his heart rate returned to normal. "Mark . . . the last time anything like that happened to you, you were in junior high. What's up with you, my friend? What's it mean when watching a science documentary with a woman beats the best sex you've ever had?" He shook his head. "Oh well, whatever it means, you can't just hide out in the washroom all day."

Taking a few deep breaths, he grabbed a paper towel and dried off his face. Then, feeling more or less composed, he headed back to his classroom. Giving Ms. Anderson a quick smile as he walked in, he went straight to his desk and tried to grade some more papers.

On the video, the narrator was describing all of the various perils facing a sperm on its epic journey to fertilize the egg: the odds of being defective, the vagina's dangerous and hostile acid environment, having to swim against the current, being attacked by the woman's defense systems as an invader, the chances of getting lost on the way, or stuck somewhere, or trying to fertilize the wrong cell, etcetera, etcetera, etcetera . . .

Yeah, yeah, Mark mused, glancing at the TV screen. So, it's tough to be a sperm. Being a single, *almost* middle-aged, horned-up male high school teacher at the turn of the new millennium is no picnic, either.

The program droned on. Through conception . . . fetal development . . . labor . . . and, finally, the birth.

The end, *thank God.*

Getting up, he crossed to the wall switch and turned on the lights.

"Well, that was an amazing film," Ms. Anderson said, standing up and smoothing her skirt. "I can't imagine anyone seeing it and not gaining a deeper appreciation for the miracle of life. Would you like me to give you Cameron's permission slip today?"

"Sure. If you'd like to," he said.

Taking it from her purse, she signed it and handed it to him. Then she asked, "How much time is left in the period, Mr. Edwards? I told Cameron I'd meet him here."

Putting the form on his desk, Mark glanced at the clock. "The bell's going to ring in about two minutes," he said.

Then it hit him. Soon she'd be gone. And even though he felt relieved that the film had ended, he didn't want her to go.

Gazing intensely at the woman, he tried to drink in as much of her as he could in the precious moments that remained. Her auburn hair . . . her large, hazel-green eyes . . . her plump lips—

The lower lip trembled. Or, did it?

One thing was certain. She was looking at him just as intensely as he was looking at her.

How easy it would be to reach out and—

The bell signaling the end of the school day sounded across the campus, breaking the spell. And seconds after that, Cameron knocked at the door.

"Hi, Mr. Edwards," the boy said, stepping into the room. "Hi, Mom."

"Hi, Cameron," she replied with equanimity, as if she and Mark had been having an ordinary parent-teacher conference. "Are you ready to go?"

He nodded at her. Then, turning to Mark, he asked, "Did you tell her, Mr. Edwards? Did you tell her about my model?"

Mark palmed his forehead. "Oh . . . no. I'm sorry, Cameron. I forgot. But, I'll tell her now." Turning to her, he said, "I asked Cameron to bring in his geologic column cross section and display it here in the classroom. I hope you don't mind."

She eyed her son. "Did you tell Mr. Edwards how enormous it is?"

"Yeah."

"Well, okay," she said, looking back at Mark, "it's certainly all right with me." Then she laughed. "Of course, we'll never be able to get it in my little VW."

"No problem," he told her. "I have a pickup, and I'd be more than happy to—"

"Mr. Edwards?"

Recognizing the principal's voice, Mark glanced at the intercom. "Yes, Mr. Caruthers."

"Can I see you in my office, please?"

"I'll be right there, sir."

When he turned back to Ms. Anderson, she flashed him a fetching smile and held out her hand. "Well, we don't want to keep you, Mr. Edwards. I'm sure you and Cameron can work out the details of getting his model to school sometime soon. Thank you so much for letting me come in."

Relishing the feel of her skin as they pressed their palms together, he smiled in return. "Believe me, it was my pleasure."

"Later, Mr. Edwards," Cameron said, waving.

"Yeah. See you, tomorrow. Good-bye, Ms. Anderson."

"Bye, now," she answered, beginning to leave.

But at the last moment, Mark saw her turn to glance back at him, and he held her gaze for one more exhilarating instant before she continued out the door. Then his heart sank again as he watched her and her son disappear into the departing sea of high schoolers.

Slowly he shook his head. Even though the woman's visit had been an emotional roller-coaster ride for him, he did have one consolation. The image of that fetching smile of hers was now permanently etched in his mind. And, that's just exactly what he concentrated on as he hurriedly buttoned up his classroom, grabbed his briefcase, and headed out into the after-school pandemonium on his way to the school office.

"How do all these students have the energy for so much craziness at the end of the day when I have so little?" he heard a voice call suddenly.

Startled from his reverie, Mark turned to see a young, heavyset woman coming down the sidewalk behind him. Heavyset, yes, but not unattractive. And although he tried not to stare, he couldn't help but notice her enormous bosom and the little silver cross resting in the cleft.

"You're one of our new teachers, aren't you?" he asked, waiting for her to catch up. "I'm sorry. I don't remember your name."

"Mary Shepherd, sophomore social studies," she answered, joining him. "And, yes, this is my first year."

"Well, no wonder you're out of energy," he said as they continued to the office together. "Even when it goes well, the first year is always tough. I'm Mark, by the way. Mark Edwards. I teach freshman science."

She frowned. "Science, huh. Not one of my interests I'm afraid."

Opening the faculty-lounge door for her, Mark gestured at

the campus. "Well, you did mention the students' crazy behavior and, you know, science just might have an explanation for it. After all, our DNA *is* 99 percent identical to that of a chimp." He winked.

Instead of the customary chuckle he expected, the woman turned on him. "Maybe *your* DNA, but not mine," she answered, scowling. "And if those are the sort of 'facts' science is teaching our children today, no wonder there's a lack of discipline." Abruptly, she stomped off.

"Ohh-kay," Mark said, staring after her.

Still shaking his head in bewilderment, he passed through the lounge, into the school office, and over to the open door marked CLAUDE CARUTHERS: PRINCIPAL. Knocking, he stuck his head in.

"Come on in, Mark," Caruthers told him, looking up from his computer screen. "Shut the door and have a seat."

Bald and overweight, the most prominent thing about Claude Caruthers's pockmarked appearance was his thick graying moustache and, almost as soon as Mark sat down, he noticed flecks of something white clinging to its corners. Powdered sugar, he guessed, judging from the donut box on top of the file cabinet.

Leaning back in his chair, Caruthers started the conversation the way he almost always did. "Had a couple of calls from parents, Mark."

Yeah, go on.

"One was from a Mrs. Brown. Says her daughter's name is Karrie, or Kathy, or . . ."

"Kelly?"

"Yes, that's right, Kelly," Caruthers said. "Anyway, she doesn't want Kelly seeing that live-birth video of yours."

Mark frowned. "Well, that is the idea behind the permission slip concept, isn't it, Claude? I mean, if Mrs. Brown had called *me* before calling you, I could have explained it to her and saved you the trouble."

"I know, Mark," Caruthers said, scratching at his potbelly.

"But, you know how some of these parents can be. Anyway, she wanted you to get the message from me and now you have."

"Actually, Claude," Mark said, seeing an opportunity, "I've been wanting to talk to you about Miss Brown anyway. She wore something to school the other day that I considered inappropriate and I thought I should probably run it by you."

"What did she wear?"

"Well, we started the year in my class the way we always do, studying the various theories of how the universe began, and she wore a religious T-shirt that, in my opinion at least, undermined my curriculum."

"What was on it?"

"Well, it said something like, 'I believe in the Big Bang theory . . . God spoke and *Bang!* it was.'"

For a few moments Caruthers just sat there, rocking in his seat. Then he straightened up. "You know, Mark, in all honesty—"

Instantly, Mark's built-in BS-o-meter sounded its alarm. At Mesquite High, everyone knew when Caruthers said, "in all honesty," it usually meant exactly the opposite.

"—I'm personally inclined to agree with you on this," Caruthers continued. "But the law, I'm afraid, says differently. In relation to student garb, students may display religious messages on items of clothing to the same extent that they are permitted to display other comparable messages—*unless* they are blatantly disruptive to classroom instruction. Did she disrupt classroom instruction, Mark?"

"Well . . . no, not really," Mark answered.

"Then, there you are," the principal said, turning back to his computer screen.

Taking his cue, Mark shrugged and stood up. "All right, then. Thanks, Claude."

But Caruthers wasn't finished. As Mark pulled open the door, the principal said, "You know, the way the climate is in the country today, Mark, I wouldn't be surprised if things like school prayer weren't right around the corner. You'd probably be a whole lot better off if, instead of fighting it, you started getting used to the idea."

"Oh, no, Claude," he answered, shaking his head. "That's where I draw the line. The First Amendment to the Constitution guarantees the separation of church and state and it does so for good reasons. No, the day I'm told I have to pray anywhere, but *especially* in school, is the day I throw in the towel. I'll quit first."

Caruthers scoffed at him. "C'mon, Mark, you don't mean that. If I give you a directive, you'll follow it. You always have before, and you always will. After all, you're a team player, one of my best, and you'd never let anything as petty as a personal conviction stand in the way of that. That's not who Mark Edwards is."

Thinking about it, Mark frowned.

"Now, close the door on your way out, please," Caruthers told him. "I'm never going to get all this work done if I have any more interruptions."

"Okay. See you tomorrow," Mark answered, starting to oblige him. But then he pushed the door open again. "Wait a minute, Claude. Didn't you say you had a 'couple' of parent calls? Who was the other one from?"

"Oh. That's right. Sorry," Caruthers replied without looking up. "John Wright was the guy's name. Said his son's name was Cameron. He doesn't want his kid seeing the movie either."

Mark grimaced. "But I just met with Cameron's mother. She already signed the permission slip."

"I don't know what to tell you, Mark," Caruthers said, sighing in annoyance. "You know how these divorce things go. Now, have a good evening."

Shaking his head, Mark shrugged and pulled the door closed behind him, all the way this time. Then he waved good-bye to the office secretaries and headed out into the school parking lot, anxious to leave for home.

And that's when two thoughts struck him:

First, the nagging possibility that Claude Caruthers might just be right about Mark Edwards, "team player."

And second, *that name*.

For some reason—and not merely because he was Cameron's father—"John Wright" sounded awfully familiar to Mark.

But, at that moment, he couldn't remember why.

Part 3
September

Chapter 7

"Oh, Ms. Anderson! *Hola*! I didn't know you worked at G. B. Shaw's."

Looking up from her shaded garden workbench and the fourteen-inch flower bowl she just finished arranging, Harmony waved at the squat Mexican woman who had called to her from outside the fence. "Well, hello, Mrs. Morales. It's so nice to see you," Harmony called back. "Please, come in. Come talk to me."

"I was just on my way to the market when I saw you, Ms. Anderson," Mrs. Morales explained, stepping through the yard gate on her way to the bench. "How long have you been working here?"

Harmony leaned close as soon as the woman reached her. "Well, don't tell anybody, Mrs. Morales, but actually I own the place."

"The whole nursery?!" Mrs. Morales said gleefully. "I don't believe it. That's so nice. Cameron's *mamá* owns a nursery. No wonder that *muchacho* knows so much about landscaping."

"How are you enjoying the tile roof he put on for you, Mrs. Morales?" Harmony asked.

The woman clapped her hands together. "Oh, we love it! And you know what? Even with all these summer rains we've been having, *it doesn't leak*! Oh, you have such a good *hijo* there, Ms. Anderson. Tell me, when will his Eagle Court of Honor be? My family is so anxious to come."

Glancing down at the flower bowl, Harmony frowned. "Soon, we hope."

When Mrs. Morales didn't respond right away, Harmony looked back up at her. To her surprise, a single tear was slowly making its way down the woman's dark cheek. "Why . . . Mrs. Morales. What's wrong?"

Shaking her head, the woman smiled and wiped it away. "Oh, I'm just being silly, Ms. Anderson. But every time I think about Cameron, I just want to cry. He did such a special thing for my children and me. He's an *ángel*, Ms. Anderson. Just an *ángel*."

Harmony smiled. "Well, Mrs. Morales, I guess you aren't aware of our shoppers' rules here at G. B. Shaw's plant nursery. There's no crying allowed here, of course. And, I'm afraid, anyone who's caught doing it is obligated to receive one complimentary flower bowl. Here, take this one. I just finished it." She nudged it across the bench to the woman.

"Oh, no, Ms. Anderson, I couldn't," Mrs. Morales said, gasping. "But *muchas gracias*, anyway."

"Please," Harmony insisted. "I've been wanting to give you a house-warming gift and now seems like the perfect time. Really. Take it."

Mrs. Morales gazed at the flowers and Harmony could tell she was thinking it over. Glancing back at her finally, the woman said, "Oh, they're so lovely. What kinds are in here?"

"Well, we have quite a variety," Harmony said, pointing them out. "There are marigolds here, petunias there, some snapdragons over here, and some sweet alyssum down there, some false heather, and purple robe. . . . Just lots of good stuff."

"Well . . . okay," Mrs. Morales said. "If you're sure."

"I am," Harmony said, nodding.

"Oh, but wait," Mrs. Morales exclaimed, her eyes growing wide. "I'm walking. On my way to the market. I can't carry this."

"No problem at all, Mrs. Morales," Harmony assured her. "We'll deliver it. Are you going to be home this afternoon?"

"*Sí.*"

"Then it's settled. Now, you go and have yourself a nice time shopping at the market."

"Okay. . . . *Un millón de gracias*, Ms. Anderson," Mrs. Morales answered, taking one last look at her new flower bowl. "Oh, it's so lovely . . ." Then she turned away. "Say *hola* to Cameron for me, *por favor. Adiós*."

Waving, Harmony watched her go. "*Adiós*, Mrs. Morales," she called after her. "Please, come back and see us, now . . ."

"You know, you're never going to get rich *that* way," a voice behind her said suddenly.

Startled, Harmony spun around. Then she laughed. "Oh, Dr. Paul, you scared me," she said, clutching at her chest. "How long have you been hiding back there?"

"Long enough to see that nice thing you did," the man answered. "And I wasn't exactly hiding. I wanted to check the price on that beautiful park bench you have. I thought it might go nicely on the church grounds, over under our big paloverde shade tree."

"Well, that's okay then," Harmony said, grinning warily. "Just as long as *you* don't start crying on me, too. I'll go broke if I have to start giving my park benches away."

They both laughed.

Then, Harmony noticed the name tag on the man's western-style shirt. DR. PAUL DREYFUSS-CAMPBELL it read. Pointing at it, she asked, "What's that for?"

"Oh . . . ," he answered, chuckling in embarrassment. "I just gave a talk on Humanism over at the public library. I guess I don't need this anymore, do I?" Peeling off the sticker, he crumpled it up and put it in his pocket.

For the first time that morning, Harmony took a good, long look at Dr. Paul. At his curly gray hair, and his close-cropped beard, and his striking blue eyes. Then she smiled to herself. If he'd been single, and just a little bit younger, she'd have gone after him a long time ago.

"So, Harmony," Dr. Paul said, looking serious, "just what *is* the story on Cameron's Eagle Court of Honor anyway?" Evidently he'd heard *that* part of the conversation, too.

Harmony bit her lip while she considered whether or not she should say anything. Finally, she let out a sigh and shook her head in resignation. "Well, Dr. Paul . . . there may not be one."

"Why not?" the minister asked, frowning.

"Because he failed the board of review he had two months ago, that's why not," Harmony answered, reaching for another fourteen-inch plastic bowl. Filling it with potting soil, she added, "And get this. . . . It's *because* he told them he didn't believe in God."

Dr. Paul's jaw muscles flexed. "I'm sorry to hear that, Harmony," he said. "But, you know, considering what Cameron's been going through lately, and *other* things, I was afraid something like this could happen."

"*What* 'other' things?" Harmony asked.

Now it was Dr. Paul who seemed unsure as to whether he should say anything or not. Reaching over, at last, he took her gloved hand. "Well, forgive me if I'm being presumptuous, Harmony, but . . . did John have anything to do with this situation?"

Harmony's mouth fell open. "How did you know that?"

"Come on, Harmony," Dr. Paul answered, looking knowingly at her. "It's hardly a difficult conclusion to draw."

"I guess," she said, frowning. "Even though it did shock *me*, at first."

"And unfortunately," Dr. Paul went on, "John and the Scouts do have a few recent court rulings in their favor. The case of the Randall twins in '91 and the Welsh case in '93 were very similar to the problem Cameron's facing now. The Scouts won both, I'm afraid."

Harmony nodded thoughtfully. "Yes, that's what Mr. Smith, Cameron's Scoutmaster, told me, too." Then, she cocked her head. "Dr. Paul, it sounds like you've already been doing a little research on this behind my back."

The minister didn't answer but the coy smile on his face told Harmony she was right. Grabbing a six-pack of vincas, she started transplanting them in the bowl. "Well, one way or the other, I hope my little darling figures out where his head's at, and soon."

The smile on Dr. Paul's face left as quickly as it had come. "If I may, Harmony, a word or two of Chinese wisdom: 'He who thinks he knows, doesn't know. He who knows that he doesn't know, knows.'" Smiling again, he added, "And remember, it's like I'm always saying on Sunday. It's not the destination that counts, it's the journey."

"I know, Dr. Paul," Harmony said, shaking her head. "But it just seems that if Cameron doesn't get his Eagle award, the last three years will have been a big waste."

"I think that lovely Hispanic lady who was here before might just disagree with you on that, Harmony, you know why?" Dr. Paul asked. "Because I think she knows what I also know. She knows that celebrities live for self, and heroes live for others. And, since we *are* speaking about Cameron . . . well, let's just say that I suspect you have yourself a little hero there."

"Thank you for saying so, Dr. Paul."

"You know, I'd be more than willing to talk to him, anytime," Dr. Paul offered. "If you think it would be helpful, that is."

"Oh, he knows that, Dr. Paul," Harmony answered. "And I'm sure at some point he probably will come to see you. When he's ready."

"Okay," the minister said, nodding. Then he looked at his watch. "Well, Harmony, it looks like I'll have to get back to you about that park bench there. I'm running late *again*. But before I go, there's something I just have to ask you. You have a . . . *look* about you today. Is there anything *else* you want to tell me?"

She felt herself blush. Sometimes her minister's perceptiveness seemed downright uncanny. "Well, actually . . . ," she answered, plucking a vinca blossom and twirling it between her fingers, ". . . I met someone."

"I knew it," Dr. Paul said, grinning. "Anybody I know?"

Harmony shook her head. "Probably not. *And* it's really too soon for me to be talking about it. I mean, we haven't even seen each other socially, or anything. It's just that . . . he's always on my mind lately. In fact, today, before you and Mrs. Morales got here, I daydreamed about him all morning. I can't tell you the last time I felt this way."

"Well, I'm really very happy for you, Harmony," Dr. Paul said, taking her hand again. "And I'll be keeping my fingers crossed for you. Now," he checked his watch a second time, "I really have to go."

Harmony watched as Dr. Paul exited the nursery through the yard gate. Then, to her surprise, he came back and put his face between the wrought-iron fence bars. "Don't worry, Harmony," he called. "I have a feeling this one's going to work out for you. You're gorgeous, you're brilliant, and you're loving. Why, if I wasn't happily married already, and you were just a little bit older . . ."

Harmony blushed again as she waved good-bye to Dr. Paul.

Now, if only Mark Edwards felt the same way.

Chapter 8

The stucco home, complete with bell tower, looked like a Spanish mission church nestled at the base of the mountain foothill at the end of the gravel road. And as Mark Edwards pulled up in his '64 Chevy pickup, ejected the Sting CD he'd been listening to, and glanced around at the tall grass, oak trees, and century plants surrounding it, only one word came to mind.

Peaceful.

Then he remembered who lived here and started getting nervous again.

Closing the truck door, he took a deep breath of high desert air in an attempt to steady himself before starting up the brick sidewalk to the entry arch where two heavy wooden doors stood open. And that's when he first heard the singing.

Chant and polyphony. In women's voices only. Simple . . . lovely . . . exquisite . . . and positively medieval. Like angels.

It beckoned him. From the courtyard, beyond the archway. So, without thinking about it, he walked up and stepped through . . .

And saw her.

For a moment, he thought his heart might stop. Bathed in a halo of heavenly light that streamed through the branches above her, she was the most serenely beautiful thing Mark Edwards had ever seen in his life.

But . . .

. . . she was also standing knee-deep in a fishpond, with handfuls of what appeared to be slimy green algae draped from her fists. Smudges of something brown splotched her cheeks and chin and, noticing the thin tank top she had on, it was immediately obvious to him she wasn't wearing a bra.

No, something was definitely fishy here—besides the pond, that is. Apparently—despite Cameron's assurances to the contrary—she wasn't expecting his visit. He knew it. He should have called first. But, oh well. It was a little late to worry about that, now.

"Uh . . . Ms. Anderson," he said, trying not to startle her.

From her present position in the pond—bent all the way over with her perfectly proportioned derriere pointing directly at him—and from the horrified expression on her face as she looked back between her legs, he knew he was right. He was the last thing she expected to see right then.

"*Mr. Edwards?!*"

Quickly, she straightened and turned toward him. Flinging the globs of oozy green scum off her fingers into a plastic bucket beside the pond, she stepped barefooted out of the water onto the flagstone patio.

The scene practically mesmerized him. And, between the brightly colored goldfish and lush vegetation, the beautiful music and celestial light, the woman's thin tank top and her oh-so-short shorts, and the glistening water droplets on her silky, shapely legs, Mark Edwards was shocked and embarrassed to find his body responding to her at yet another inappropriate time.

"As you must have already guessed," she said, breaking his reverie, "I had no idea you were coming."

Thrusting his hands deep in his pockets and bouncing on his toes, he asked, "Cameron didn't tell you?"

"No, he didn't. But that's all right. I'll kill him later."

Mark glanced around awkwardly. "So . . . what are you doing anyway?" Instantly, he knew it was a lame question. It was obvious she was cleaning her pond. But under the circumstances, he couldn't think of anything else to say.

She smiled flirtatiously at him. "Well, actually . . . I was praying," she said.

What? Mark thought. Praying? While scraping pond scum? Just what was he getting himself into here? Could it be this unbelievably luminous woman was some kind of crazy religious kook? Well, that would be just his luck, now, wouldn't it?

There was some good news. He wasn't aroused anymore. But on the other hand, he had absolutely no idea how to respond to her "praying" remark.

Luckily, he didn't have to. At that very moment, Cameron showed up in the archway with a large German shepherd at his heels. "Hey, whose cool old truck is that parked—"

As soon as the boy got a good look at his science teacher standing next to his scantily clad mother, his expression showed he knew he'd made a big mistake. "Uh, Mom . . . ," he said sheepishly, glancing at Mark. "Mr. Edwards is coming after my model today."

Ms. Anderson put her hands on her hips. "Oh . . . well, how nice. Thank you for letting me know, dear." Then, she shot the boy a look. "You and I will discuss this later, Son. For now, help Mr. Edwards load your project in the back of his truck, please. I have to go put some clothes on."

Watching her disappear through one of the sliding glass doors that opened onto the courtyard patio, Mark and Cameron exchanged knowing glances. "Hey, who's your buddy there?" Mark then asked, kneeling down to scratch the German shepherd behind its ears.

"This is Barkley, Mr. Edwards," Cameron answered. "He must like you. Usually he barks like crazy at people he doesn't know."

"Yes . . . good boy. . . . What a good boy," Mark said, giving the dog a final scratch. Then he stood back up. "Okay, so, where's this rock-layer replica of yours?"

"It's right back here," Cameron answered, leading the way to the card table in the corner of the covered patio. "Let me know if I need to change anything."

"Oh, Cameron. . . . This is great," Mark said with admiration, bending down to take a closer look. "This'll be *the* perfect visual aide when we study about geologic history, and evolution, and paleontology later in the school year. Why, I think it's every bit as good as those models they have in the museums up at the canyon itself."

"Really? I wouldn't know. I've never been to the Grand Canyon."

"You're kidding," Mark said, frowning. "Well, you have to go. It's the most awesome place in the world."

Tentatively, Cameron asked, "So, Mr. Edwards . . . is the information on all my little labels there *correct*?"

Studying them a moment, Mark shrugged. "Everything looks good to me, Cameron. Why?"

"Oh, well . . . it's just that . . . my dad said I made some mistakes on the ages of some of the rocks, that's all. But he's not a scientist, so . . ."

"Hey . . . ," Mark said, pointing to the papier-mâché river in the center of the model. "That blue-green paint you picked out for the Colorado really works. It's a nice contrast from the tans and reds and browns you used for the rocks. Really sets it off."

"Thanks," Cameron said.

Straightening up finally, Mark glanced at his watch. "Oh well, Cameron, I have my karate club tonight so I guess we'd better get this puppy loaded. Why don't you take that side there, and I'll take this one."

"Okay."

Lifting the project up by its plywood base, he and Cameron carefully carried it to his pickup and then slid it into the bed. As Mark closed the tailgate, Cameron stepped back to admire the truck.

"I like your Chevy," the boy told him as Mark took out his keys and circled around to the driver's-side door. "It's really beautiful."

"My dad bought her when I was six years old," Mark answered, smiling. "I even learned to drive behind that very wheel. When I got out of college, I bought her from him, and I've tried to keep her looking good as new ever since."

Cameron nodded. "Well, you've done a good job."

"I'll just bet, if that old truck there could talk, she'd have some fascinating stories to tell about *you*, Mr. Edwards . . ."

Turning to see the boy's mother standing in the archway, it was immediately obvious to Mark that she'd quickly gussied herself up. And although the denim dress she now wore was far less revealing than her tank top and shorts, she still looked unbelievably sexy to him. Plus, there was no doubt in his mind that that last comment had been a blatant flirtation.

"You're not leaving, are you?" she asked, staring provocatively at him.

"Well," he answered, "as I was just telling Cameron a little while ago, I do have this karate thing to go to—"

"We'd really like you to stay for dinner," Ms. Anderson said, cutting him off.

Stepping out halfway between the arch and his truck—so he could get a better look no doubt—she stopped and waited for him to answer. And *she looked good*.

"Okay," he said, slipping his keys back in his pocket. "But, I'll need to use your phone. I should give my brother a call."

That fetching smile of hers lit up her whole face. "Cameron, show Mr. Edwards your room, Hon. He can use the phone in there. Then, show him where the bathroom is. It's time for you two to get washed up for dinner. I hope you like spaghetti, Mr. Edwards."

"Love it," Mark answered, smiling back at her.

"Come on," Cameron said.

Leading Mark into the house, Cameron pointed out the guest bathroom, then continued down the hall to his bedroom. Decorated in a basketball motif, the room's focal point was a large poster over the bed depicting GODZILLA VS CHARLES BARKLEY.

Crossing to the desk, Cameron said, "Here's the phone, Mr. Edwards." Then he headed back out again. "Well, I'm gonna go get ready for supper now. See you in the dining room."

"Thanks, Cameron," Mark answered, watching him go.

Picking up the receiver and dialing the phone, he waited for it to ring.

"Hello?" his brother's voice answered.

"Hey, Justin."

"Hey, Bro."

"Listen, Justin, sorry to do this to you on such short notice but I'm not gonna be able to make it tonight."

"What?"

"Sorry."

"You're gonna leave me high and dry with all those karate assholes?"

"You can handle it, Justin."

"So . . . what's up, Mark? Why can't you go?"

"You're not gonna believe this, Justin. Do you remember that stunning redhead who came into your shop that day? You know, the day I bought the starship model?"

"You mean, the stunning redhead who made *fun of you* for buying the starship model?"

"Yeah, Justin. That's the one."

"Of course, I remember her. What am I, comatose?"

"Well . . . I'm having dinner with her tonight."

Silence.

"Justin? Hello, Justin?"

"Mark, you lucky sonovabitch. How in the hell did you finagle *that*?"

"Her son's in my science class. I didn't tell you before because I wasn't sure she was interested. But now, well, I'm pretty sure she is."

"You lucky sonovabitch . . . ," Justin repeated.

"Yeah? Well, she did make one weird comment about 'praying' that has me kind of con—"

"You lucky sonova-*bitch* . . . ," Justin said for the third time.

"Ohh-kay," Mark said. "Well listen, Justin, gotta go. Dinner's almost ready. Talk to you later."

"You lucky *sonovabitch* . . . ," Justin said yet again.

"Justin, gotta go . . ."

"You *lucky sonova*—"

Mark hung up the phone. "Poor guy must be in shock, or something," he said to himself, shaking his head. Then he shrugged and went to dinner.

Ms. Anderson served them salad, garlic toast, spaghetti, and red wine, and Mark thoroughly enjoyed every bite. Stuffed at last, he glanced first at Cameron, then at the boy's mother. Wiping his mouth with his napkin, he grinned. "Wow, that was one delicious meal, Ms. Anderson."

"Thank you," she said.

"I'm curious," he asked her, taking a sip from his wine glass, "what is this music we're listening to? It's so . . . ethereal."

Putting her fork down, she rested her chin on her hands. "Do you like it?"

"Very much."

"The singer's name is Enya," she answered. "And the album is called *The Memory of Trees*."

"Well, it's entrancing."

"My mom likes classical," Cameron said, rolling his eyes.

"*And* jazz, *and* New Age, *and* movie soundtracks," Ms. Anderson said, shooting the boy a look. "I've even been known to listen to Gregorian chant on occasion."

"Is that what I heard playing in the courtyard when I first got here this afternoon?" Mark asked.

"Similar," she answered. "Actually, that was English Lady-mass, from the thirteenth and fourteenth centuries. By a vocal quartet called Anonymous 4."

"Well, I liked *it*, too," he told her.

Twirling spaghetti onto her fork, she asked, "Are you a music lover, Mr. Edwards?"

"Oh, you bet. But, I must admit, I'm more of a rock fan myself."

"Yes!" Cameron exclaimed.

Glancing briefly at her son, Ms. Anderson turned back to Mark. "Well, whatever name you call it doesn't really matter to me. It's how the music makes me feel that's important."

"And how's that?" Mark asked.

Her sea-foam eyes looked deeply at him. "I like to listen to music so beautiful that it makes me want to cry," she said. "Tell me, Mr. Edwards, haven't you ever cried from just listening to music?"

Her gaze was so intense that, for a moment, Mark almost forgot to answer. Finally he said, "I'm not sure."

Looking a bit disappointed at his reply, she sighed and inspected their plates. "Well . . . it looks like everyone's finished with dinner. Why don't we step out onto the back patio and watch the sun go down? Mr. Edwards, would you like a little more wine?"

"Please."

Pouring some for the both of them, she got up from the dining table and slid open the glass patio door. Following her out, they all took seats on the terrace's chaise longues just as the sun was touching the mountain horizon.

"Nothing like a good old Arizona sunset," Mark said, sipping his wine.

Quiet minutes passed as they watched the fiery orb disappear completely. Above them, the stars slowly brightened, shimmering through the growing lavender twilight. Nighthawks and bats, shooting stars and satellites put on a show for them as the night grew absolute.

Finally, as they were gazing up at the starry desert sky, Cameron's voice intruded on the stillness. "Mr. Edwards," he asked, "what did you mean exactly that time in class when you said we were 'born of the stars'?"

Mark smiled to himself. As a teacher, it always felt good finding out that sometimes students did listen in school after all. Considering the question a moment, he turned to the boy. "Well, you see, Cameron," he began, "all the heavy elements in the universe—the ones important for building things like planets, and lifeforms like us—well, they were made in the centers of stars, as a by-product of nuclear fusion."

Pointing up at the luminous band stretching through the darkness above, he continued. "Just think of it, Cameron. The very atoms in your body could have been made by the explosion of a star halfway across the Milky Way Galaxy there. It boggles the mind."

"Cool," the boy said. Then he scoffed. "Sure makes a lot more sense to me than some old man up there in a long white robe with a beard."

"Come on, Cameron, there's no need to be sacrilegious," Ms. Anderson said, scolding him gently. "Besides, I don't really think most people see God that way, anyway. We should probably change the subject, dear."

Turning to Mark, she said, "So, Mr. Edwards, Cameron tells me you're very interested in space exploration and that you're even a *Star Trek* fan. Would that make you a Trekkie, then?"

Even though Mark couldn't see her face very well, he could imagine her expression. After all, he'd been asked that question many times before. "Actually, these days they like to be called

Trek-*kers*," he answered. "And, I don't really consider myself one. I do think *Star Trek* is good—as far as TV shows go, I mean—because it does offer kids a lot of positive role models.

"And as far as space exploration goes, I think since we are, in essence, starstuff pondering the stars, returning to the cradle of our existence is only natural. So in that way—just like all other sciences— the exploration of the universe is a voyage of self-discovery."

"But don't you think all the truly important answers could be found right here . . . in *us*?" Ms. Anderson asked, putting her hand to her breast.

Mark nodded at her. "I agree that looking 'in,' as you put it, is important. But so is looking *out*. In fact, I think science, in its search for knowledge, should continue to look in *all* directions. The important thing for us as a species is that we continue to move beyond the ordinary, out of the known into the unknown, stop thinking one way and start thinking a different way. . . . You see?"

"Makes sense to me, Mom," Cameron said.

"Oh, it does, does it?" From the tone of the woman's voice, Mark could tell she'd said it with a twinkle in her eye.

"Mom?"

"Yes, Cameron."

"Uh . . . I need to go use the phone. Is it okay if I go do it now?"

"Sure, Hon," Ms. Anderson replied. "But don't stay on too long."

"Thanks, Mom," he said excitedly, bouncing up from the chaise longue. "Night, Mr. Edwards. See you tomorrow."

"Okay, Cameron," Mark answered, sitting up. Turning toward Ms. Anderson, he put his feet on the patio and waved at the boy. "See you in class in the morning. Good night."

As soon as Cameron had disappeared through the sliding door behind them, his mother leaned close and put her hand on

Mark's knee. In a hushed voice, she said, "I think he's going to call his new girlfriend—his *first* girlfriend—but he's been very tightlipped about her, so I'm not sure. Her name's Mandy Ross, I think. Do you have her in one of your classes by any chance?"

"Oh, yes," Mark answered, nodding. "In Cameron's class, as a matter of fact. Yeah, I thought there might be something going on there. He's got good taste, that's for sure. Mandy's really lovely. And *smart*. Maybe the smartest student I have this year—except for Cameron, of course."

"Nice save, Mr. Edwards," she said. To his delight, her hand was still on his knee. And now she was patting him.

"She can be a bit too precocious at times," Mark went on. "And I've seen some of the kids react negatively to that. But not Cameron. No, he saw past that right away. You should give your son a lot of credit, Ms. Anderson. They make a really cute couple."

"Well, I am excited for him, of course," she said. "But there is one thing I don't like about it. He seems to have her on his mind *all of the time*. And he's been very scatterbrained lately. I think that's why he forgot to tell me you were coming today."

Mark decided to be bold. After all, *she* was the one with her hand on his knee. "Well, Ms. Anderson," he said, "something tells me you know just exactly how your son must be feeling. You know as well as anyone, when you first find a new love it's very hard to think about anything else. I know for me, personally . . . it's almost impossible sometimes."

She didn't answer. She just looked at him. He wished he could see the details of her face, to get a read on how she must be feeling at this moment, but it was too dark. If he'd had just a little more courage, he would have kissed her anyway.

But, he didn't. With a final squeeze, she took her hand away.

Well, he had his chance and blew it. Sensing it was time to go, he stood up. "Well, it is a school night, Ms. Anderson. I guess I better hit the road. There is one more thing I've been putting off telling you, though, and I should probably tell you now."

"What's that?" she asked, allowing him to help her off the chaise.

"Well . . . ," Mark said hesitantly, "Cameron's father called my principal the other day and told him he didn't want Cameron seeing that reproduction film you previewed. And since you already signed the permission slip, I'm not really sure how to handle it."

"Well, I'm sorry to say I'm not surprised, Mr. Edwards," she said. Then she cocked her head. "When were you planning to show the video anyway?"

"Not until fourth quarter."

She put her hands on her hips. "Well, we have plenty of time then. Let me talk to John. I'll try to straighten it out."

"Speaking of your ex-husband, his name sounds awfully familiar to me," Mark said. "Where do you suppose I've heard it before?"

"Oh, let's see," Ms. Anderson replied, crossing her arms. "He's a realtor . . ."

"No, that's not it," Mark said, shaking his head.

"He's an elder at one of the Lutheran churches in town, and he's on a Scout troop committee . . ."

"No."

She sighed. "Well, then I don't. . . . Wait. Oh, yes. He's also a Christian Coalition member in—"

"That's it. That's it," Mark repeated, nodding. "He's the guy who organized those protests down at the Planned Parenthood office by my brother's shop. *Oh* . . . Justin doesn't like him *at all*."

"He's not the only one," Ms. Anderson said. "But that's much too long a story to get into tonight. Come on, Mr. Edwards. Let me walk you out to that cool old truck of yours."

"You don't have to do that," Mark said, trying to be polite.

Taking his arm, she looked up at him. "*Yes*, I do."

Circling around to the front yard with her at his side, Mark gasped when he saw the lights of the cityscape shimmering in the valley below. "Boy, I don't believe the view you have up here," he said. "It's not often Mesquite, Arizona, looks so good."

"Actually," she answered, "if you were to come up here regularly, you could see this pretty much any night." Then she laughed. "Oh, you know what I mean. It's just like John always used to say. 'Location! Location! Location!'"

"Well," Mark said, as they strolled to his truck, "you'd be hard pressed to beat this location anywhere. I mean, with the Milky Way stretching above us and those city lights spread out below, it almost feels like we're floating here, doesn't it? Right in the middle of a whole sea of stars." Turning away, he started to reach for his door handle.

Taking his arm firmly again, she stopped him. And as he turned back to her, she said, "I hope what I'm about to do doesn't scare you off, Mr. Edwards. But you see, the thing is, I just can't stand waiting any longer."

And that's when she kissed him, her lips unexpectedly soft against his own.

And it wasn't just a peck. It was a real kiss.

Her mouth was open, so he opened his.

Instantly, he realized she liked to kiss just exactly the same way he did, and that discovery fueled his passion even more.

It was intense, and deep, and probing. And it was long.

As they held each other tight, Mark felt the firmness of her breasts pressing against his chest and he had the overwhelming urge to . . .

No. This was only their first kiss so he fought the desire, limiting himself to the safer parts of her glorious body.

Her shapely hips . . . her slender waist . . . the small of her back . . . her shoulder blades . . . her bare arms . . . her soft shoulders . . . the nape of her neck . . . her fragrant hair . . . her hot cheeks . . .

And all the while, while he was touching her, she was touching him back.

It felt like paradise.

Yet he knew that, even if he wanted to, they couldn't keep kissing forever.

And, finally, regretfully, he stopped.

With his heart still beating out of his chest, Mark squeezed her and whispered in her ear, "*Oh, Ms. Anderson.*"

Pulling back only slightly, she put her hands on her hips as if to scold him. "You know, Mr. Edwards," she said. "I really think it's about time you started calling me Harmony."

Then they laughed, and started kissing again.

Chapter 9

"How's this one, Cam?"

Looking up from reading his Scout handbook, Cameron checked Ricky McGee's taut-line hitch, *again*. "It's perfect, Ricky," he said. "Just like the last one. They've all been perfect. Now why can't you do 'em that way for your Tenderfoot board?"

"I dunno," Ricky answered, peering at Cameron through his thick glasses. "I get nervous, I guess. Sometimes . . . your dad makes me nervous. Sometimes I think he doesn't like me."

"I know, Ricky," Cameron said, nodding. "But that's just the way he is. With everybody. Try not to let him get to you, okay?"

"Okay," the boy answered. "But sometimes it seems like he's even worse with me."

"Just keep practicin', Ricky," Cameron assured him, handing the knot back. "You'll get your Tenderfoot. You'll see."

Leaning back in the wooden pew, Cameron took a deep breath and gazed up at the high vaulted ceiling of the church sanctuary. Gradually, he smiled. Whether God existed or not, you couldn't find a much better place to sit and think than in a church.

Oh, outdoors beneath a starry desert sky, maybe . . . or, perhaps, on the brink of a great canyon like the Grand . . .

Glancing over to his left, Cameron suddenly noticed the colorful stained glass window that was the pride and joy of his Scout troop and of the congregation here at Mesquite Evangelical Lutheran Church.

Below it, a plaque read: TO THE GLORY OF GOD AND IN LIVING TRIBUTE TO TROOP 424 AND SCOUTMASTER RALPH SMITH ON THE OCCASION OF THE THIRTIETH ANNIVERSARY OF THE TROOP, 1968–1998.

The window itself depicted a Scout on one knee holding a troop flag, with the motto, slogan, and Oath encompassing him. And naturally, it being a church window and all, the words TO DO MY DUTY TO GOD stood out prominently from the rest.

Shaking his head, Cameron looked back down at his Scout handbook, at the chapter that talked about the Oath and the Law. Try as he might, he just couldn't quite reconcile what he read there.

Basically it told him, in order to be reverent and do his duty to God, he had to follow the religious teachings of his family and church. Well, he was doing that. His mother's church encouraged each individual to develop his or her own personal faith, and that's just exactly what he was trying to do. His minister, Dr. Dreyfuss-Campbell, said sometimes the process took a lifetime, so Cameron wondered why he was being forced to make a decision now.

Also, Scouts were always supposed to be morally straight. In other words, trustworthy, honest, and open. Cameron always tried to tell the truth and that's just exactly what he'd done at his Eagle board.

And one more thing bothered him. His handbook said Scouts should always respect and defend the rights of others to have their own religious beliefs. It even went on to say the United States Constitution guarantees everyone complete freedom to believe and worship as they see fit without fear of punishment. So, if that was true, why was he being punished now? Why wouldn't they give him his Eagle badge?

"Ricky? Cameron? We're about to start the meeting, boys."

Turning around, they saw Mr. Smith standing at the back of the sanctuary. Without delay, Ricky bounced up and headed down the aisle toward him, but Cameron remained seated, still thinking.

As Ricky departed the room, leaving them alone, Mr. Smith approached Cameron, a look of concern on his face. "Is there something wrong, son?" the Scoutmaster asked. "Why the frown?"

Getting up from the pew, Cameron glanced at the stained glass window, then looked back at the man. "Mr. Smith," he said, "there's something I've been meaning to ask you."

"And what's that?"

"Well," Cameron answered, "I know you believe in God and all, the kind of God who actually listens to your prayers I mean, and I was just wondering. . . . Well, *why* do you believe in that kind of God? I mean, there's really no proof that one exists, is there?"

Mr. Smith smiled that slow smile of his. "Well, Cameron, let me answer your question with another question, if I may. Then we really must get to the troop meeting."

"Okay," Cameron said, nodding.

"Think about this, son: If there were a way, by science or any other means, to absolutely prove the existence of God, then what in the world would be the value . . . of *faith*?"

Putting his arm around Cameron's shoulder, Mr. Smith looked up at the stained glass window one more time and then Cameron did the same. Silently, at last, they turned and walked out of the sanctuary together.

By the time they reached the church's troop-meeting room, the senior patrol leader had already conducted the meeting's opening and was now talking about their upcoming fall encampment.

Taking a seat with the rest of the troop, Cameron listened as the older boy said, "As you all know, this year's district encampment is being held at West Cochise Stronghold Canyon in the heart of the Dragoon Mountains over there by Tombstone. And I know what you're all thinking. You're thinking, 'Yes! We're gonna get to climb around on all those cool boulders and rock formations over there.' Well, we probably will get to do some of that. But, remember, that's *not* the main reason we're going over. The main reason we're going is to win another one of these . . ."

Stepping over to the big awards display case at the front of the room, the SPL pointed to the long line of large trophies sitting on the top shelf, each one consisting of an axe, painted gold, and stuck in a base with a shiny plaque on it. "*This* is the main reason we're going to Cochise Stronghold, gentlemen," the SPL said. "To win ourselves yet another . . . *Golden Axe*."

Waiting a few moments for his words to sink in, he stepped back to the front of the group. "Now, each of your patrol leaders has already been given an encampment information packet with all the necessary stuff you'll need to prepare for this year's competition. Remember, the main event is a timed race where your patrol has to set up a campsite, cook a meal, and then break camp following the strict guidelines listed in those packets. You have to pack your gear, carry it on your backs, pick a campsite, avoid safety hazards, set up a shelter tarp, dig a latrine, cook a meal on a backpack stove, break camp, and do it all in a low-impact, no-trace way *as fast as you possibly can*. Any questions about that?"

Cameron glanced around. It seemed everyone understood.

"Well, okay then," the SPL said. "Use your time meeting with your patrols tonight to get organized so you can start practicing in the next few weeks. Remember, the encampment's in

November. That leaves us a little more than a month and that's not much time. Ready? Break."

"Okay, Pigs . . . ," Cameron called, getting up from his seat. "Let's head to our patrol corner. We have a lot of work to do."

Thinking about their patrol name as he went, Cameron smiled to himself. Officially, they were the Javelina Patrol, after the wild boar of the desert. But the general consensus among his patrol members was that it was much cooler to call themselves "Pigs." So, to keep them happy, he did.

As soon as all the boys had gathered at their table, Cameron had the patrol scribe take attendance and collect dues. Once that was done, he turned to the real business at hand: the campsite competition duty roster. For the most part, everything went smooth as he divvied up the responsibilities. Until he got to the last two names on the list, that is.

"Okay, that leaves Ricky McGee and Randall LaRue," Cameron said, gazing at the bottom of the roster. "Let's see . . . Ricky, your job will be to tie the cords to the shelter tarp grommets—using taut-line hitches, of course. And Randall, you'll be digging the perfect latrine."

"*What?!*" Randall LaRue screeched, his chubby cheeks flushing with indignation. "You mean to tell us Scrub Boy there is gonna tie all the knots while *I* dig the shitter? Well, that's crazy. First, tying knots takes brains, something the Scrub just don't have. And second, why do *I* hafta dig the shitter? I'm a First Class Scout, after all."

"First, Randall," Cameron said, doing his best to remain calm, "stop saying 'scrub' and 'shitter.' It's 'Ricky' and 'latrine.' And second, *I'm* the patrol leader. It's *my* job to organize the duty roster and I did the very best I knew how. Now, I'd appreciate it if you could show a little Scout spirit around here."

Turning to Ricky—who appeared to be in shock over the responsibility he'd been given—Cameron said, "So, Ricky, Randall doesn't think you have what it takes to tie all those taut-line hitches. But, if you *can,* there's no way they'll be able to keep your Tenderfoot from you anymore. What do you think about *that*?"

Slowly, Ricky nodded at Cameron. "Well . . . if it'll get all these guys to stop calling me the Scrub, then you bet I will. *I'll do it*." Looking straight at Randall, he added, " 'Cause I'm *not* a scrub. Sometimes, ya know, it's just like Cameron says. Slow and steady *can* win the race. Maybe it's true that I am a tortoise some of the time, but I'm *no* scrub."

"Ooo . . . nice comeback," Randall said sarcastically, making a face at the boy. "Where ya gonna work when you grow up, Ricky, a *slow*-food restaurant?"

"Okay, that's enough," Cameron said, stepping in.

"No, not quite, Mr. Patrol Leader," Randall answered, turning his venom on Cameron. "You know what I heard about *you*? I heard you're *never* gonna get your Eagle. You know why? 'Cause you're not a Christian, that's why. Is that true, Cameron? Are you not a Christian?"

Caught off guard by the question, Cameron didn't know what to say and, as the eyes of his patrol watched, he just stared. What bothered him most as he sat there was the fact that Randall LaRue knew about his problem. How in the world did he find out?

"Guess what else," Randall went on. "You know that new Christian Club they're starting at Mesquite High? Well, I'm in it. And guess who else is in it, Cameron. Just guess."

Cameron shook his head.

"Your new little girlfriend, Cameron," Randall said, sneering. "Mandy Ross. Mandy Ross is in the club. So, not only is Little Miss Know-it-all *black,* she's also Christian. And you're *neither*. You two are kind of an odd couple, aren't you?"

Cameron frowned. He didn't want to believe what Randall was saying. Trying to hide his surprise, he said, "I haven't heard anything about any Christian Club at the high school, Randall."

"We had our first meeting last week," Randall answered. "Miss Shepherd, the new social studies teacher, is sponsoring it. You know, that teacher with the humongous hooters."

"Hooters?" Ricky asked.

"God, what a doofus," Randall said, shaking his head. "*Boobs,* Ricky. Tits, melons, jugs, ta-tas, mammos. Ever heard of 'em?"

Cameron checked his watch. "Okay, okay, Randall. I think we all get it. Now, if you're quite through acting 'Christian' over there, it's about time to go play Snatch the Bacon with the rest of the troop. Let's go, guys," he said, getting up.

The rest of the Scout meeting went by like a big blur for Cameron and, as the other boys faced off one by one to try and steal a neckerchief from the center of the floor before being tagged, he instead fretted over what Randall LaRue had told him.

Could it be true? Could Mandy Ross really be in a Christian club? But she liked science so much. And she seemed so much like himself . . .

Before he knew it, eight-thirty rolled around. Closing time. And as all the Scouts formed a circle with everyone facing each other, Cameron watched his father come out of his office to take his traditional place in the center.

"Please bow your heads," John Wright said. "And now. . . . May the Great Master of all Scouts be with us till we meet again."

As the circle disbanded and the Scouts started leaving to go home, John Wright put his hand on Cameron's shoulder. "Son," he said, "I have some paperwork to finish up in my office. It'll be a few minutes."

"Okay, Dad," Cameron answered, nodding. Then, unconsciously, he stepped over by the big trophy display case to stand while he waited.

Glancing down, the line of Golden Axes suddenly caught his eye. They'd won so many that some people were starting to call

424 the Golden Axe Troop. Personally, Cameron had mixed feelings about that. As a new patrol leader, of course, it'd be very nice to win one. But on the other hand, the fact that he knew his father *expected* it of him tainted the prospect a bit.

Then something else in the case captured his attention: the TROOP 424 EAGLE SCOUTS plaque listing all the Scouts who had earned the rank of Eagle since the troop began in 1968. Slowly, for fun, he read over all the names and dates. Then he wondered, would *his* name ever be inscribed there?

"Cameron, I'm ready," John Wright's voice said suddenly, breaking his reverie. So, with a sigh, Cameron joined his father and together they walked out of the church and climbed into the Suburban Silverado.

On the way to Cameron's house, John Wright turned to him. "Son," he said, "will you explain something to me. During the closing, I've noticed you no longer bow your head when we pray. Can you explain that to me, please?"

But Cameron barely heard his father because something else was occupying his thoughts. Something that had dawned on him only this moment.

On the Eagle plaque. One of the names there. He remembered vaguely something that was said in that hobby shop back in July, but he never dreamed . . .

What a coincidence! Cameron thought, shaking his head.

The inscription on the TROOP 424 EAGLE SCOUTS plaque had read: 10–25–75 MARK EDWARDS.

Part 4
October

Chapter 10

"Mr. Edwards, wait!" Cameron called as he hurried down the sidewalk toward the teacher's room. The lunch bell had just rung and, around him, everyone else was headed for the school cafeteria.

Mr. Edwards stood outside his door with his keys in his hand and appeared to be locking up on his way out. As Cameron approached, the man said, "Well, hi, Cameron. I was just heading over to the teacher's lounge for lunch. What's up?"

"Yeah, I'm sorry to bother you now, Mr. Edwards," Cameron answered. "But, I really need to talk to you about something and it's kind of important."

"Well, okay then. Not a problem. Let's go back inside while we talk." Unlocking his door and propping it open, the teacher stepped back into his room and then sat down on the edge of the table nearest the doorway.

Following his lead, Cameron took a seat on the low cabinet counter opposite him.

"What can I do you for?" Mr. Edwards asked.

"Well," Cameron began, "I have a few questions to ask you and I hope you won't mind answering them. They're kind of . . . personal."

Mr. Edwards smiled. "If I don't want to, I just won't. No harm will be done. So . . . ask away."

"Okay," Cameron said, bolstering his resolve. "Well, first, I need to know if you were in Troop 424 back when you were in Scouts."

The teacher's eyes widened. "Now how did you know—wait . . . Cameron, are *you* in Troop 424?"

Nodding at the man, Cameron repeated himself. "So . . . 424 *was* your troop then?"

"Sure was. Hey, I don't suppose Ralph Smith is still the Scoutmaster?"

"Yep, he is."

"Wow. Amazing. And you still meet at Mesquite Lutheran?"

Cameron nodded again.

"Well, I'll be darned," Mr. Edwards said, shaking his head. "I guess ol' Mr. Smith is the one who must have told you I was in the troop then, huh?"

"Nope," Cameron answered. "I saw your name on the Eagle plaque in the trophy case."

"Oh . . ."

"So, did you like bein' in Scouts back when you were a kid?" Cameron asked.

"Best thing that ever happened to me, Cameron," Mr. Edwards answered, smiling. "I think I probably learned more from Scouts than I did from either high school or college. In fact, it was my experiences teaching Scout skills to the younger boys in the troop and then, later, counseling merit badges during my college summer vacations that made me finally decide to become a teacher. Yeah, I was thinking about becoming an astronomer until I found out how much I enjoyed working with kids."

Cameron cocked his head. "So, as a kid, you wanted to be a scientist? Have you always liked science?"

"Since I was in diapers. My parents tell me I knew how to count backward from ten before I could count forward, because of watching all the space shots on TV. My mom tells this story that once, during Alan Shepard's suborbital launch, I threw my baby bottle across the room at the same time his Redstone missile lifted off the pad. Milk went everywhere. Luckily, Shepard's splashdown was more successful than mine."

They both chuckled. Then, a bit too abruptly he feared, Cameron asked, "Are you Lutheran, Mr. Edwards?"

Hearing the question, the teacher's face turned serious. "Well . . . no, Cameron, I'm not. But, why—" Suddenly, his eyes lit up. "Oh, you mean because Troop 424 is sponsored by Mesquite Lutheran. I see. No, I'm not Lutheran. But, as I'm sure you know, lots of kids join that troop who don't necessarily go to that church. Probably because they hear Mr. Smith's such a good Scoutmaster."

"Well, what church *do* you go to?" Cameron asked, finally getting to the core of why he'd come to talk to Mr. Edwards in the first place.

Hesitating a moment, the teacher smiled warily at him. "Well, you did warn me you were going to get personal, didn't you? May I ask why you want to know that?"

Starting to get frustrated, Cameron frowned. "Well, you like science, right? But also, you're an Eagle Scout. Well, Mr. Edwards, what I need to know is, did any of your boards of review ever ask you if you believed in God?"

Standing up, Mr. Edwards stared thoughtfully at Cameron as if, maybe, he had started to get the picture. Then, sitting back down next to him, he said, "You know, thinking back, I'm not really sure if anybody ever came right out and asked me that or not. . . . But, getting back to your 'church' question, I will tell you that I guess I'm what you'd call 'nonaffiliated.' "

"What?"

"I don't belong to a religion," Mr. Edwards explained. "Not to any organized religion, anyway. I never have. I guess it just hasn't ever been something I've needed in my life."

"Well . . . do you believe in God?" Cameron asked.

"You know what, Cameron?" Mr. Edwards said, standing up again. "Now, don't get me wrong, because I really would like to discuss this with you further. But, just to be on the safe side, I think I should touch base with your mom on this before I do. Okay?"

"Okay," Cameron answered, shrugging. Getting up, he started for the door.

"Cameron?"

He turned. "Yes, Mr. Edwards?"

"You know, your mother and I *will* be seeing each other this coming Sunday. I could ask her about this then."

"All right."

"Cameron?"

"Yes?"

Looking intently at him, Mr. Edwards said, "I've been wanting to ask you how you feel about your mother and me going out on our date this weekend. I mean . . . are you okay with it? Are you okay with your mom dating one of your teachers? I know it has to feel kind of weird. At least, it does for me."

Leaning back in the doorway, Cameron thought a moment. Then he nodded. "Sure, Mr. Edwards, I'm okay with it. From what I can tell, she likes you a lot, and, well . . . so do I. It's just that . . ."

"What?"

"Well, since my parents split up and all, my mom's been very picky about who she goes out with and . . . well, to tell you the truth, she doesn't get out much. Mostly, she just stays at home and takes care of all her plants and watches old movies and listens to her music. So, I don't know what you're expecting, but . . ."

"Well, Cameron, you want to know what *I* do?" Mr. Edwards said, smiling. "I go to karate once a week . . . or maybe I'll work on my truck some . . . or maybe I'll work on one of my models or do some reading . . . or maybe I'll watch a science documentary on the Discovery Channel . . . or maybe I'll listen to some of *my* music. You see? Not so different. And I haven't been on a date in months, so . . ."

"Sounds like you're made for each other then," Cameron quipped. "There is one thing, though."

"What's that?"

"Well, should I keep calling you Mr. Edwards, or can I call you Mark, now? Seein' as how you're a friend of the family and all. Oh, you know what I mean."

The teacher winked at him. "Yeah, I know what you mean. . . . Well, in front of other students, you should probably continue saying Mr. Edwards. But, when it's just us, like now, Mark'll be just fine."

"Okay. Great," Cameron said, nodding. "Well, I'll let you get back to your lunch break then." Deciding to try their newfound familiarity on for size, he added, "See ya later . . . Mark." Then, he turned away.

"Bye, Cameron," Mark's voice called after him as he headed out the door.

Then, suddenly, from down the sidewalk, someone else called to him. "Hey, Cameron! There you are, boy. I've been looking all over campus for you."

Oh no, he thought. Just the person he *didn't* want to run into. Mandy Ross. And, she was coming over to him. Now what was he gonna do?

"So, what's going on, Cameron?" she asked, walking up. "With the way you've been acting in science class lately and your mysterious disappearances around school, I'm starting to get the feeling you're trying to avoid me."

Looking into those gentle almond eyes of hers, lying was

totally out of the question for him. So, instead, he just kept his mouth shut.

Right away, she got the message. But rather than leave as he expected her to, she took his hand. "Come over here, Cameron," she said. "Tell me what's wrong."

Allowing Mandy to lead him to a nearby bench, he sat down with her and then tried to figure out what he was going to say.

"Come on, Cameron," she said, still holding his hand. "Tell me."

"Well, Mandy," he answered finally, struggling to find the right words, "the other day I found out something about you. Something I didn't know before. And I'm just afraid it's gonna make us . . . incompatible."

Looking away for just a moment, Mandy asked, "Whatever it is, Cameron, did finding it out make you not like me anymore?"

"Oh no," he said. "Actually, I'm worried that, when you find out, you won't like *me* anymore."

Frowning, Mandy shook her head. "Look, Cameron, I have absolutely no idea what you're talking about. So just tell me, *please*."

She was right. Enough beating around the bush. He'd just come right out and ask her. "Okay, Mandy, here it is," he said. "Randall LaRue told me the other night that he saw you at a Christian club meeting. Is that true?"

She made a face. "Yeah. So?"

"Well, there ya go," Cameron said, deciding to just blurt it out. "I'm not. Christian, I mean."

"And why is that a problem?" Mandy asked simply.

"Well . . . ," Cameron didn't know exactly how to answer that question because he hadn't expected her to ask it. He had expected the problem to be as obvious to her as it was to him.

Before he could say anything more, Mandy gave his hand a squeeze. "Look, Cameron," she said, gazing into his eyes.

"When Jesus said, 'Love thy neighbor as thyself,' he didn't mean, 'Love just thy *Christian* neighbor,' or, 'just thy *white* neighbor,' for that matter. He meant *all* neighbors. If I stopped liking you because you weren't Christian, well that'd be like you not liking me because I'm black. It'd just be plain wrong, and I'd never do it."

Smiling at him, she added, "Cameron . . . you're one of the few people in my life, black *or* white, who truly treats me as if color doesn't matter *at all*. That's why you're so special to me. And you know what else? I already know who you are. Your religion doesn't matter to me. Not at all."

Looking back at her, Cameron slowly shook his head. "You make me feel so stupid, Mandy."

Giggling, she held his gaze.

Still feeling as if he owed her an explanation though, Cameron said, "You know, Mandy, right or wrong, religion *can* be a problem. A *big* one. At least, it was for my parents. And now they're divorced. And since I started being completely honest about my own beliefs about God, some people aren't treating me the same as they did before. They're treating me worse. I think, for the first time, I'm really starting to find out a little bit of what it's like to be a minority."

"And what are your beliefs about God?" Mandy said. "If you don't mind me asking, I mean."

"Well," Cameron answered, chuckling ironically, "I'm just not at all sure there *is* one, that's all."

"Oh . . ."

"Are you shocked and appalled?"

She nodded at him. "Shocked . . . a little bit, I guess. But listen, Cameron, can you tell me why you feel that way?"

"You're not gonna try to talk me out of, or into, anything . . . are you, Mandy?"

She shook her head. "I just want to understand, Cameron, that's all."

"Well, okay then," he said, glancing at his watch. "Well, there're lots and lots of reasons but we don't have time to talk about 'em all. So, I'll just tell you *one*. I'll tell you the first time I started really wondering about this stuff. But, you're probably gonna think it's stupid."

"No I won't, Cameron," she said, squeezing his hand again.

"Do you have a dog, Mandy?" he asked.

"No. But my family does have a cat. Simba." She giggled.

"Well, I have a dog," he said. "Barkley. Named after the Chuckster, of course. He's been my best friend ever since I was a little kid. And I know this is gonna sound sappy, but I love him. And there's absolutely no doubt in my mind that he loves me back."

She smiled.

"Well, one day, my dad sits me down and tells me, according to doctrine, animals like Barkley don't have souls so it's impossible for 'em to go to Heaven when they die. Well that sounded pretty cheesy to me. And to tell you the truth, I think Barkley deserves to go a lot more than some of the people I know. So anyway . . . that's what first got me to thinkin' that all this God stuff isn't really what it's cracked up to be . . ."

Mandy sighed and shook her head. "Yeah, you're a thinker, Cameron, that's for sure. And that's part of why I like you. But," she frowned at him, "there are some things you just can't think through. Some things you have to *feel*, you know."

"I agree, Mandy," Cameron told her. "And it's all those feelings I have for my dog, Barkley, that're makin' me wonder."

To his relief, she smiled at him again.

"So," Cameron asked, changing the subject, "how do you like bein' in that Christian Club, anyway?"

"Oh . . . I didn't join," Mandy answered. "I only went to that one meeting."

Surprised, he asked, "Well, why didn't you? Why didn't you join?"

Mandy shook her head. "They were planning to protest Halloween. Can you believe it? Said it was satanic. I *like* Halloween. In fact—" She stopped, as if suddenly embarrassed by something.

"What?"

"Well, I was just gonna say there's a school Halloween dance coming soon, and since it seems like we're not gonna be breaking up—"

"Wait a minute," Cameron interrupted. "You just said, 'we're not gonna be *breaking up*.' Does that mean . . . we're *going out*?"

"Well, aren't we?" Mandy asked.

"Well, I don't know," Cameron said. "I haven't ever gone out with anyone before." Then, noticing a look of disappointment starting to creep onto her angelic face, he added quickly, "But I'd like to. With you, I mean."

Thankfully, her brilliant wide smile returned. Then, leaning close, she said, "Well that's good, boy. 'Cause there's a first time for everything . . . including *this*."

The next thing Cameron knew, Mandy Ross's soft, dimpled lips were pressed against his own and his body felt like it was melting.

Now, he was more mixed up than ever. Perhaps, there *was* a God.

After all, his mother *had* always told him, "Remember, Cameron . . . God *is* love. And love is the meaning and the high point of life."

Chapter 11

"Now who is this we're listening to again?" Harmony asked, glancing at Mark through the darkness of the truck cab as she softly stroked the top of his scalp with her fingernails.

"Sting," he answered, switching to his low beams, preparing to pass another car.

"Is that the name of the singer . . . or the group?"

"The singer," he said, hitting his left turn signal. "Haven't you ever heard of Sting, Harmony? He *used* to be in a group. The Police. They were very popular. But now, he's even more popular since he went solo. He's even a movie star. This is his greatest hits CD, *Fields of Gold*."

"I like it," Harmony told him, nodding.

"Yeah?" he said, glancing over as he accelerated past the other driver. "Well, I haven't seen any of the songs make you *cry* yet."

She pulled her hand away. "Are you making fun of me, Mr. Edwards?"

"Never," Mark answered, pulling back into the right lane. "And, please. *Please* don't stop rubbing my head. It feels *so good*."

"Well, okay," she said, resuming his massage. "As long as we're clear you're not making fun."

Glancing over at her again, he said, "Not much up there anymore, is there, Harmony? I gotta tell ya, male pattern baldness is a real bitch."

"I like it," she told him. "It's like baby hair. And it does go with your baby face." Reaching down, she brushed the backs of her fingers against his smooth cheek.

"Careful, Harmony," Mark said. "Comparing me to a baby isn't gonna do much for my masculinity, you know."

She smiled coyly. "Oh. . . . Something tells me we don't need to be too worried about that, Mark."

Putting her head on his shoulder, Harmony closed her eyes and listened to the music playing on the car stereo. Then she sighed contentedly. It felt so good to finally have a real man in her life, a man like Mark Edwards. And as they drove on through the night, she basked in the warm memories she already had of him . . .

His kindness and generosity when they first met, that day in the hobby shop, and the priceless look on his face when she made the crack about grown men building spaceship models.

The thrill she experienced from simply reading his name for the first time on a school permission slip and then the burning desire, a desire she was sure they *both* felt, as they watched that science film alone in his classroom together.

The pride she had for her son when Mark wanted to display Cameron's Grand Canyon model at school, especially after his own father made him feel so bad about it.

And the feelings she had when kissing him . . . *kissing him*. . . . Well, she could hardly wait till they got home so they could finally do *that* some more.

Smiling to herself, she suddenly remembered their flirtatious phone conversation earlier in the week. He'd called to ask her out for the first time, for this very date.

"What are you doing?" he asked when she answered the phone.

"Oh . . . praying," she'd told him for the second time since they met, hoping once more for some kind of revealing reaction.

But he made a joke instead. "You're cleaning out your fish-pond *again*?" he asked.

"No. . . . This time I'm cooking," she answered. "Oriental salad. Hot, *spicy* . . . oriental salad."

"Spicy, huh? Sounds delicious. Is it as *spicy* as your spaghetti?"

"*Spicier*," she answered in a low, sexy voice.

Silence.

Finally, he said, "Listen, before I'm completely overcome from hearing your provocative dinner menu, I called to ask you out on a date. I know you must be very busy with your nursery and all, but it's Columbus Day weekend coming up and I was hoping—"

"How 'bout Sunday afternoon?" Harmony said, so anxious she interrupted him. "But I wouldn't be able to see you until around fourish. I'll go to my early morning church service that day and then close up the nursery a few hours before I usually do. Just what did you have on your mind, sailor?"

"Well, I know a little place in Tucson that serves some pretty spicy dishes of its own. And four o'clock sounds just perfect."

"Taking our new romance outta town, are we? Sounds like a good plan to me, Mr. Edwards. See you Sunday at four. Bye, Mark."

"*Wait* . . . Harmony?"

"Yes?"

"So . . . all this seems okay to you? Appropriate, I mean? Cameron being one of my students and all."

"Well, you're not dating Cameron, are you, Mark? You're dating *me*. I'll see you Sunday. At four."

"Okay. . . . Bye, Harmony."

"Bye, Mark," she said.

And as she remembered hanging up the phone after that first call, all the happiness and excitement she felt then came rushing back. But it wasn't just the effect Mark Edwards had on *her* that made her feel that way. It was also seeing the impact he was having on Cameron.

That very afternoon for example, when he came to pick her up, Cameron was watching one of those *Star Trek* shows on TV, something he never did before Mark became his teacher.

"Mark," her son had said, greeting the man at the door, "*Star Trek: Deep Space Nine*'s on. You're gonna miss it. Don't you want to sit down and watch it with me before you two take off?"

"I'd sure like to," Mark answered. "But your mom and I really need to hit the road."

"Oh . . . okay," Cameron said, looking disappointed. Then his eyes lit up. "Hey! I could tape it for you. How 'bout that? Then you guys could watch it when you get home."

"Okay, sure," Mark told the boy, winking knowingly at Harmony as they headed out to his truck. "That'd be just great . . ."

And after that, she recalled, it was Cameron who continued to be the main focus of their conversation during the hour-and-a-half-long drive to Tucson that followed.

"He asked me if I believed in God, Harmony," Mark told her when they pulled onto I-10 and headed west past the saguaro-dotted foothills of the rugged Rincon Mountains. "But I thought I'd better check with you before discussing anything so personal with him."

"Well, if you're asking my permission, Mark, you have it," Harmony answered, confident that anything the science teacher might tell her son could only be helpful. "You see . . . oh, how should I put this? Right now, Mark, Cameron's on a . . . a spiritual search. A search for ultimate meaning, I guess you'd call it. And I'm very proud of him for making that search. I only hope it doesn't take him too long."

"What do you mean?" Mark asked.

She explained the situation with Cameron's Eagle badge to him. Then he squinted at her.

"Don't you think your expectations that he'll be able to resolve these questions quickly are a little unrealistic, Harmony? I mean, they are *big* questions. He's only fourteen."

She stared back. "Yes. . . . That's pretty much what our minister told me, too." Then she let out a heavy sigh. "It's just that. . . . Well, I'll just be sick if he doesn't get his badge."

Unexpectedly, her eyes started to fill with tears and, even though she tried to hide it from him, he must have noticed. "Come on, Harmony," he said, patting the bench seat. "Slide on over here."

Obliging Mark as a tear ran down her cheek, she cuddled up next to him and he gave her a reassuring squeeze. From that point on, they spent the rest of the highway miles that remained in silent closeness.

Arriving in northwest Tucson, before they went to dinner, Mark surprised her with an uplifting stroll through the beautiful Tohono Chul Park desert preserve. And when she smiled appreciatively at him for doing so, he shrugged modestly. "I knew you liked plants," he said.

Walking down the winding nature trails through the lush paloverdes and numerous garden displays, they soon forgot they were in the middle of a city. And as they marveled at the varieties of desert plants and cacti and wildflowers surrounding them, Harmony began to feel as if they were the only two people in the world.

Oh, and the birds. It was like being in an aviary without walls. With no effort at all they spotted pyrrhuloxia, curve-billed thrashers, phainopepla, cactus wrens, Gambel's quail, Inca doves, and even a black-chinned hummingbird. But the very best thing about their bird watching, for Harmony at least, was the fact that they did it while holding hands.

Then just before leaving the park for the restaurant, they were relaxing by one of several pools on the grounds when, suddenly, they got a thrilling glimpse of a mother javelina and her adorable baby pigs as the animals stopped for an evening drink. Mark kissed Harmony then, making an already memorable moment absolutely unforgettable.

Now, after an experience like that, Harmony wouldn't have been too surprised if dinner had been somewhat anticlimactic. Well, it wasn't. Mark took her to the Terra Cotta, a casual café specializing in southwestern cuisine, where the menu read: ARIZONA'S COOLEST RESTAURANT.

At first, she was skeptical. But after thoroughly enjoying her poblano chiles stuffed with Mediterranean couscous, vegetables, and tamale—and sampling Mark's, stuffed with chicken and shrimp—she became a believer. The Terra Cotta was a cool restaurant indeed.

And then, it was after dinner, she remembered, while sipping their microbrewed pale ales, that the conversation eventually rolled back around to Cameron again. And, inevitably, to John Wright.

"So, Harmony," Mark said, the first to broach the subject, "you mentioned before your ex-husband had something to do with Cameron's Eagle badge situation. I don't understand. Why on earth would he do something like that?"

Staring at her glass of beer, Harmony said, "Well, the nice answer would be that John is concerned about his son's religious growth, and I'm sure that's the answer *he'd* give. But it wouldn't be true. The real answer is he's doing it out of revenge."

"You mean, because you divorced him?" Mark asked.

She nodded. "He never wanted it. He doesn't *believe* in it," she added, rolling her eyes. "And now Cameron's the one who's paying the price."

"Well . . . what happened to your marriage, anyway?"

"John's ridiculous biblical literalism is what happened to it," she answered, shaking her head. "Deuteronomy and all that. The fall of the city and the rape of the women, etcetera, etcetera. You see, to ultraconservative Christians like John, women are mere booty and, eventually, that's exactly how he started treating me."

"You mean . . . he was abusive?" Mark asked.

She didn't answer. She didn't have to. She was sure he could see it in her face.

"Well, then I'm curious, Harmony," Mark said, frowning. "If John was like that, why in the world did you—"

"Marry him?" Harmony said. She sighed. "Well . . . he can be very charming when he wants to be—in a manipulative kind of way, that is. And I was very young at the time." Smiling, she stared at her beer again. "From my first name you probably already guessed that, when I was born, my parents were hippies. Anyway, you can do the math. I was a teenager when I met John and, before long, I was very pregnant. *That's* why I married him."

"Now wait a minute, Harmony," Mark said. "Didn't good ol' righteous John consider premarital sex a sin?"

"You bet he did," she answered. "And he's the first to admit that he's not without sin. But that's the thing about people like John. Whatever they choose to do in their daily lives, they can always repent on Sunday. And as long as they accept Jesus as their Savior, their eternal salvation is always secure."

Mark smiled ironically. "So, they get to have their cake and eat it, too. I guess you can't blame 'em. It's a pretty nice setup."

"Well . . . one more thing and then we'll stop talking about John," Harmony said, finishing her beer. "I checked with the video stores in Mesquite and several of them have that science video of yours for rent. When I told John that *I'd* show it to Cameron if he didn't let him see it at school, he backed off. I don't think you'll have any more trouble with him."

"Wow, that was pretty sly, Ms. Anderson," Mark said, reaching over to take her hand. "I can see right now that I'd better keep a close eye on you."

Winking at him across the table, she replied, "I really hope that you will." . . .

Suddenly, something in the lyrics playing on the car stereo caught Harmony's attention, dissolving her memories of their evening together and bringing her back to the present. Lifting her head off Mark's shoulder, she asked, "Mark . . . in that song . . . who's the 'you' he's talking about?"

"What?"

"In the song, Mark," Harmony repeated. "He's singing about losing faith in all these things. In science and religion, and in the media, and in politicians and the military. But, he *hasn't* lost his faith in 'you.' Who *is* the 'you'? Is it a lover? A parent? God, maybe?"

"I don't know," Mark answered. "I guess it could be God, but I doubt it. Maybe . . . it's himself. Maybe Sting's saying faith in self is what's most important. . . . Yeah. That's the answer I like, and I'm goin' with it."

"Maybe . . . ," Harmony said, nodding thoughtfully. Then she pointed excitedly out the window. "Hey, I forgot to show you on the way out of town earlier, but that's my nursery over there. See it?"

Glancing at the lighted sign above the entrance gate as they drove by, Mark asked, "Why is your place called G. B. Shaw's, Harmony? Why did you give it that name?"

She squeezed his thigh. "Ask me again when we get to my house, Mark, and I'll show you."

But by the time they actually did pull up and park in Harmony's dark driveway, it seemed Mark had lost all interest in her nursery. Now it was her lips that occupied his full attention. Consequently, the two of them stayed in his truck cab a long time gazing at the city lights, listening to his music, and kissing and caressing one another.

Not surprisingly, their passionate necking eventually lead to something more as Mark's hands started to roam over Harmony's body. And when they did, she liked it.

But . . .

. . . she stopped him anyway.

A little out of breath, she captured his hands and held them. Then she said, "You know where this type of behavior is going to get us, don't you?"

He kissed her forehead. "Well . . . I know where I was *hoping* it might get us."

"Is that the way you want our first time to be, Mark? Across a bench seat? In a truck cab?"

He answered jokingly. "Well, I'm sure it wouldn't be the first time such a thing has happened in a pickup."

"Or *this* pickup for that matter, eh, Mark?" Harmony said, cocking her head at him.

"Is *that* what's bothering you about it?"

"Don't be silly," she answered. "It's just not the right time yet, that's all. You know, we aren't teenagers anymore. If and when it does happen, I don't want us to be rushed or . . . constrained in any way. I don't want to be worried about Cameron or anything else. I just want to be able to enjoy it."

"We could go back to my place," Mark said seductively, kissing her neck. "Come on, Harmony. Let's go. We won't be sorry."

"Ohhh . . . Mark," she moaned, sorely tempted as she let her head roll back for another glorious moment when he continued to shower the side of her neck with kisses. But finally, gaining control again, she gently pushed him away.

"You're a persistent little devil, I'll give you that," she said, squeezing his hands. "Come on. Let's go in for a little while and watch at least part of that show Cameron taped for us. I'll make some herb tea. It'll be nice."

"As nice as what we're doing now?" Mark asked.

"Well, no . . . ," Harmony answered. "But nice."

"Well, okay," Mark said.

So, putting their desires on hold again, they went in the house and, while Mark got comfortable on the sofa, Harmony checked on Cameron—who was either asleep or *pretending* to be asleep—and then made them their tea. Finally, curled up together with Barkley at their feet, they started to watch *Star Trek*.

"Oh, wait!" Harmony said, bouncing up before pushing PLAY. "There was something I was going to show you, remember?"

Going to the bookcase, she pulled out a small, hardcover volume and then returned to the sofa. Thumbing through its pages, she asked, "So, Mark, are you familiar at all with George Bernard Shaw?"

"Vaguely," he answered. "Wasn't he an Irish playwright or something?" Suddenly, his eyes lit up. "George Bernard Shaw . . . *G. B. Shaw*." Glancing at Harmony, he smiled.

Finding the right page, she handed him the book. "Here, Mark. Read this part," she said.

" 'The best place to seek God is in a garden. You can dig for Him there,'" Mark said, reading out loud. Then, his smile became a full-blown grin. "Very good, Harmony. I understand. . . . What is this anyway?"

She watched as he closed the book and read its front cover. The title said: ADVENTURES OF THE BLACK GIRL IN HER SEARCH FOR GOD.

Still grinning, Mark handed it back to her. "You know, Harmony," he said, "you really ought to have Cameron read that book. Considering what he's going through, it might be just the ticket for him."

"That's a good idea, Mark," she said thoughtfully, setting the book on the coffee table in front of them.

Then, starting the VCR with the remote, laying her head on Mark's shoulder, and patting his chest, she gazed at him and said it again. "Yes, a very good idea, indeed."

Chapter 12

"Okay, Mr. Edwards. It's almost five o'clock and, since not enough of my *teachers* volunteered to chaperone, I have a Halloween dance in the gymnasium to get to. Whatever it is, you're gonna hafta make it fast."

This time, Claude Caruthers had some kind of pinkish goo in the corner of his gray moustache—hamburger secret sauce judging from the fast-food bag on top of his file cabinet—and, for a moment, Mark couldn't help but stare.

"Mr. Edwards?" Caruthers said impatiently.

"Oh . . . yeah. Right," Mark said, trying not to look at the goo as he gathered his thoughts. "That demonstration at the flagpole this morning, that's why I'm here. I thought I should come over and voice my concerns about that new Christian Club of ours picketing against Halloween."

"Well, take a number," Caruthers said, leaning back and scratching his belly. "I've had teachers in and outta here all day long about that, and I'll tell you the same thing I told them. This *is* America. If the students here at Mesquite High want to have a 'see you at the flagpole' gathering before school to protest this or that, I'm gonna let 'em. Nothin' wrong with it."

"Actually," Mark replied, "it's not really the protest that bothers me so much as the fact that we have a Christian Club in the first place. I mean, we are a public high school, after all. What about the separation of church and state?"

"Well now, think about that a minute, Mark," Caruthers answered, somewhat condescendingly. "The reason the Founding Fathers created that separation was they wanted to make sure the state didn't *interfere* with the church. And that's why I'm not gonna interfere with the club."

"I'm afraid you have that backwards, Claude," Mark said matter-of-factly.

"What?"

Mark sat up in his seat. "The reason there's a separation of church and state, Claude, is because the Founding Fathers didn't want any particular religion interfering with the state. *Not* the other way around."

"Look, I'm not gonna debate history with you, Mark, because you're a science teacher," Caruthers said disdainfully. "I, on the other hand, *did* teach history a few years back, and I think I know a little about our First Amendment. Now under the Equal Access Act, student religious activities are accorded the same access to public school facilities as secular activities. And since this *is* a club, and since it *is* voluntary, and since there *are* no grades given for it, then I see nothing wrong with it. After all, nobody ever said our public schools should be religion-free zones, did they?"

Without thinking, Mark asked, "Well . . . what if some of our students wanted to have an atheist club? Or a satanist club, for that matter? Would you allow that, too? I mean, they are the flip side of the same coin, aren't they?"

Getting out of his chair, Caruthers went and closed the office door. He turned to stare at Mark with anger in his eyes. "What kind of question is that, Mark?" he asked scornfully. "You know, you're really starting to piss me off. What do you want to rock the boat for? I'm gettin' sick and tired of you teachers comin' in here and trying to tell me how to do my job. Well, *I* make the policy decisions around here, not you. You go teach."

Now it did concern Mark that he'd managed to anger his principal. After all, the last thing he needed was bad blood between him and his boss. But he did have one more question and, since it seemed like an important one, he decided to take the risk and ask it anyway.

"But, Claude," he said, "what about the fact that our Christian Club is sponsored by a *teacher*? An official of the *school*? A *state* employee? Surely, that can't be right. Can it?"

All at once, the principal's demeanor mysteriously changed. Now he acted downright conciliatory. "Look, Mark," he said, smiling, "in all honesty, and just between you and me, we're *all* Christians anyway, aren't we? I mean, here in this room at least? We both have Christian values, don't we? Let's just put this little disagreement to rest. I have a dance to get to."

Oh well, Mark thought, getting up from his seat. He hadn't really expected Caruthers to take him seriously anyway. After all, he never did before.

But still, Mark knew he was right about this one. And as he headed out of the school office toward the parking lot, it continued to bother him. He knew no teacher had any business sponsoring a religious club at a public school.

Then, all of a sudden, he started feeling bad about himself. Why didn't he have the courage to stand up for his convictions more forcefully? If he did truly believe he was right, then why not try to sponsor an atheist or satanist club in order to make his point? Why not just come out and say he didn't consider himself a Christian?

Because he knew he was chicken shit, that's why.

And he knew something else . . .

If people like him continued to allow religious conservatives to influence the schools, democracy was in real trouble.

Shaking his head dismally as he thought about that, he glanced up as he approached his truck. Then he smiled.

Coming down the sidewalk, headed for the Halloween dance no doubt, were Mandy Ross and Cameron Wright. And they were holding hands.

Now, as outlined in the Mesquite High Code of Conduct, PDAs—public displays of affection, including hand-holding—were definitely against the school rules and it was part of Mark's job to ask the two students to disengage.

But he decided not to this time.

Because seeing Mandy and Cameron holding hands that way suddenly gave him something he really needed to feel at that particular moment. Something talking to Claude Caruthers had all but taken away.

Hope.

Hope for the future.

Part 5
November

Chapter 13

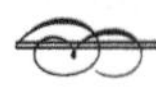

"Mark . . . ," Harmony said softly into his ear as soon as they finished kissing hello. "Wouldn't you feel more comfortable . . . in the bedroom?"

"*What?*"

Seeing the look of total shock grow on Mark's face as the full implications of what she asked him sank in, Harmony giggled with delight.

"What about Cameron?"

"Oh, he's not here," she answered, batting her eyes at him. "He's on a Scout campout."

"Well . . . what about dinner? And the movie?"

Shrugging teasingly, she started to turn away. "Well, if you'd really rather go to dinner and a movie, then—"

"No, no, no," Mark said, spinning her back around. "The bedroom—" he kissed her "—sounds just—" he kissed her again "—perfect." And he kissed her again.

Moments later, with their lips hovering only inches apart,

Harmony smiled. "Good choice, Mr. Edwards," she said. "For a minute there, I was afraid you might be getting stupid on me."

Then, kissing him once more as passionately as she could, she winked at him, took his hand, and, without any further discussion, led him down the long hallway to her bedroom.

"I have a surprise for you, Mr. Edwards. A couple of them, actually," Harmony said, releasing him as they stepped through the doorway. Going over to the night table, she picked up the small wrapped gift she had waiting there. "Here," she said, handing it to him, "this is the first."

She watched as he inspected the wrapping paper she'd chosen—a floral print of Georgia O'Keeffe lilies—and, from the glint in his eye, she knew the erotic quality of the images hadn't been lost on him.

Tearing off the paper, Mark smiled knowingly as he read the unwrapped box. "Twelve ultra-thin condoms, eh? Why, Ms. Anderson, I do believe you're trying to seduce me."

"Well, since I did kind of spring all this on you tonight," Harmony answered, "I wanted to make sure we were prepared."

Tossing the box of condoms onto the bed, he reached out and pulled her to him. "Well then, let's start making sure your wise prior planning doesn't end up going to waste."

Again, he kissed her. And as he did, she let him unbutton her blouse. Finishing with the last button, he pulled her tucked shirt up out of her denim jeans and then slid it off her bare shoulders, dropping it to the floor. Reaching behind her, he searched blindly for the hooks that would unfasten her brassiere. But they weren't there.

She giggled.

"Hey," he said, "this isn't a bra."

"That's what you get for trying to undress me with your eyes closed, Mr. Edwards."

"Well . . . what is it?" he asked, nibbling at her ear as he tried to pull the shiny black undergarment out of her pants the way he had the shirt. "Is it a camisole or something?"

"Uh, that won't work, Mr. Edwards," Harmony answered in a singsong voice as his tugging grew more and more frantic. "It's your *second* surprise, because I wanted to feel as sexy as possible tonight. It's a teddy, and it has a thong. Step back, please . . ."

When he obliged her, she slowly undid her button fly, allowing her blue jeans to slide to the floor. Then, stepping out of them, she did a gradual pirouette so he could enjoy the tantalizing black thong teddy from every angle.

Satisfied that he more than liked what he saw, Harmony decided it was finally time for the *coup de grâce*. So, slipping the straps from her shoulders, she slowly and deliberately peeled off her last remaining article of clothing.

Standing there dumbfounded, watching her every move, Mark Edwards had only one thing to say.

"*Oh . . . my . . . God . . .*"

• • •

Glancing at the digital clock, Harmony couldn't believe her eyes. "Mark . . . do you realize it's after eleven o'clock? We've been in bed over *six hours*."

"Well, you know what they say about time flying when you're having fun," Mark answered, stroking her hair as she lay next to him. "And actually, we weren't in bed the whole time. We were on the floor for part of it, remember? And then there was that time leaning against the wall over there. And the time in your rocking chair. And the—"

"Okay, okay," Harmony said, putting her finger to his lips. "I guess I should've said bed-*room*."

"Well actually, there *was* that time when we both went to the kitchen, and while we were standing naked by the sink you started to—"

"I remember," she said, quickly kissing him to shut him up.

But after the kiss, Mark went right on. "Well," he said, "at least the most important question *was* finally answered tonight."

"And what's that?"

"Well, a while back, Justin bet me the color of your hair wasn't natural. I guess he just couldn't believe any woman could have hair *that* red, I don't know. Anyway, *I* of course said it was. And now, after seeing . . . well . . . after seeing *all* of you, I know I was right. And it's satisfying."

"Mark Edwards!" Harmony said, scolding him. "I can't believe grown men have conversations like that."

"It's a guy thing," he replied, shrugging.

"You know, Mark," Harmony said, running her fingernails up and down his chest, "there is something I've been wanting to ask you about your brother."

"What?"

"How did he lose his arm?"

For a long time, Mark didn't say anything. Then he sighed heavily. "Well, it was really stupid, Harmony. And, it was my fault."

"What happened?"

"Well, I don't know if you knew this or not, but back when Justin and I were kids, there used to be a drive-in theater here in town. And back by the theater snack bar there was a playground. Well, the most popular ride there was this heavy iron merry-go-round that all the big kids used to run and push to get it to go faster and faster. . . . That's where it happened."

"Well, *how* did it?" Harmony asked softly. "Why did you say it was your fault?"

Sighing again, Mark shook his head. "Well, the merry-go-round was poorly maintained and it wasn't safe. One side of it was way up off the ground, while the other was actually cutting a . . . a big gouge in the dirt as it spun around. My dad knew it was dangerous, and he told us not to ride it."

"But you guys did anyway, is that it?"

"Not 'guys,'" Mark answered. "Just me. I was the oldest and, when I took Justin to the playground during intermission, I made him stand and watch while I broke my father's rule and got on."

"Well . . . if you were the one on the merry-go-round," Harmony asked, confused, "then how did *Justin* end up getting hurt?"

"That's the really ironic part . . . ," Mark answered.

Something in his tone made Harmony look at him. In his eyes, by the light of the digital clock, she thought she saw tears.

"I got dizzy," Mark went on. "The high school boys had the thing going so fast that I lost my balance and slipped off—very close to where that spinning edge was digging into the ground. Well—" his voice cracked "—little Justin saw me fall. He realized that I was probably going to be caught under the merry-go-round and . . ." He stopped to clear his throat and then she heard him sniffle. "Could you hand me a tissue, please, Harmony?"

Getting one for him, she kissed his shoulder while she waited for him to blow his nose.

"I can't believe telling you this is affecting me this way," Mark said finally, still not fully under control. "I mean, it happened over thirty years ago."

"I know," Harmony whispered, giving his arm a squeeze. "I know."

"Anyway," he said, struggling to finish his story, "Justin, who was only about six at the time, rushed over and yanked me out from under that damn spinning thing. . . . But when he did, *he* got caught. By his arm. And then . . . I heard him scream . . ." Sniffling more than ever now, he had to stop again. "I'm sorry, Harmony. Could you give me another tissue?"

Handing him one, she waited silently until he was ready to resume the conversation.

"*I* was the big brother, Harmony," he told her. "It was my job to look after *him*, not the other way around. But, because I couldn't do a simple thing like follow my dad's rules and watch my little brother on the elephant slide and the zebra swings,

Justin has had to spend his entire life with only one arm. And you know what else? Even though he's turned out to be kind of a bitter person, mostly due to the accident I think, he never once blamed me or threw it in my face. And that's much better treatment than I deserve."

"Come on, Mark," Harmony said softly, kissing his shoulder again. "You were just kids. Kids do really dumb things sometimes. Actually, when you think about it, it's kind of amazing any of us ever survives childhood."

Looking over, she saw Mark close his eyes and nod at her.

"Speaking of kids, Mark," she said, deciding it was probably a good time to change the subject, "I have another question I'd like to ask you. About Cameron, this time."

"What?" he asked, wiping the corner of his eye as he turned to face her.

"Well, I still haven't met his young lady friend yet. This . . . Mandy Ross. And maybe it's my imagination, but I'm starting to get the feeling he doesn't want me to. Can you think of any reason why he might be afraid I wouldn't like her?"

"Hmmm," Mark said. "No . . . I can't— Oh, wait. Maybe . . . Harmony, I told you she was black, didn't I?"

"No, you didn't. I mean . . . she *is*?"

"Is that a problem?"

"Well, no, not for me. In fact, the idea of it makes me feel kind of proud. Of Cameron, I mean."

"Well, then, could it be possible that Cameron *thinks* it might be a problem?"

"I don't know. Maybe," Harmony replied, sighing. "I guess I better have a talk with him about it when he gets home."

"And speaking of Cameron getting home," Mark said, patting Harmony on her bare thigh, "I guess I'd better get up and get dressed and head home myself. I'd hate to accidentally fall asleep and then have him come back tomorrow morning with me still here."

"Now wait just a darn minute, Mr. Edwards," Harmony said, wrapping her arm around him. "Who ever said anything about Cameron coming home tomorrow? For your information, he's not coming home until late Sunday afternoon, *and* I also made arrangements for someone to cover things for me at the nursery. That means we can spend the entire weekend just enjoying each other—if you want to, that is. You don't have to *go* anywhere."

"Well then, by all means," Mark answered, moving his hand to the inside of her thigh, "Let's not waste another precious moment. Let's start 'enjoying each other' *right now . . .*"

"Why, Mr. Edwards! *Again?!* What stamina! But I was just thinking I might get up and take a shower."

"Well . . . we could do *both* then," Mark suggested, slowly sliding his hand up her leg. "As long as we do them at the same time, of course."

Shaking her head in amazement as she took a deep breath, Harmony grabbed the wandering hand and then quickly led Mark to the shower.

"Okay, Mr. Edwards," she said, stepping in and turning on the water. "Here we go again . . ."

Chapter 14

The starter pistol fired.

"Pigs! Don't run!" Cameron shouted at the boys of the Javelina Patrol as they took off from the line with the rest of the competing teams. "Remember, if the judges see us running with our backpacks on, they'll deduct safety points. Just walk fast and watch your step. Our designated area's over that way. Let's go!"

Leading them up the grassy slope toward the spectacular rock formations beyond, Cameron did his best to concentrate on the campsite selection checklist he'd memorized. Unfortunately, the words his father said to him only minutes before kept getting in the way.

"Obedience, Cameron, the seventh Scout Law," John Wright had reminded him. "Now, I'm telling you to play it safe and let Randall LaRue tie those shelter tarp knots, not Ricky McGee. Ricky can do something he's more suited for, like digging the latrine. And don't disappoint me, boy, because there's a lot riding on this. There are over fifty patrols here at the encampment, but they're only going to award the Golden Axe to one of them—and it better be yours. So, what's it going to be, Son?"

At the time, to avoid a confrontation, Cameron hadn't given his father an answer. But he did know what his answer was. His father's instructions changed nothing as far as he was concerned. After the initial shock of being given so much responsibility wore off, Ricky actually started looking forward to today, and Cameron wasn't about to spoil it for him. After all, he'd given his word. No, his only real choice was to stay with his original plan, even if it was the dreaded "disappoint Dad yet again" option.

So, with that question resolved—in his mind, anyway—Cameron turned his attention to his more pressing problem, finding a good campsite among the gnarled oak trees and enormous granite boulders that his patrol was fast approaching.

Scanning the hillside ahead for a suitable spot, Cameron simultaneously went over the necessary requirements in his mind: an already established site, so no fresh marks would be put on the land; no safety hazards like overhanging dead limbs, arroyos that could flood, lightning targets, or game trails; shade from the sun and wind protection, both a must; gently sloping ground for good water runoff; and lastly, relative seclusion, to respect the privacy of other people in the area.

Just as Cameron started to think they'd never find a location to satisfy all their needs in the time allotted, an area off to the right caught his eye. Gradually, a smile grew on his face. He couldn't believe it. At first glance, it looked like the perfect campsite.

"Over here, guys!" he shouted, heading for it. "It's exactly what we're looking for. Already trampled down . . . a nice oak tree for shade . . . that big boulder there a natural windbreak . . . I mean, what could be better?"

Arriving at what seemed a good kitchen area, Cameron wasted no time. Hoisting the pack off his back, he yelled to his patrol as he unzipped the front flap and took out his backpacking stove. "Okay, guys, you all know what to do. Let's go to work!"

"C'mon, Cameron. Let me tie the knots. Make the Scrub dig the latrine," Randall LaRue said suddenly, striding to his side.

"For the last time, *no*, Randall," Cameron answered, pumping up the stove. Looking around, he saw Ricky McGee had the blue nylon tarp out of his pack and was already working on his first knot. Glancing back at Randall, he said, "Now, you better get goin' or Ricky's gonna have all those hitches done before you even have your shovel outta your pack."

Shooting a hateful look in Ricky's direction, Randall turned and headed up the hill, grumbling as he went. Not a happy camper, Cameron thought, watching him go.

Lighting the stove, Cameron put some water on and then checked to see that all the rest of his patrol members were efficiently doing their jobs. They were. And even better, Ricky McGee was on his *third* taut-line hitch already.

The competition required that all the patrols cook macaroni and cheese and, as Cameron waited for his water to boil, he went about organizing the various ingredients and utensils he needed to prepare the meal. But as he worked, something began to distract him.

Up in the rocks, on the hillside behind their campsite, Randall had finally started digging the latrine. But what worried Cameron was that the boy didn't seem to be paying too much attention to what he was doing.

Instead, every time Cameron glanced at him, Randall had that icy glare of his leveled directly at Ricky McGee. And with each additional taut-line Ricky finished, that glare grew a few degrees colder. By now, Ricky was on his sixth knot with only *two* to go and, as a result, Randall's expression was downright frigid.

Noticing his pot boiling at last, Cameron dumped in the bag of pasta tubes he'd prepared and gave them a stir. Then, just as he started to chop up the big block of cheese he had out, he heard Ricky yell with glee.

"I'm done! Hey, Cam, I'm done with my knots! Now I need somebody to help me put up the tarp! Quick!"

Yes, Cameron thought. This was the moment he'd been waiting for. And now, with a little luck, Randall LaRue just might learn something. Glancing back up the hill, he called, "Hey, Randall. Come on down here and help Ricky with the shelter."

From his expression and body language, Cameron could tell Randall was both shocked and disgusted that Ricky McGee finished at all, let alone before him. But within just a moment or two, much to Cameron's chagrin, those two lesser emotions gave way to outrage.

"*Shit!*" Randall exclaimed, flinging his shovel angrily as he started down the hill. Fixated on Ricky, the boy still wasn't paying any attention to what he was doing.

And that's when it happened.

As Cameron looked on in horror, Randall LaRue fell to the ground, screaming in agony, holding his leg. Somehow he managed to hurt himself. Hurt himself *bad*.

As fast as he could, Cameron got the first-aid bag out of his pack and then rushed to Randall's side, but not before Ricky McGee got there first.

Holding Randall's hand, Ricky was talking very softly to him, trying to calm him down. And amazingly, it seemed to be working. Then, as Cameron reached them, Ricky shot him a look and pointed.

"Snake, Cameron."

He saw it. About two yards from them. Headed *away*, thankfully. A rattlesnake. It had a black tail and snout, with light-colored scales and dark markings on its back.

"It's a black-tail," Cameron told Ricky with confidence, unzipping the first-aid bag. Then he yelled to the rest of his patrol. "Guys! Get the medics! Tell 'em snakebite. *Black-tailed rattler*. Tell 'em to bring a stretcher. Hurry!"

Turning his attention back to Randall as the others scurried away, Cameron felt a twinge of emotion as he watched Ricky tenderly stroking the crying boy's forehead. Then and there, something told him that Randall had called Ricky the Scrub for the very last time.

"Okay, Randall," Cameron said, removing the boy's neckerchief, "let's slide you around this way just a little bit so your legs are pointed downhill. We've gotta get that bite lower than the rest of your body."

"You're . . . you're not gonna . . . you're not gonna *cut me*, are you?" Randall asked between sobs.

"No," Cameron assured him. "Nothing I do is gonna hurt you at all. Now, just try to relax, Randall. Close your eyes and try to take long, deep breaths."

Rolling Randall's pant leg up to his knee, Cameron used the neckerchief as a constricting band, placing it about three inches above the two oozing fang marks. Then, as Ricky continued to stroke and reassure Randall, Cameron got his snakebite kit out of the first-aid bag.

"Ricky . . . Cameron . . . my leg *burns*," Randall cried, grimacing. Then he opened his eyes wide as he heard Cameron pop open the plastic snakebite box. "*What're you gonna do now*?"

"Don't worry, Randall," Cameron answered calmly. "I'm just gonna get as much of that poison out as I can before the medics get here to take care of you, that's all. Just lie back. I'm not gonna hurt you, I promise."

"Just lie back," Ricky repeated, gently pushing Randall's head down as he continued to stroke him. "There . . . that's good . . . that's real good . . ."

Finally getting the chance to do for real what he'd practiced so many times in Scout first-aid training, Cameron went to work. Donning his rubber gloves, he first used the kit's safety razor to remove the leg hair from the bitten area. Then, selecting the right size suction cup, he fitted it to the kit's small hypodermic-like vacuum pump and prepared to extract the poison. Pulling the pump's plunger out, he placed the suction cup over the bite. Now he was ready for the final step. Holding his breath, he slowly pushed the plunger back in—and felt the suction begin. He checked his watch. It would take at least three minutes for the pump to do its work. It was while he was waiting that, to his profound relief, the medical corpsmen arrived.

"You're quite a pair," one of them told him and Ricky as the team of medics took over Randall's care. "You guys did a heck of a job here."

"Thanks," Cameron said.

"Would one of you boys like to go with us on the ride back to Mesquite?" another medic asked. "It might help keep him calmed down."

Shrugging, Cameron answered, "Sure. I'll go."

"Wait," Ricky piped up, still holding Randall's hand. "I'd like to be the one. If it's okay, I mean."

Cameron looked at him, then at Randall, and then Randall nodded up at him. It seemed it was what they both wanted. Shaking his head at the irony of it all, Cameron smiled. "Sure . . . I think that'd be great. Just great."

"Thanks, Cam," Ricky called excitedly as the medics lifted the stretcher and started carrying Randall down the hill. "See ya later."

"Bye, Ricky," Cameron shouted after him with a wave. Then, watching them go, he shook his head again. "Whodda thunk it?" he said to himself.

Suddenly, from up in the rocks behind them, to the mob that had gathered to see Randall taken away, John Wright's voice boomed down. "It's okay, everybody. You can all relax now. I've killed it."

Looking up, Cameron saw his father standing like some victorious Apache warrior with the limp body of a rattlesnake held high over his head.

"Gentlemen!" John Wright shouted at the medics. "Shouldn't you take this with you?"

"Naw . . . that won't be necessary, sir," one of them called back. "The kids had it pegged, all right. That's a black-tail. No doubt about it." And with that, the medical team hurried away.

All of a sudden, with the crisis over, Cameron started to feel a little giddy. And as the rest of the Scouts went over to get a closer look at the dead snake, he took his water bottle and sat down against the trunk of the nearest shady oak tree. Laying his head back, he closed his eyes and took a drink.

"I thought I told you to have Ricky dig the latrine," his father's voice said suddenly, interrupting the moment.

Without opening his eyes, Cameron decided to ignore the remark. Instead, he had a criticism of his own. "You know, Dad, black-tailed rattlesnakes are a protected species. It's against the law to kill one."

"I don't believe it. You're worried about the *snake*?" John Wright asked, incredulous. "Well, you know what I'd be worried about if I were you? I'd be worried that, by allowing Randall to get bitten by a rattlesnake, you threw away any chance of winning the Golden Axe. That's what I'd be worried about."

"Okay, *that's it*," Cameron said, finally losing his temper. Bouncing up, he yelled at his father. "You know what, Dad? I don't care about any stupid Golden Axe. You wanna know what I *do* care about?"

Rushing over to where the blue shelter tarp still lay on the ground, he pointed down at one of the taut-line hitches Ricky tied. "What I *do* care about is that Ricky McGee tied every one of these stupid, stinking knots all by himself. So, quit screwing around with him, Dad, and give the poor kid his *goddamn Tenderfoot* already."

Cameron was so mad now he was actually shaking but, from the way John Wright's dark eyes drilled into him, he knew his father was probably even madder.

Marching over to him, John Wright grabbed him by the collar and then took him behind one of the granite boulders, out of sight. Cameron knew what was coming and he braced himself as his father raised his hand and backhanded him full in the face.

Reeling from the pain of the blow, Cameron forced himself not to cry. After all, over the years he'd had lots of practice at that.

He and his mother both had.

Chapter 15

As Mark Edwards turned off the street into the church parking lot, he scanned the sign out front. It read: MESQUITE UNITARIAN UNIVERSALIST CHURCH. Suddenly, he felt his tie start to choke him. Glancing over, he said, "Oh, no . . . Harmony. This isn't the church that weirdo guy, Reverend Moon, started back in the seventies, is it? Please tell me you're not a Moonie."

She laughed. "No, Mark. That's the Unification Church. *This* is the Unitarian Church. They're two entirely different things."

"Thank God," he told her as he pulled into a space and switched off the pickup. Turning to her again, he frowned. "Well, then . . . what exactly *is* the Unitarian Church?"

"Well, I'd really rather you discovered that for yourself, Mark, so I won't tell you too much," Harmony answered as she rolled up her window. "Let's just say Unitarian Universalism is a faith that stresses individual freedom of belief, reason, a united world community, and liberal social action. Beyond that, I think you should just see for yourself. Okay?"

"Okay," Mark answered, nodding.

Getting out of the truck, he circled around to the passenger's side and opened her door. Watching as she gracefully slid off the seat in the short pleated skirt and high heels she had on, he bit his lip. No doubt about it. Harmony Anderson had the most beautiful legs of any woman he'd ever seen.

"Mark?" she said as he closed the door for her.

"Yeah?"

"If you wouldn't mind, I need a few minutes to myself right now. It's kind of a Sunday morning ritual I go through. Why don't you go over to that building over there and take a look at the things they have hanging in the hallway. I think you'll find them interesting. I won't be long."

"Well . . . where will you be?" Mark asked.

"Oh, I'm just going to walk through the grounds and maybe sit on a bench for a bit. I'll just be a few minutes. You don't mind, do you?"

"No. Of course not," he said, smiling.

Standing on her tiptoes, she reached up and gave him a quick peck on the lips, then winked at him. "See you in a little while, Mark," she said.

"Okay. Bye."

Watching her walk away, Mark finally turned and headed for the church wing she pointed out to him. As he approached, he saw a sign over the entrance: THE HALL OF GREAT UNITARIAN UNIVERSALISTS. Jogging up the stairs, he pulled open the glass door and went in.

Strolling down the long hallway, the first set of framed portraits he came to were American presidents. It seemed John Adams, John Quincy Adams, Millard Fillmore, Thomas Jefferson and William Howard Taft had all been Unitarian Universalists, members of a religion Mark Edwards had never even heard of before today. His curiosity more than aroused, he shook his head and continued on.

WRITERS headed the next section and, again, Mark was intrigued to learn that Emerson, Hawthorne, Longfellow, Lowell, Thoreau, and Whittier had also all been Unitarians.

Then, he came to the great Unitarian women of history, with Susan B. Anthony, Clara Barton, Dorothea Dix, Mary Livermore, Florence Nightingale, and Julia Ward Howe just some of the names he recognized.

But most interesting of all to Mark were the great Unitarian scientists represented in the hall. And they were many, including Locke, Linus Pauling, Priestley, and Charles Steinmetz to name but a few.

Finally, upon reaching the hall's end, Mark noticed that some of the famous Unitarians defied easy categorization, like the patriot liberal Ethan Allen, child-care expert Dr. Benjamin Spock, and the leaders Albert Schweitzer and Adlai Stevenson. All in all, a very impressive list, indeed.

Suddenly he remembered Harmony and, glancing at his watch, realized fifteen minutes had already slipped by. Thinking he should probably go, he spun around and hurried up the hall, back through the doors, and out into the bright morning sun. Finding her sitting on a park bench in the shade of a big paloverde with her eyes closed, he walked up quietly and sat down beside her. "So . . . what are you up to?" he asked.

"Praying," she answered softly.

With a devilish grin, Mark said, "Well, Harmony, I don't see any fishponds that need cleaning out here. And it doesn't look to me like you're doing any cooking either."

"This time I'm *praying* praying, smart guy," she said, her eyes still closed. But even though she was trying hard not to, Mark could see the beginnings of a smile playing at the corners of her mouth.

Her mouth, he thought. He couldn't resist. Taking her by surprise, he kissed her.

Reaching up, she caressed the back of his head, holding him

to her as they enjoyed the moment. When they were finished, she opened her eyes and gazed at him. "*Amen*," she said.

"We better go, Harmony," Mark told her, brushing a strand of auburn hair back from her face. "Didn't you say the service starts at ten?"

"Oh, that's right. We are here for the church service, aren't we?" she answered, teasing him. "Well, okay. Let's get going."

Getting up, Mark offered Harmony his arm and, when she took it, they headed toward the main church entrance, joining the others filing in from the parking lot.

Glancing at the marquee on their way in, Mark raised his eyebrows at the title of the day's sermon which read: STUCK ON THE METAPHOR—THE NEED FOR A NEW MYTHOLOGY. "Hmm . . . ," he said as they headed down the aisle. "Sounds interesting."

Taking seats in the church's cushioned pews, Harmony turned to him and smiled. "Mark, do you recognize the music that's playing?"

Pausing to listen more closely, he nodded. "Isn't this the singer you played for me the night we had spaghetti at your house? Enya, I think her name was?"

"Very good, Mr. Edwards. You passed that test with flying colors. We'll make a New-Ager out of you yet." Leaning closer, she whispered in his ear. "And by the way, don't look now but all the women in the congregation are watching you, checking you out. I've never brought a man to church with me before. They must be very curious."

"Well, thanks for bringing it to my attention, Harmony," Mark said, feeling himself blush. "As if I wasn't nervous enough already. You know, I haven't been to church since I was a kid and I bet they can tell. In fact, that's probably why they're watching me."

Giggling, Harmony patted his thigh. Then, she quickly sat up. "Oh, here comes Dr. Paul."

Mark watched as a gray-haired, bearded man in a western-style suit and bolo tie stepped up onto the front stage and crossed to the podium. And even though he and Harmony were sitting a fair distance back, it was impossible not to notice the man's striking blue eyes. Checking the program someone handed him on the way in, Mark looked for his name. It read: DR. PAUL DREYFUSS-CAMPBELL.

"Good morning," the minister said into the microphone as the music faded.

"Good morning," the congregation answered in unison.

"God . . . ," he said, beginning dramatically when the church grew quiet again. "Why is there such a problem with this word? The problem," he explained, answering his own question, "is that, in our language, the word 'God' is an ambiguous one. You see, it seems to refer to something that is known. But the problem is, how can that which is truly transcendent ever *be* known? No, the mysteries of life and the infinite universe are beyond our finite human conception. And, after all, that's what mythology has always been about."

Glancing at Harmony, Mark nodded at her. So far, this guy seemed to be making sense.

"You see, the myths, to include all those stories in the Bible," Dreyfuss-Campbell continued, "are metaphorical representations of the grand mystery of our world and of the spiritual potential of every human being. But the key word here is . . . 'metaphorical.'

"You see, metaphors are images that suggest something else. They are . . . poetry, *not* prose. And the symbols of all our religious systems must be interpreted, not as facts, but as metaphors. Otherwise, we end up with all the crazy problems we have today where, everywhere you turn, people are worshiping, loving, and, tragically, dying for their metaphors. And that's exactly what has happened with our own biblical tradition.

"You see, here in the Western world, Christianity is still based on a view of the universe that should have been left to the first millennium B.C.E., a view that belongs in another age, to another people, to a whole different set of human values. But, it no longer belongs here.

"You see, all religions *are* true, but only when understood metaphorically. It's when they get stuck on their own metaphors, interpreting them as facts, that they get into trouble. There never was a real Garden of Eden, after all. It's a metaphor for innocence. And science has shown us there is no physical Heaven anywhere in the universe. It's a metaphor for turning inward, returning to the source. But the most tragic example of Christianity getting stuck on its own metaphors, in my opinion at least, has been its attitudes toward the natural world and, ultimately, toward life itself . . ."

Mark listened intently as Dreyfuss-Campbell went on to describe how, because of the serpent seducer and the Fall in the Garden of Eden, the biblical tradition has always condemned nature as corrupt and impure. What this amounted to then was a refusal to affirm life and a loss of appreciation for planet Earth itself contributing to global problems like the destruction of the rain forests, the polluting of our oceans and air, the greenhouse effect, and overpopulation. And with that said, Dreyfuss-Campbell finally came to the main point of his talk.

"What humankind needs then," the minister said, using a remote to dim the lights and switch on a slide projector, "is a *new* mythology, one that will hopefully save the Earth and, in turn, save ourselves. A new mythology that just might use *this* as its symbol . . ."

On the wide screen which had electronically lowered behind the man, a huge picture of Earth from space flashed on. For Mark, it was hard to believe that anything so breathtakingly beautiful could ever be condemned by anyone.

After taking a moment to gaze up at the dramatic image, Dreyfuss-Campbell turned back to the congregation. "As we are all aware," he said, "every group of people is the chosen people in its own mind. And that kind of thinking, ladies and gentlemen, will get us nowhere fast. What the new mythology to come must do is identify the person not with his local group but with the society of the entire planet at large. And so, in conclusion, *that* will be the only true salvation of humankind on planet Earth. . . . Thank you."

They applauded. Then, as the clapping gradually died down, the music came on again. *Ave Maria*. And this time, the congregation sang along.

Mark didn't know the words so he gazed around at everybody while he listened to them sing. Then, glancing over at Harmony as they held hands, he did a double take. Tears were streaming down her cheeks.

"I like to listen to music so beautiful, it makes me want to cry," he remembered her telling him. Evidently *Ave Maria* was just such a piece.

Taking out his handkerchief as the music ended, he gave it to Harmony and she dried her eyes. Then, filing into the center aisle with the others, they headed for the door.

Just outside the church entrance, Dr. Dreyfuss-Campbell was waiting to thank them all for coming. And as Mark and Harmony reached him, Harmony stopped to talk.

"Dr. Paul," she said, "I'd like you to meet Mark Edwards . . . Mark, this is Dr. Paul."

Shaking the minister's hand, Mark couldn't help but feel the man was sizing him up. But he decided to ignore it. "How do you do?" he said.

"Very well, thank you," Dr. Paul answered, smiling. "I'm very pleased to meet you finally. Harmony has had a lot of good things to say about you and, from what she tells me, we have something in common, you and I—besides a keen interest in *her*, I mean."

"And what's that?" Mark asked, opting to ignore the fact that the minister was flirting with his date.

"Well . . . ," Dr. Paul said, "it seems we are both *Star Trek* fans."

Mark cocked his head. "You know, it's really funny you should say that now. I was just thinking as we were walking out a second ago that *Star Trek*, with its positive view of the future where all races and cultures are working together, is as close to that new mythology you were talking about as anything I've ever heard."

"Excellent point," Dr. Paul agreed. "In fact, maybe I should make that the topic of my next talk."

Mark nodded at him. "I'd come."

"You know, if I remember correctly, I think they did a poll once," Dr. Paul said, frowning thoughtfully. "Anyway, from this poll, they found out over half the American public considers themselves *Star Trek* fans. That's a lot of people."

Nodding again, Mark suddenly grinned. "Well, I guess that means if we could somehow convince the other half to watch the show, then your work here would be done. Heck, you'd be out of a job."

"And I could spend the rest of my days fly fishing," Dr. Paul said, smiling at him. "Listen, Mark, it was really good to meet you. And Harmony—" he hugged her "—I'm very glad for you. I really hope to see you both next week. Take care now."

Telling Dr. Paul good-bye, they walked out to Mark's pickup and got in. Then, as they pulled out of the church parking lot onto the street, Harmony asked, "So, Mark, did you really mean what you said back there? Do you really want to go again?"

He smiled. "You mean, when Dr. Paul gives his talk about *Star Trek*?"

She gave him one of her scolding looks. "I mean *anytime*, Mark."

"Sure," he told her, nodding. "I liked it. I think I'd enjoy going back."

Glancing over, Mark saw Harmony beaming at him, obviously happy. And knowing she was happy made him happy. It seemed just being together made them both feel happy. What a concept, he thought.

"Mark," Harmony said suddenly, breaking his reverie, "I was just wondering. . . . What are your plans for the holidays?"

Pulling up to a red light, Mark stopped the truck, shifting into neutral. Turning to her, he answered, "Well, for Thanksgiving, Justin and I are traveling to Oregon to visit relatives. But we don't have any plans for Christmas yet. Why?"

For a few moments, Harmony seemed to be mulling something over. Then, as the light turned green and they took off again, she said, "Yeah . . . Cameron and I are going to be gone for Thanksgiving, too, spending it with my folks up in Sedona. But we don't have any Christmas plans yet, either, and . . . well . . . we were both really hoping you and Justin could spend Christmas Day with us."

"Christmas, huh?" Mark said, taking a breath. "This is starting to sound serious, Harmony."

"Well . . . *isn't it*?" she asked him.

Holding her gaze while they both considered the question, Mark felt like some kind of powerful electric current was passing between them. Finally, grinning at her, he patted the seat next to him. "Get over here," he said. And for the rest of the ride home, he held her as close as he possibly could.

But when they arrived back at Harmony's house, Mark knew full well John Wright could be bringing Cameron home from their campout at anytime. And he thought it would be best not to be there when he did. So kissing Harmony passionately and thanking her for one of the best weekends of his entire life, he started to leave.

"Oh, but wait, Mark!" she said, grabbing his arm at the last moment. "I want to give you something first."

Spinning around, she rushed into the house, returning less than a minute later holding what looked like a cassette tape. "Here," she said, handing it to him. "Another little test for you, Mr. Edwards. I want you to listen to this from beginning to end and if it doesn't happen by the time you've heard it all, then you and I need to sit down and have a serious talk." With that, she kissed him one last time and hurried away.

Not at all sure what she was talking about, Mark shook his head, got in, and started the truck. Then he looked at the tape box in his hand. LES MISÉRABLES it read. Popping the cassette in the car stereo, he started down the road.

Now of course Mark Edwards had heard *of* the famous Broadway musical *Les Misérables*. But seeing as how he'd never really been into Broadway shows much, he hadn't ever *heard* it before. To his complete surprise, it captivated him instantly.

Whether it was the pathetic story of extreme social injustice that got to him, or simply the beauty of the music itself, he wasn't really sure. All he did know was that it touched him. So much so in fact that, when he finally got to his house, he didn't even go in. He just sat in his carport with the engine off, listening.

Then, near the end of the tape, a song called *Bring Him Home* came on in which the hero, convict Jean Valjean, pleads with God to take his life rather than that of young Marius, his adopted daughter's true love. Earlier, Mark recalled, the same character had chosen not to let an innocent man be wrongly condemned for a crime he himself committed.

For some reason, the selfless nature of those two acts suddenly hit home—hard. And before he knew it, Mark Edwards started to cry.

Reaching up, he wiped his cheek with the back of his hand and, as he did, it finally dawned on him what Harmony had been talking about.

"Well, I'll be damned," he said.

Part 6
December

Chapter 16

"Okay, Mom," Harmony heard Cameron say. "Take one last guess. What do you think your present is?"

Tilting her head back as inconspicuously as she could, she started to—

"Hey, Harmony!" Mark's voice exclaimed. "No fair trying to peek under the blindfold."

"Sorry," she said with a giggle. Then she shook her head. "Okay, I give up. I have absolutely no idea what could've possibly taken three men the better part of an hour to set up in here. Can I look now? *Please*?"

"All right," Cameron told her. "Go ahead. Take off the scarf."

Pulling the cloth down around her neck, she blinked a few times while her eyes adjusted to the light. Then, glancing around the family room, she saw it. By the Christmas tree, in its own beautiful wooden cabinet, was a brand-new stereo.

"Merry Christmas, Mom!" Cameron said, giving her a hug. "We all helped. While Mark and I put the cabinet together, Justin ran the wire to the speakers in the corners over there. He says that's where we'll get the best sound from. Then we hooked her up. It even has a CD player!"

"Oh, thank you, Hon," she told Cameron, kissing him on the cheek. "And thank you, too, Justin. Oh, we're so pleased you could be with us today."

From the sofa, Justin nodded back solemnly.

Then Harmony stepped over to Mark, wrapping her arms around his waist. Looking up at him, she said, "*You* I'm mad at. That's much too expensive a gift, Mr. Edwards."

"Oh, come on," Mark answered, smiling. "Cameron did kick in some of it, after all. Besides, a music lover like you deserves a good system." Then, pulling her close, he added softly, "And, Harmony, compared to the gifts you've given me in the past two months, something material like a stereo is really precious little."

That did it. Feeling tears starting to well up suddenly, she kissed him.

"Okay, break it up, you two," she heard Justin say behind her. "Enough with the mushy stuff, already. That high-tech electrical job worked up a real appetite and Cameron and I are starved, aren't we, Cameron? When's dinner, anyway?"

"Well, I'm happy to report the Christmas ham is ready and waiting," Harmony answered, wiping a smudge of lipstick from the corner of Mark's mouth. "Let's put a tape on, shall we? Then everybody up to the table. It's time to eat!"

As the four of them dined to the lush renditions of classic holiday chamber music wafting from her new stereo, they all conversed pleasantly. Pleasantly, that is, until Cameron broached his question, the question Harmony knew had plagued him ever since last July.

"Mark," Cameron asked, between forkfuls of his cherry pie à la mode, "do you remember that thing I wanted to know back when I first found out you and Justin had been in my Scout troop?"

"You mean, when you asked me if I believed in God?" Mark said.

"Yeah," Cameron answered.

"Sure, I remember that. Why?"

"Well," Cameron said somewhat hesitantly, "you never really answered. And since it's Christmas and all, and since we're all friends and everything, I thought today might be a good time to ask you again."

Harmony watched as Mark looked first to Justin, then to her, hoping for some kind of cue as to how to proceed. Even though she knew religion wasn't the safest topic for polite dinner chat, she didn't say anything. After all, now was probably as good a time as any to find out where everybody stood.

"Well, Cameron," Mark said finally, realizing he was on his own, "I don't know if you're going to understand this or not, but I consider that an irrelevant question."

"What do you mean?" Cameron asked, frowning.

"Well," Mark said, "since I'm basically a scientist, and since the concept of God lies outside the bounds of probable knowledge, I don't really see any reason to consider the hypothesis."

Harmony couldn't help it. Now she was frowning too. Justin, on the other hand, looked amused by his brother's comment.

"Well . . . does that mean you're an atheist?" Cameron asked.

"No, not at all," Mark answered, shaking his head. "I think it's ludicrous to say there's no God. It's just that, well, I think it's equally ludicrous to say there is. Understand?"

"Then you mean you're uncertain?"

"Exactly, Cameron. That's exactly what I mean," Mark said, smiling. "And after all, every good scientist is."

"So what about Heaven, or Hell, or an afterlife?" Cameron persisted. "What do you think about those things?"

"Well, I've never seen any scientific proof of any of them," Mark said with a shrug. "So I don't see any reason to believe in them."

Cameron frowned again, cocking his head. "Well then, Mark, what do you think *made* everything? And *why*?"

"Well now, that's *the* question, isn't it?" Mark replied, taking a bite of pie. Chewing a few times, he used his napkin and continued. "But the problem with that question is, if *anything* must have a cause, then God, too, must have a cause. Therefore, it's a question that can never ever be answered. *But*, if we're even going to come close to answering it someday, science will be the way. Not religion."

"And so that's why you don't belong to one, huh, Mark?" Cameron said, glancing at Harmony. "A religion, I mean."

"That's right," Mark answered. "The way I see it, science is the search for truth and art is the search for beauty and together those two things are really all the religion I need . . . or want."

Harmony watched as Cameron nodded thoughtfully at Mark. It seemed her son finally understood what he meant. But when she glanced at Justin, he still appeared unsatisfied. And Mark must have noticed it, too, because immediately he started to explain himself further.

"Let's put it this way, Cameron," he said, leaning back in his chair. "If what you're talking about is a *personal* God—that 'old man up there in a robe and beard' you mentioned to me once—then no, I don't believe in that. I mean, a God that creates entire galaxies looking like *us*, bothering with *our* prayers? Get real. But, if you're using the word 'God' to mean nature or the universe, then yeah, I think I could go for that. After all, Stephen Hawking himself did refer to the laws of nature as the 'mind of God.'"

"Now just wait a damn minute there, big brother," Justin said suddenly, jumping into the conversation. "I'm sorry, but I can't sit here any longer being a good boy listening to all your wishy-washy BS. As everybody here knows, Cameron has a decision to make and, frankly, I don't think you're helping him very much."

"Oh, you don't?"

"No, Mark, I don't," Justin repeated emphatically. "Listen, for the word 'God' to be of any use at all, you have to be talking about a personal string-puller in the clouds. Otherwise, if you're talking about nature, then call it 'nature.' If you're talking about the universe, then call it the 'universe.' But don't call those things 'God.' I mean, why muddy the waters?"

"Well, what about 'love,' Justin?" Harmony asked, looking across the table at him.

"What?"

"Well, Justin," she said, glancing at Cameron and Mark before turning back to him, "*I* think it's like Jesus said. God *is* love . . . the center of life . . . the ground of all being. God's present everywhere, in all things and in all persons and at all times. Don't you think?"

"*Thinking* has nothing to do with a point of view like that," Justin answered flatly. "I mean, you sound like Yoda, or Obi-Wan, or somebody. 'Use the Force, Luke,' and all that. Sorry. That's much too metaphysical . . . too mystical for me. Besides, if it's love, then call it 'love.' Don't call it God."

"Well then, what do *you* believe, Justin?" There was an edge to Cameron's voice now and Harmony suspected it was because her son didn't like the way Justin had just spoken to her.

"Well, thanks for asking me, kid," Justin answered, staring back at him. "And I'll be more than glad to tell you, too. The sad truth is *there is no God*. It's just a crutch. A fiction created by wishful thinkers to console themselves. An irrelevant, even harmful, concept. I mean, all you have to do is ask yourself a few simple questions. Like if God could make angels, why did he bother with us? And if God did make us, such as we are, then why did he damn us for being so? I mean, it makes no sense, does it? It's all BS to me."

A little bit shocked by Justin's bitter outburst, Harmony turned to Mark who merely shrugged at her. Evidently, he'd heard all this from his brother before.

But Cameron, much to Harmony's chagrin, didn't seem shocked at all by Justin's remarks—more like intrigued. Cocking his head again, he asked, "So what about religion? Do you consider yourself an atheist, then?"

"You bet I do," Justin fired back. Glancing at Mark, he went on. "And I'm not afraid to admit it either. Religion? Well, as Edison said, it's all bunk. As Freud put it, it's childhood neurosis. Collective insanity, born of fear, and a source of untold misery. Nothing but a tax-sheltered money maker, really. It'd be a much better world if there were no religion in it."

"And what about an afterlife? Prayer? Stuff like that?" Cameron persisted.

"Kid," Justin answered, shaking his head, "the entire hope of any particular religion is the salvation of its members and the damnation of everybody else. Now I ask you, is that *right*? No, there's no Heaven. And there's no Hell, either, for that matter. As I'm sure you know, there's plenty of Hell right here in this world without creating an imaginary one someplace else. And prayer? Well, if God really did listen to our prayers, then all of us would be in some real deep shit because most of us are praying for something bad to happen to all the people we don't like. No. Prayer is nothing more than a form of group thought control used by the churches."

"Now, come on, Justin," Harmony said gently, unable to contain herself any longer. "Not everyone sees prayer the way you seem to think they do. At our church, for example, many of us see prayer more as a way of taking stock in ourselves . . . as a meditation, really. Personally, I like what Emerson said, that 'all honest work is prayer.'"

"Yeah, yeah," Justin said, nodding. "Mark told me a little bit about your church and I have to admit it does sound better than most. *But*, I still say churches are just places for lazy sheep and lambs to turn to in times of trouble so they won't have to rely on themselves. And in the end, I don't think that's a good thing."

"And . . . faith?" Cameron asked.

Justin smiled at him ironically. "No more than a belief in something you know can't possibly be true, kid," he said.

For the next few moments, they were all silent. But then, when Justin realized the three of them were staring at him, he turned to Harmony again.

"You mentioned Jesus a little while ago," he said to her. "So tell me, Harmony, do you really believe in him, or what?"

"Yes, Justin, I believe in him," Harmony answered without flinching. "But not because he was God, but because he was a human being, a human being at his best. But if you mean, 'Do I believe he was the *Son* of God?' then I only know one way to answer that question. After all, we're *all* the Children of God, aren't we?"

He didn't answer. He just frowned at her.

"Okay, come on, Cameron," Mark said suddenly, getting up from the table. "I think we've all pretty much exhausted this topic. How 'bout you and I clearing the table and getting these dishes done?"

"Wait. I have one more question," Cameron said. Turning to Mark's brother once again, he asked, "So, tell me, Justin. I'm curious. Do you think you feel the way you do because of what happened when you were a little kid? I mean, do you think it has anything to do with what happened to your arm?"

Staring blankly at Cameron, Justin stood up from his chair. Then saying, "Excuse me," he turned his back and went into the living room.

"What'd I say?" Cameron asked, concerned.

"Nothing, Cameron," Mark said, putting his hand on the boy's shoulder. "Don't worry about it, it's not your fault. It's just that, well, I can't take him anywhere, that's all—never could. Come on now. Help me with these dishes."

As Mark and Cameron started clearing the table, Harmony got up and followed Justin. She found him crouched in the corner of the living room petting Barkley. When she went over to him he stood up and, for several long moments, they simply gazed at one another.

Then, shaking his head, Justin started to say, "Harmony, I'm sor—"

But before he could finish, she kissed him. Full on the lips.

Stunned, Justin stammered, "Wha—what in the world was that for?"

Clasping his one hand in both of hers, Harmony smiled at him. "Without you, Justin," she explained, "Mark wouldn't be in any of our lives today. And because of that fact, you will always be a hero to Cameron and me. Now we may have our differences but that's okay. Because one thing will never change. Here in this house you will always be loved."

Suddenly, as Harmony watched, the ever-present tension in Justin's face seemed to ease a little. Then, clearing his throat, he gave her hand a squeeze. "I said it before and I'll say it again now, Harmony," he told her. "That big brother of mine is one lucky sonovabitch."

"Thanks, Justin," she answered, ". . . I think."

The phone rang then, but only once.

And glimpsing a blur moving fast down the hallway, Harmony knew why. Cameron had picked up in his bedroom before it had a chance to ring again.

"Justin, would you excuse me, please? That might be one of my relatives calling."

"Sure, Harmony."

Following her son into his room, Harmony asked him, "Who is it, dear?"

"Hang on a sec," Cameron said into the phone. Covering the receiver with his hand, he answered, "Mom, it's Mandy Ross. She wants to know if I can come over to her house to meet her parents tonight. She says she has a present for me, too. Can I go?"

"Tell Mandy you'll call her back, Cameron. We need to discuss it first."

"But Mom . . . ," Cameron complained.

She put her hands on her hips. "Cameron . . ."

"Oh, okay, Mom," he answered, shrugging. Uncovering the receiver, he said, "Mandy? Hi. I'm gonna hafta call you back. . . . No, she probably will. . . . Yeah. . . . It's just that we hafta 'discuss it first.' Yeah . . . okay . . . okay. Bye." Hanging up the phone, he turned back to her. "Okay, Mom, let's 'discuss it.'"

Crossing to the bed, Harmony sat down and patted the spread next to her. "Come sit here, Cameron," she said. When he obliged her, she asked, "Now if I let you go over there, Mandy's parents *will* be there, right?"

He rolled his eyes. "I already told you, Mom. That's why I'd be going. To meet them."

"Well then, let me ask you this," Harmony said, reaching over and touching his knee. "Maybe it's my imagination, but I sometimes get the feeling you're afraid to have *me* meet *her*. I mean, you have had several opportunities. Like when I picked you up after the Halloween dance, for one. Tell me, Cameron. Is there some reason why you haven't introduced us yet?"

He didn't answer her. He didn't have to. The look on his face told her she was right.

"There *is* something, isn't there, Cameron?"

With his eyes downcast, he nodded.

"Well, Cameron," she said, coaxing him gently, "is it because Mandy is black?"

"No, Mom!" he exclaimed, frowning. "It's not 'cause she's black."

"Well then, why?"

"It's not 'cause she's black," Cameron repeated. "It's 'cause she's . . . Christian."

"What?" Harmony said, stunned.

"She's Christian."

Harmony was confused. Shaking her head at Cameron, she said, "Well, that's no problem, silly. Most people we know *are*, after all. In fact, some of the people who go to our church consider themselves Christians. Why on earth would you think I'd have a problem with that?"

"Well," Cameron answered, "you had a problem with Dad being one, didn't you?"

All of a sudden, the pieces fell into place and Harmony finally understood why Cameron had been so secretive about Mandy. But her son had the wrong idea. "Cameron," she said, taking his hand, "it wasn't because your father was Christian that he and I got a divorce, you know."

"Well, why did you then?" he asked.

She sighed. "I think you already know that, Son. Think about it. It wasn't because he was Christian. It was the *kind* of Christian he was that was the problem. You know as well as I that your father was a very intolerant person. He still is. That's why I couldn't live with him anymore. While we were together, I bent and bent and bent as far as I could. But finally, I couldn't bend anymore. I knew I would break if I stayed with him. I think you and I both would have. Don't you?"

Slowly, he nodded at her again.

"Well, okay then," she said, smiling at him.

"Well, what about it, Mom?" Cameron asked suddenly, returning to his original question. "You know, Dad and I *are* leaving for our San Diego trip tomorrow. If I don't see Mandy tonight, I'll hafta wait till school starts again. Come on, Mom. Can I go? *Please*?"

"Oh, all right," Harmony said, getting off the bed. "But you won't be able to stay more than a couple hours. You have a big day tomorrow, remember. Call Mandy back and then hurry up and get ready while I go tell Mark. Then I'll run you over."

"Thanks, Mom!" Cameron said excitedly.

Turning, Harmony headed back up the hall when she unexpectedly ran into Mark coming out of the kitchen. He had a funny look on his face. "What's wrong?" she asked him.

In a hushed voice, he answered, "Well, do you have any idea what just got into Justin? I mean, I thought he was mad when he left the dinner table a little while ago but he just came in to the kitchen and told me *he* wanted to do the rest of the dishes. Very strange."

Harmony smiled coyly and gave him a hug. "Oh, I wouldn't worry about it too much if I were you, Mark," she said. "Justin and I just came to a sort of mutual understanding, that's all."

"Hmm . . . ," he said, raising an eyebrow at her.

"Listen, Mark," Harmony told him, "I have to take off for a little while and run Cameron over to Mandy Ross's house. She just called and invited him. Will you and your brother be able to keep yourselves occupied till I get back?"

Taking her hand, Mark winked. "I have a better idea," he answered.

Leading her into the family room and over to the Christmas tree, he reached behind the tree stand and produced one last unopened present.

"What's this?" Harmony asked, grinning.

"Well, it just so happens that Justin asked me to run *him* home as soon as he finishes those dishes," Mark said. "So why don't you let me take Cameron, too. While I'm gone, you can relax and open this and, hopefully, enjoy it. Then I'll hurry back here and we can spend some 'quality' time together, if you know what I mean."

She did. And she liked the idea—a lot.

"Oh, and by the way," Mark added, placing the present in her hand before starting out of the room, "the *last* selection is the reason I picked this particular item out for you. Hope you like it." Then, winking again, he was gone, taking Justin and Cameron with him.

As soon as Harmony was alone, she lost no time unwrapping

the mysterious gift. And she smiled when she saw it was a CD to go with her new player, an Elton John album called *Goodbye Yellow Brick Road*.

Popping in the disc, she fast-forwarded to the final song and then curled up on the sofa to listen. And almost immediately, she started to cry.

But in this case, it wasn't so much the beauty of Elton John's music that made the tears come as it was the uncanny appropriateness of the song's lyrics and title. It was a love song, of course. And its title and the name of the woman in the song were the same.

They were both called *Harmony*.

Chapter 17

On his bed in their motel room, Cameron Wright channel surfed with the remote while his father took a shower. But he wasn't really paying much attention to what was on the television. Instead, the dismal day he and John Wright had kept playing over and over again in his mind.

They didn't go to Sea World, or to the zoo, or to the wild animal park, or to any of the places Cameron hoped to see. They didn't even go to the beach.

Rather, his father took him to a place he had never heard of before called the Institute for Creation Research where 'creation scientists,' as his father called them, worked to try and reconcile science and the Bible.

"Creation *scientists*?" Cameron said as they pulled into the institute's parking lot. "Isn't that what they call an 'oxymoron,' Dad?"

Not surprisingly, John Wright didn't appreciate that little remark one bit. And, as it turned out, that first disagreement seemed to set the tone for their entire day.

According to his father, the whole idea of touring the place was to help Cameron by showing him how 'scientific creationism' had bonded scientific evidence with the concept of direct special creation. But the more he saw, the more Cameron realized it was practically all religion and no real science whatsoever.

For example, one exhibit maintained that, as described in Genesis, the universe was created in only one week, a totally ridiculous idea as far as Cameron was concerned. He asked his father a few questions about it.

"Look at this, Dad," he said. "It says here that on the second day the atmosphere was created and then, on the third day, the plants were created."

"Yeah. So?"

"Well, they've got it backwards, Dad," Cameron tried to explain. "I mean, I've known ever since middle school that it's the green plants that are responsible for the atmosphere we have today. They *made* all the oxygen. Don't you see?"

"You don't say."

"And look at this," Cameron went on. "They've got the sun created on the fourth day. That's backwards, too."

"How so?" his father asked.

"Well, photosynthesis, Dad," Cameron answered. "I mean, everyone knows plants need sunlight to make their food. To live. How in the world could the plants have come *before* the sun? It makes absolutely no sense, that's all."

"It was God's will, Cameron," his father told him, frowning.

"But, Dad," he persisted, "I thought you said this place was going to integrate scripture and science *together*. So far, I don't see that happening."

"Let's just continue," John Wright said.

Next they came to a room totally devoted to a reconstruction of Noah's ark and to the worldwide flood in Genesis, which included an exhibit on how creation scientists thought the flood formed the Grand Canyon in a matter of weeks. But since

Cameron and his father had already gone round and round over that one, he thought it best not to say anything about it.

Finally, near the end of their tour, they saw a display that tried to argue against Darwin's theory of evolution by natural selection. But again, after studying it carefully, Cameron simply shook his head and shrugged.

"What, Son?" his father asked.

"Well, Dad," he said, "it's just like all the other stuff in here. It's wrong."

"What do you mean 'wrong'?" John Wright asked, glaring at him. "What about the case it makes here that no missing links have ever been found in this fossil record of yours? Unless, of course, you want to count ridiculous hoaxes, like Nebraska man or Piltdown man. What do you say to that?"

Cameron smiled. "That's not fair, Dad," he said. "After all, it was scientists who eventually *exposed* those hoaxes. And it's not true that no intermediate life forms have ever been found. Thousands have. *Archaeopteryx*, for example."

"What?"

"The missing link between dinosaurs and birds, Dad," Cameron explained. "*Archaeopteryx* is the perfect example of evolution caught in the act. We learned all about it in Mark's—I mean, Mr. Edwards's class."

For what seemed an eternity, John Wright stood scowling at Cameron. Then he shook his head. "It was a mistake to bring you here, boy," he said, turning for the door. "I see that now." And as Cameron followed him out, so ended their ill-fated trip to the Institute for Creation Research.

And now, as Cameron continued to flip through the channels on their motel room TV, he wondered when the *real* San Diego fun would begin. So when his father stepped out of the bathroom finally, he asked him, "Dad, are we going to Sea World tomorrow?"

No answer.

"Not Sea World, huh? Oh, I bet we're going to the zoo, aren't we?"

Again, no answer.

"Well, how 'bout the wild animal park then?"

Still no answer.

"Well," Cameron persisted, sitting up, "then it's gotta be the beach. That's where we're going, isn't it? We're gonna spend the day at the beach, aren't we, Dad?"

Slowly, John Wright turned to him, unexpectedly piercing Cameron with his cold, dark eyes. And then, with just a hint of a smile playing on his thick lips, he spoke. "Boy," he said, "after what happened today, the only place you're headed tomorrow is straight through that godforsaken desert *back* to Arizona."

Incredulous, Cameron stared silently at his father.

"Oh, and by the way, Son," John Wright added, "Merry Christmas."

Chapter 18

As Mark Edwards worked, meticulously applying the secondary color of paint over the base coat of his *Next Generation Enterprise* model, he glanced up at the clock on the wall. It read: 3:07 A.M.

Then, from behind him suddenly, he heard, "What's the matter, Mark? Couldn't you sleep?"

Turning around in his swivel chair, he saw Harmony standing in the doorway of the hobby room, wearing nothing but an old shrunken T-shirt of his. If he'd ever seen anything sexier, he couldn't remember when.

"Mark?" she said.

"Oh, I'm sorry, Harmony," he answered, catching himself staring at her body again. "Please, come in. Come see what I'm working on."

Joining him at his worktable, Harmony sat across from Mark and then gestured at the saucer-shaped command module of his miniature starship. "Oh, Mark," she said, "I love the color of that paint you're using. Oh, and that pattern! It's so intricate. You know, it looks a lot like an Aztec calendar. Don't tell me you're doing all that by hand, with that little tiny brush there."

"Yep. All by hand," he answered. "Hey, watch this!" Reaching over, he flicked the switch on the model's external battery power pack and simultaneously hundreds of pinpoint windows lit up all over the spaceship.

"*Ohh, Mark*," she said, delighted.

He grinned. "The magic of fiber optics."

Reaching across the table, Harmony took his hand. "Mark, you *do* realize what it is you're doing here, don't you?"

"Uh . . . building a model?"

"Mark," she said, frowning. "Don't you remember what I told your brother the other day? You know, that all honest work is . . ."

Suddenly, he got it. "Oh, yeah," he answered, nodding. "Good old Emerson, wasn't it? 'All honest work is prayer,' he said. I remember. But, Harmony, you don't really believe putting together and painting plastic space models is the same thing as praying, do you?"

"Well," she said, "I guess that depends on why you do it. Why *do* you do it, anyway? What do you think about while you're working on these models of yours?"

"If I tell you that, you'll think I'm silly."

"Try me."

Hesitating a moment, he shrugged. "Well, Harmony," he said, "I guess what I think about mostly is what it might be like to be a real space explorer, to be a crew member aboard an amazing ship like this one. Pretty juvenile, huh?"

"Not at all," she answered, smiling at him. "Don't you see, Mark, in a way you're fulfilling one of your dreams by building these models of yours. And by doing that, you *are* praying. You know, there's an old hymn that goes 'Prayer is the soul's sincere desire, uttered or unexpressed.' What I think that means is, anything we do that's constructive, anything we do that's helping us follow our bliss, well then that's prayer. Just look at this little starship of yours, Mark. It's beautiful! *Love* went into it. No, there's no doubt about it, Mark. You were praying when you built this. That's for sure."

He smiled back. "Okay, Harmony. If you say so."

"Oh, I just love this color, Mark," she said again, taking a closer look at his paint job. "What's it called, anyway?"

"Well, it's really kind of funny you should like it so much because. . . ." He handed her the little paint jar. "You see, it's the same paint Cameron used on his Grand Canyon river water. The same color he needed in Justin's hobby shop that day when we first met."

"You're kidding," Harmony said, surprised. Then reading the label, she cocked her head. "Duck egg blue. Huh. . . . Very pretty."

"Well, Harmony," Mark told her, resuming his painting, "I better get back to this. I'm almost done with this section I'm working on and I'd like to finish it."

But instead of leaving him alone, she started stroking his bare leg with her foot under the table. "Mark," she said, "you know you never answered me. What's the matter anyway? Why couldn't you sleep?"

Without looking up, he shrugged. "It's no big deal, Harmony, really. It's probably just all the excitement of having you spend the night at my house for the first time, that's all. It's certainly nothing for you to worry about."

Getting up from her chair, Harmony circled around behind Mark and, the next thing he knew, he felt the weight of her breasts and the hardness of her erect nipples pressing on his bare shoulders. Then she whispered in his ear, "I guess I didn't tire you out enough before we tried to go to sleep, Mark. But I'm more than willing to give it another shot."

Without a moment's hesitation, Mark said, "This painting

can wait," and then he got up. He didn't even stop to clean his brush. He simply took Harmony's hand and led her into the hallway. On their way to his bedroom, he asked, "You know, speaking of 'following your bliss,' I think we're about to follow *mine*. Does that mean what we're about to do could be considered praying, too?"

"Well," Harmony answered, hugging him, "even though some might say it's sacrilegious, I would answer definitely 'yes.' I think what we're about to do could most explicitly be called prayer."

Mark hugged her back. "You got the *explicit* part right, that's for sure." Then, just as they reached the bedroom doorway, the phone rang.

Harmony looked shocked. "Who in the world could that be at *this* hour?"

"I have no idea," Mark answered. "Listen, you go get the bed warmed up for us and I'll be right back." Kissing her quickly, he added, "But you better not start without me."

"I'll try not to," she teased. "But you better hurry."

He did. Jogging into the kitchen he flicked on the light switch and then picked up the phone. "Hello? Well, hi. What's the matter, is there something wrong? *You are*. . . . Uh huh. . . . Uh huh. . . . Yeah, she's here. . . . Okay. . . . Okay. . . . Okay. Bye." Hanging up, he left the light on and slowly walked to the bedroom.

"Well . . . was it a wrong number, Mark?" Harmony asked when he walked in.

"I'm afraid we've been found out, Harmony," he said, standing in the dark.

"What do you mean?"

"Well," Mark answered, "guess who's at your house this very minute, home from San Diego four days early after having a really shitty time?"

Silence.

"I better get dressed," Harmony said.

Part 7
January

Chapter 19

Mark Edwards had had a particularly dismal day and beneath his expressionless facade he seethed with frustration. He managed to hide it from everyone else at the tai kwan do karate club, but his brother knew him too well.

"What's wrong, Mark?" Justin asked.

"Nothin'," he answered, tightening the black belt at his waist. "Just hold the pad for me."

"Okay, I'm ready," Justin said. "Hit me with your best shot."

Mark began with a series of side stamp power kicks which he delivered at a target on the large practice pad Justin held up in front of him. When he'd finished, his brother looked out from around it.

"Is that really the best you can do?"

"Just hold the damn pad, Justin," Mark repeated sullenly. "I'm gonna do my forward stamp kicks next."

"So do 'em," Justin said.

One after another, Mark smashed the sole of his foot directly into the target on the pad. A few times, he thought he could hear his brother groaning with exertion behind it.

"Now that's more like it," Justin said, peeking around the edge of the pad again when Mark had finished. "Snap kicks next?"

"Hold the pad," Mark told him.

"I'm holding, I'm holding."

Focusing on the target, Mark took a deep breath and prepared to strike. But suddenly, something else popped into his mind. Replacing the target were the faces of Kelly Brown's parents and, as Mark remembered the upsetting conference he'd had with them earlier in the day, his anger grew.

Snapping his kicking leg outward, he slashed sharply with the edge of his foot. As he did, Justin groaned repeatedly and loudly from behind the pad. Finally, when Mark had finished his series, Justin started to drop it.

"Man, those were good ones, Bro," he said. "Hey, I need a little breather. My shoulder kind of hur—"

"Get that damn pad up!" Mark ordered. "Roundhouses next."

Inhaling deeply, he tightened his abdominal muscles and tried to focus. Now Principal Caruthers's fat, pockmarked face appeared on the pad, making him madder than ever. Delivering high roundhouse after high roundhouse, he pummeled the annoying hallucination with the ball of his foot, grunting, "*Huh! Huh! Huh!*" as he kicked.

Then, to his surprise, Justin went down.

For a few moments, Mark just stood there in stunned silence. But, as the other karate students started coming over, he snapped out of it. Reaching down quickly, he grabbed the pad and threw it off his brother. Seeing that Justin's eyes were open and rolled back in his head, Mark dropped to his knees and leaned over to listen for breath sounds. Thankfully, he was breathing.

"Don't worry, Mark," the karate class teacher told him as he joined Mark on the floor. "Justin's just unconscious. He'll be okay in a couple minutes or so. I've seen this a million times."

"Well . . . what happened?" Mark asked, concerned.

"You kicked him in the head, that's what happened," the teacher answered. "I was watching you. Every time you kicked, your roundhouses got higher and higher. Finally, you totally missed the target. Your concentration seems off tonight, Mark. Are you all right?"

"No . . . not exactly," Mark said, holding his brother's hand.

• • •

"So, are you sure you're okay, Justin?" Mark asked across the coffee shop booth as the pair waited for their orders. "You sure you don't want to go see a doctor?"

"Come on, Mark," Justin answered, smiling. "Would I have asked for dessert if I didn't feel perfectly fine? Really, I'm all right."

"Well, *I* feel terrible," Mark said.

"And well you should," Justin replied. "Now, Mark, are you going to finally tell me what happened today that compelled you to kick the holy shit out of a one-armed man?"

Mark took a deep breath and let it out slow. Then he shook his head. "Well . . . it's just that I had the parent conference from Hell after school today, that's all. It put me in a really bad mood."

"So . . . what happened?"

The waitress brought their orders then and Mark waited for her to leave before starting to tell his brother the details. Finally, adding cream and sugar to his coffee, he said, "Well, Justin, I'm afraid worrisome things are afoot at Mesquite High School. If you recall, I already told you we have a Christian club down there, now."

"Yeah," Justin said, nodding. "You know, I really can't believe that. And sponsored by a teacher, no less. At a *public* school."

"Well," Mark continued, stirring as he talked, "the students in the club aren't exactly keeping a low profile. One in particular, a young lady in my science class, has been making things kind of difficult for me since the very beginning of the school year. She wears all kinds of religious T-shirts and makes sarcastic comments in class and, sometimes, she's even been excused from participating altogether. Like during our sex education unit, when we talked about birth control and AIDS. That's some of the most important stuff I teach."

Taking a quick sip of his coffee, Justin shook his head and set down the mug. "And so, what happened today, Mark?"

"I'm getting there," Mark went on. "You see, about a week or two ago in class, we started talking about the evolution of life on Earth. And ever since then, it's just been one sarcastic remark after another from my young Miss Brown. So finally, it got to the point where it was becoming disruptive and I referred her to the principal's office. That's what provoked the Browns to schedule their conference."

"Okay. I see," Justin said, taking a bite of pie. "So what happened at the conference then?"

"A lot," Mark said, smiling ironically. "First, the Browns demanded that disclaimers be pasted into our science textbooks calling evolution 'controversial,' and 'just one theory among many.' And they want 'creation science' and something else called the 'intelligent-design theory' to be taught right alongside natural selection. They had these two books with them, *Darwin on Trial* and *Of Pandas and People*, which they said explained the so-called theories."

"Sounds like a load of crap to me," Justin said, frowning. "So what did you tell 'em? I mean, you're not teaching a class in religions, after all, you're teaching a science class. And no matter how you slice it, 'creation science' *isn't*."

Mark nodded. "Well, of course, that's exactly what I said to them. But then *they* said they were gonna go to the school board over this and, considering we have a very conservative board right now, well . . . I just don't know what to think."

"What did your principal say?" Justin asked.

Mark shook his head. "That's the worst part. I mean, you know Caruthers. The guy's a spineless wonder. He always takes the path of least resistance and, to him, that usually means pandering to the irate parent. The 'wrong' or 'right' of it doesn't really matter to him."

"So he sided with the Browns."

"Yeah," Mark said. "And he told me if the board of education does also, then he'll give me a directive—that's his favorite word these days, 'directive'—and then that'll be that."

Justin rolled his eyes. "No wonder America's becoming scientifically illiterate. . . . Well, what're you gonna do, Mark? You're gonna fight it, aren't you? Are you gonna go to the school board meeting?"

"Oh, Justin," Mark replied, his head in his hands, "I just want to teach science. I don't want to get involved in a whole bunch of political bullshit. And I don't want to lose my job either."

"Come on, Mark," Justin said, grinning. "They're not gonna fire you. As you've told me so many times before, the only way a public school teacher gets fired these days is by killing a kid or sleeping with one. Isn't that right?"

"I guess."

"That's right," Justin said. "Now I know you don't like to hear this, Mark, but sometimes it is necessary to stick up for yourself. Sometimes you just have to take a stand. I think the reason you're feeling so bad is, inside, you already know that's true. And if you don't fight this, Mark, you'll never feel one bit better."

Mark glanced up at Justin. "Please," he said. "Don't start psychoanalyzing me now. Not tonight. I don't think I can take it. I have a splitting headache."

"Okay, Bro," Justin answered, smiling. "But remember, you're not the one who got kicked in the head an hour ago. Hey, drink some of your coffee there. You haven't even touched it yet. Would you like some of my apple pie? It's really good."

Ignoring his brother's offer, Mark sighed heavily. "You know, there's one last thing I haven't told you yet, Justin," he said, rubbing his eyes. "Guess who the Browns said gave them those two books they had *and* encouraged them to go to the board."

"Well, I don't know," Justin replied, frowning. Then his eyes lit up. "Unless . . ."

Mark nodded at him. "That's right, Justin. You see, it seems the Browns just so happen to be Christian Coalition members, and their spiritual guru is none other than an old buddy we both know and love."

"John Wright?" Justin asked.

"John Wright," Mark answered, nodding.

"Oh, boy," Justin said.

Chapter 20

"Boy, that was one great movie," Mark told Harmony as the end credits of *Inherit the Wind* began rolling across the television screen. Then he said, "You know, as a science teacher, I was of course familiar with the Scopes 'monkey trial' of 1925. But I can't believe I've never even heard of that movie before."

"Well," Harmony answered, patting his leg, "it's actually been made into a movie *twice*, the version we just saw and then a TV movie. And it was a stage play before that."

"Huh . . . ," Mark said, nodding. Then he asked, "When we went to the video store, what made you pick that one out?"

Teasing him, she said, "You mean besides the fact I'm madly in love with Spencer Tracy?"

"Yeah," Mark answered, smiling. "Besides that."

"Well, to tell you the truth, Mark," she said, gazing into his eyes, "I thought seeing it might somehow help you with the problems you're having at school. I hate seeing you so upset all the time."

"Thanks," he told her, squeezing her hand. Then he shook his head. "You know what amazes me most, Harmony? My whole career, I've been under the erroneous impression that the John Scopes trial all but resolved this whole creation versus evolution debate. But boy, was I wrong. Lately I feel like we're living in the nineteenth century again. It's just that I thought we were way past this nonsense a long time ago."

"Hey, that's exactly how I felt at my Eagle board," Cameron said, glancing up from petting Barkley on the family room floor. "Just like that."

Harmony gave Mark's leg another pat. "You know, Mark, I suggested this to Cameron already but he hasn't taken me up on it yet." She shot the boy a look. "What you both might think about doing is talking to Dr. Paul about these situations of yours. You never know. He just might be able to help you in some way."

"Maybe," Mark answered.

"Well," Cameron said, as he crawled over and hit the VCR'S REWIND, "now that the girls' video is over, are we about ready to pop in the guys' pick now? I mean, we better start it soon or Mom's gonna wimp out and fall asleep on us."

Harmony frowned. "I beg your pardon, young man."

"You know you probably will," Cameron said, grinning.

"Actually, Cameron," Mark said, "there's something I want to run by you first. An idea I had."

Taking her cue, Harmony got up from the sofa, grabbed the large bowl off the coffee table, and headed out of the room. "I'm going to pop some more corn," she called from the hallway. "You *men* go ahead and make your manly plans." Once in the kitchen, she hurried to put a bag of corn in the microwave so she could eavesdrop on their conversation.

"What was she talking about, anyway?" Harmony heard Cameron ask Mark.

"My idea," the man answered. "You see, I already ran it by your mom."

"Oh," Cameron said. "Well, what is it?"

"Well, Cameron," Mark replied, "do you remember that day we were loading your Grand Canyon model in the back of my truck and you told me you'd never been there?"

"To the canyon, you mean?"

"Yeah."

"Yeah, I remember that. Why?"

"Well," Mark asked, "how would you like to go?"

In her mind's eye, Harmony could clearly see the excited expression growing across her son's freckled face, and the thought of it made her smile.

"Really?!" Cameron exclaimed. "We're going to the Grand Canyon?! When?!"

"Well . . . how does spring break sound?" Mark asked. "I was thinking we'd backpack. You and your mom and Justin and I. Down to Phantom Ranch and back. You could even ask your friend, Ricky, if you want to. I've already taken the liberty of sending for the permits. I hope spring break is good for you."

"Are you kidding?" Cameron said excitedly. "Spring break is great for me. I can't wait to see the look on Ricky's face when I ask him."

"Do you think he'll be able to handle the hiking all right?" Mark asked.

"Well," Cameron said, "you know they finally did give him his badge and he's a bona fide Tenderfoot now. Yeah . . . I think he could handle it."

The microwave beeped, startling Harmony.

Taking out the bag of popcorn, she dumped it in the bowl and then headed back into the family room. "Well, okay," she said, placing it on the table. "I've taken care of the *women's* work and it sounds like you two have our upcoming adventure well in hand, so what do you say we start the next movie. What was it you guys picked out again, anyway?"

"*Star Trek V: The Final Frontier*," Cameron answered,

ejecting the first video and inserting the second. Pushing PLAY, he added, "I haven't seen this one before. This oughtta be good."

"Yeah, *Star Trek*," Harmony said, rolling her eyes at Mark. "It oughtta be *real* good." Then, cuddling up next to the man, she yawned, fully expecting to do just as her son had said and rapidly fall fast asleep.

• • •

Still wide awake, Harmony stared intently at the the TV while she nibbled a piece of popcorn, totally engrossed by the movie's storyline. After being hijacked by a misguided Vulcan prophet, the starship *Enterprise* and her crew had been forced to travel to an uncharted planet at the center of the galaxy where God was believed to dwell. But, they didn't find Him there. Instead, they discovered a malevolent entity who used people's superstitions against them in order to get what *it* wanted. Well, Kirk had overcome the creature, of course, and now the movie was almost over.

Munching another piece of popcorn, Harmony watched as Kirk approached Bones and Spock who were gazing down at the planet from one of the starship's large viewports. "Cosmic thoughts, gentlemen?" the captain asked.

Looking thoughtfully at Kirk, Bones said, "We were . . . speculating. Is God *really* out there?"

Kirk smiled. "Maybe he's not out there, Bones. Maybe he's right here . . ." He tapped his chest. "The human heart . . ."

Harmony cocked her head and nodded. "Hey, Mark," she said, "maybe I will become a *Star Trek* fan, after all."

He didn't answer.

Turning toward him, Harmony's jaw dropped. *He was asleep*. Then she glanced down at Cameron. *He was asleep, too*. "Well, so much for the macho men," she told herself, shaking her head.

Using the remote, Harmony punched STOP and then REWIND.

But when she did, a commercial flashed on which was much louder than the movie had been.

"What's going on?" Cameron asked suddenly, rubbing his eyes. "Is it over?"

"Yes, dear," Harmony answered. "Time to go to bed."

Stretching his arms out next to her, Mark glanced at his watch. "Oh, boy," he said, standing. "I better hit the road."

Getting up off the floor, Cameron scratched at his ribs. "Well, *please*, Mark," he said, "don't leave on my account."

Intentional or not, the boy's comment had just a hint of sarcasm to it and Harmony flushed. "*Cameron*," she said as Mark helped her up, "that wasn't necessary."

"Well, c'mon, Mom," he answered. "I mean, it was totally obvious you guys were spending the nights together when I was in San Diego with Dad. Then or now . . . what's the difference?"

Harmony put her hands on her hips. "Cameron, the only reason you're still breathing right now is because I know you're half asleep and don't know what you're saying. Now go to bed. You and I will discuss this tomorrow."

"Okay. . . . Sorry, Mom," he said, heading out of the room. "See ya later, Mark."

"Night, Cameron," the man answered.

When he was gone, Harmony leaned against Mark, her forehead on his chest. "I'm sorry about that," she said. "I'm so embarrassed. It looks like I'm definitely going to have a little talk with him . . . about *things*."

"No," Mark told her, kissing the top of her head. "It really should be me. I mean, why don't you let me talk to him about this? I'll do it soon. As soon as possible. I promise." Then he paused, a mischievous look in his eye. "After all, Harmony," he added, "it is kind of a *guy* thing, isn't it?"

Gazing up into his eyes, she smiled. "Okay. . . . Thanks, Mark," she said.

Chapter 21

Time out . . .

Resting on the bench with the rest of the Mesquite High JV Mountain Lions, Cameron took a swig of energy drink and glanced up at the game clock. Only nine seconds remained. Then the coach came over and put an arm around his shoulder.

"Wright," he said, "it's crunch time. We're down by a bucket and I've got a hot date tonight so I don't want this thing goin' into overtime. Now you've been in the zone all evening long so, if we're gonna beat these Rincon wussies, you're my go-to guy. Take the last shot for us, Cameron . . . and make it a trey."

Cameron frowned. "But . . . I haven't hit any three-pointers tonight, Coach—"

"No buts, Cameron," the coach said, cutting him off. "The throw-in's comin' your way. Be ready, get set up, and take the three. It's all gonna be up to you."

"Okay, sir," Cameron said, shrugging. "If you say so."

"I do," the coach said, slapping him on the back. "Now get out there and make us all proud."

Crumpling his paper cup, Cameron cast it aside, bounced up, and sprinted onto the court trying to look confident. But it was merely a game face. On the inside, he just didn't like his odds. Deciding he needed a back-up plan, he found Randall LaRue and motioned to him.

Jogging over, Randall asked, "Yeah, Cameron, what's up?"

"Listen, Randall," Cameron told him, eyes darting around the gymnasium, "Coach wants me to take the three-pointer but I have a feeling those Rattler defenders are gonna be all over me. If they are, be ready. I'm gonna pass it off to you."

Randall looked shocked. "I don't know, Cameron. I've never made a game winner before."

"Oh c'mon, Randall, don't worry," Cameron said reassuringly. "You're the best three-point shooter on our team. It'll be just like drainin' threes in your own driveway. No problem."

"A little like the '97 NBA title game, eh? Only this time, you're Michael Jordan and I'm Steve Kerr."

"Exactly," Cameron said. "And on top of that, since we are playing the Rattlers, this is your chance to finally get revenge on that snake that bit you at the Scout encampment. All you hafta decide is . . . are you a scrub or a stud?"

"Okay, I hear ya," Randall called, hurrying to get into position. "I'll be ready."

Then, the whistle blew . . .

. . . and here came the pass.

Catching it, Cameron put the ball on the floor and dribbled quickly toward the three-point arc. But then, just as he feared, all five Rattlers collapsed on him, getting right in his face. The clock was ticking down and no way did he have any kind of a decent shot.

But Randall LaRue did.

Passing to him crisply, Cameron held his breath as Randall

made the catch, checked his foot placement, bent his knees, and pulled the trigger—just as the buzzer sounded.

But, as Cameron watched the ball sailing through the air on its way to the hoop, his heart sank. After years of playing this game, he knew when a shot was on the mark—and this one wasn't.

Instead of arcing neatly through the net, it ricocheted hard off the backboard causing Cameron to grimace. But then, his eyes widened again as he watched the ball hit the inside of the hoop's front rim and, miraculously, bounce *within* the cylinder. Round and round and round it went . . . until . . . until . . .

It fell!

Thanks to Randall LaRue's Hail Mary, game-saving, buzzer-beating, three-point shot, the JV Mountain Lions had just beaten the Rincon Rattlers, 63–62. The Mesquite High School gym went wild.

The band played their fight song and the cheerleaders cheered as every spectator in the bleachers started jumping up and down. Even more jubilant than the fans, the team itself hoisted Randall into the air and started parading him around.

"Hey, LaRue," Cameron yelled, grinning, as he ran to join the procession. "That has to be the ugliest game-winning garbage shot I've ever seen!"

"Yeah?" Randall shouted back. "Well then, I guess it's a good thing 'game winning' are the key words there, huh?!"

"You got that right!" Cameron said.

"Hey, Wright. I want to talk to you."

Turning around, Cameron saw the coach marching toward him with a frown on his face. "Uh-oh," the boy said to himself.

"Wright," the coach said, reaching him, "the next time I tell you to take the last shot and then you ignore my instructions and pass it off instead . . ."

"Yeah, Coach?" Cameron asked sheepishly.

"Well," the man answered, breaking into a wide grin, "after

tonight I guess I won't have a problem with it. Go right ahead, use your own judgment—*just as long as we win*." Ruffling Cameron's hair, he turned away.

"Okay, Coach . . . thanks," Cameron said, feeling relieved as he watched him go.

"Cameron! Hey, Cameron!"

Spinning around again, Cameron squinted up at the stands where his mom, Mark, and Mandy were all waving. "I'll be right there," he called to them. That's *if* he could get by all the people.

Forcing his way through the crowd, Cameron finally made it to the bottom of the wooden steps and then climbed up to where the threesome sat. As he joined them, they all congratulated him on a good game and a great win.

Turning to his mother, Cameron said, "You know, to tell you the truth, Mom, I'm really kind of surprised you and Mandy actually saw *any* of it. I mean, every time I glanced up here, you two were gabbing away. It didn't even look like you were paying attention to the game at all."

"Well," she answered, smiling, "Mandy and I did just meet—*finally*—and we had a lot to talk about. But really, Cameron, we *were* paying attention. Tell him, Mandy. How many baskets did our star player score tonight?"

"Eleven," Mandy said, without hesitation. "And that's twenty-two points. All by yourself, Cameron, you made over a third of Mesquite's total goals. Not too bad, I guess."

"You *guess*?" Cameron repeated, frowning. Mandy flashed him that wide smile of hers and he knew she was only teasing.

"Hey, Mandy," Mark said, leaning in front of Cameron's mom, "why don't you tell Cameron about our surprise."

"Surprise?" Cameron asked.

"Yeah," Mandy answered, the teasing look back in her eyes. "Mark said, if you won tonight, he'd take us all out to dinner. Wasn't that nice of him?"

"Come on, Mandy," his mother said, rolling her eyes. "That

was nice of Mark, of course, but that's not the *big* surprise. Go ahead, tell him. Tell him the big news."

"Well, ohh-kay," Mandy answered coyly. Turning to him, she took his hand. "Cameron, your mother and Mr. Edwards here have invited me to go with you all when you go to the Grand Canyon in March. I said I'd love to but I have to ask my parents first. So . . . what do you think of that?"

What did he think? *What did he think?* Well, he couldn't believe it, *that's* what he thought. It was just so cool. "Mom . . . Mark . . . ," he said, once he regained the power of speech, "this is *so cool*. This is gonna be the best trip ever!"

"Well, let's not get ahead of ourselves just yet, Cameron," his mother said. Putting her arm around Mandy, she added, "You know, she's never been backpacking before and, if her parents do let her go, Mandy's going to need a lot of help getting ready. You're going to have to give her a lot of time and attention in the next few weeks."

"Something tells me that won't be much of a problem, eh Cameron?" Mark said, winking.

Still feeling a little overwhelmed by it all, Cameron just smiled. He thought he noticed his mother and Mark exchange a look.

"Listen, Son," his mother said, getting up, "why don't you hurry and go shower and change and we'll go out and wait for you in the truck. I'm sure we're all starving. Then, over dinner, we can talk more about the trip."

"Okay, Mom," Cameron said, starting down the steps. "See you in a little while, Mandy."

"Bye, Cameron," she called after him.

In the locker room, Cameron set a new speed record for taking a shower and getting dressed. He *was* starving. But more than that, he was anxious to be with Mandy and to start telling her about backpacking. But then, as he left the locker room, he was surprised to find Mark waiting for him outside the door.

"Hey, superstar," the man said, glancing over at him. "What

do you say you and I take the long way out to the parking lot tonight? I mean, there's something I'd like to talk to you about, if it's okay. How 'bout we take a little walk on the jogging trail?"

Cameron shrugged. "Sure, Mark."

It was dark out, and chilly. Once they were outside the gymnasium, Cameron paused to get his windbreaker out of the day pack he carried. As he put it on, Mark said, "About the other night, Cameron . . ."

"Wait, Mark," Cameron told him as he zipped up the jacket. Then picking up the day pack and starting to walk again, he shook his head. "I'm sorry, but do we really have to talk about that now? I mean, what I said to you was totally out of line, I know that. What you and my mom are doing is your own business, not mine. I'm really sorry. Can't we just leave it at that?"

"But you're wrong, Cameron," Mark said.

"What?"

Heading out onto the lighted exercise trail, Mark put an arm around his shoulder. "Look, Cameron," he said, "what your mother and I are doing *is* your business. Up to a point, anyway. After all, you are her son. I mean, I'm not going to feel good about this whole situation unless you feel good about it, too. It's important to me for you to be happy that your mother and I found each other. And if you have any questions nagging at you about our relationship, then I wish you'd ask me about them."

Cameron looked at Mark.

"There is something, isn't there?"

Yes, there was. But Cameron still felt uncomfortable asking him about it.

"Go ahead, Cameron," Mark insisted sincerely. "I really want you to."

Okay, here goes nothin', Cameron thought. Struggling to find the right words, he looked up. "Mark . . . ," he said, "are you . . . I mean, are the *two* of you . . . I mean, are you and my mom . . ." Oh, forget it, he thought, shaking his head.

"In love?" Mark said, attempting to finish the thought for him.

"No."

Mark frowned. Then he took another stab at it. "Going to get married?" he said.

"No," Cameron answered again.

"Well, what then?" Mark asked, starting to sound frustrated.

Okay, you asked for it, Cameron thought resolutely. Stopping by the chin-up bars, he answered, "Listen, Mark, what I really want to know is, are you and my mother doing what you told us kids to do in that science class of yours? What I mean is . . . are you *taking precautions*?"

Slowly, a smile grew on Mark's face. "Ohh . . . you mean, are we having safe sex?"

Looking up again, Cameron nodded at him.

"Well . . . then there's no need for you to worry," Mark assured him. "Because we *are*."

"Well, that's good, Mark," Cameron answered, sighing. "That's real good . . ."

Turning, they started walking again. Then, just as they reached the parking lot, the words Mark had said a few minutes earlier finally sank in.

"What's wrong?" Mark asked Cameron as the boy stopped suddenly on the curb.

"Well . . . now that you mention it, Mark," he answered, hands on his hips, "*are* you in love with my mother? *Are* the two of you planning to get married? Or what?"

Now Mark was the one who looked uncomfortable with their conversation, as if the longtime science teacher considered sex an easy subject compared to love and marriage. And that must have been the case because, put on the spot, the only answer he could manage to give Cameron was a feeble, "Oh, boy . . ."

Part 8
February

Chapter 22

Dr. Paul Dreyfuss-Campbell steepled his fingers thoughtfully and leaned back in his chair. "Well, okay, Mark," he said, "let's see if I have all this straight. First, you're not really sure why you came here today—other than because Harmony suggested it, that is—but, since you did, you figured it couldn't hurt to go ahead and tell me about these problems you're having down at the high school . . ."

From across the minister's office desk, Mark Edwards nodded silently at him as he listened to the man talk.

"And second," Dr. Paul continued, "you're a bit shocked by this resurgent battle over teaching evolution in the public schools. You're wondering if these creationists should be taken seriously. You're thinking maybe you should just skip teaching evolution this year and that way, by avoiding the problem for a while, maybe it'll just go away . . ."

Again, Mark nodded.

"But third, then," Dr. Paul said, cocking his head, "if avoidance is truly the answer, you're wondering why it is you feel so damn bad every time you even think about that option. . . . Now, do I have all that right?"

"Yeah," Mark answered, shrugging. "That about sums it up."

Getting out of his chair, Dr. Paul went to stand by the window. Looking out, he said, "Well . . . I am glad you decided to come in to see me, Mark. And, I think there is a chance I might be able to help you in some way. In fact . . . I think maybe we can even help each other."

"What do you mean?" Mark asked.

"Well, before I explain that, let me give you a little background information first," Dr. Paul answered. "The good news is you are partially right. Evolution *is* accepted by almost all scientists and even by most religious denominations. Even the pope himself declared it didn't conflict with Catholic doctrine. In fact, Catholic schools have taught it ever since the 1950s. And, thankfully, the courts have backed evolution over and over again for years and years."

"So . . . what's the bad news?"

"Well, I'm afraid there's quite a lot of it," Dr. Paul said. "Like the fact that, against all scientific evidence to the contrary, polls show nearly half of all Americans still reject evolution in favor of the Old Testament account that says the world was created in only seven days. Now, to me, that's scary."

"That is," Mark agreed, shaking his head. "What else?"

"Well," Dr. Paul answered, turning to him, "I'm afraid I must tell you that you're wrong to think this controversy has *returned* to the classroom. Because, actually, you see, it never went away."

"But lately, it does seem to be increasing. Doesn't it?"

"Yes, it does," Dr. Paul said, nodding. "And the trend seems to be directly related to the success religious-right-oriented candidates have had starting back in 1992, primarily at the local level. Since that time, the Christian Coalition—touting its so-called family values—has become an increasingly powerful political force, especially in conservative Republican communities like ours. And by influencing local school board elections, they're waging a war across our country. It's Darwin versus the Bible, and the public school is their main battleground."

"Well . . . how widespread is this war?" Mark asked.

Counting on his fingers, Dr. Paul answered, "Already, the teaching of evolution has been challenged in Georgia, California, Washington, Pennsylvania, Tennessee, Michigan, Indiana, Ohio, New Hampshire, and Alabama. But more than that, it really goes much deeper than just the schools. You see, these biblical literalists are on a crusade, a crusade to crush liberalism in all its forms. They see us liberals as people without values and they blame virtually all of society's ills on us. To them, drugs, AIDS, violence, and crime are all the result of our 'anything goes' attitudes. And also, of course, of our belief in evolutionary theory."

Shaking his head again, Mark asked, "Well . . . what can be done about it, Dr. Paul? If anything, I mean."

From across the room, the minister's blue eyes flashed at him. "I'm glad you asked that, Mark." Returning to his chair behind the desk, Dr. Paul sat down again and then riveted Mark with his gaze. "First, it's a huge mistake for those of us who revere science and reason not to take these Darwin bashers seriously. They're much too powerful for us to do that. Second, it would be an even bigger mistake to skip teaching evolution in your class. I mean, you and I both know how important it is. It's the central organizing principle of biology after all. Teaching life science without it would be like trying to teach chemistry without using the periodic table. It just wouldn't work. And every time some timid schoolteacher stoops to doing it, it's a victory for the creationists."

Mark nodded again, frowning this time.

"Now," Dr. Paul went on, "let's talk about your specific case, this situation at Mesquite High. From what you're telling me, it sounds like the school is right on the line with this one. They're getting around the church and state conflicts by calling their Christian group a 'club.' But, what they definitely *shouldn't* be doing is allowing a teacher to sponsor it. The law is very clear that teachers are prohibited from encouraging or participating in religious activities at school. We've got 'em on that one."

"And what about the textbook disclaimers?" Mark asked. "And those two Bible-based books I told you about?"

"Well," the minister answered, stroking his beard, "I think there's a good chance we can stop them from inserting noneducational religious right propaganda into your classroom, but—and I'm not going to pull any punches here—I'm afraid you, Mark, are going to have to make some sacrifices."

"What do you mean?" Mark said. He didn't like the sound of this.

"Well, that's why I said earlier that maybe we could help *each other*," Dr. Paul explained. "You see, what we need to do here is get the ACLU involved, get them to threaten a suit. But before that can happen, you're going to have to become defiant. Tell your principal and your superintendent and your school board just exactly what they can do with their so-called alternatives to the theory of evolution."

"But . . . I could lose my job. Couldn't I?"

"That's the whole point," Dr. Paul answered flatly. "Before we can threaten them with legal action, we need to get them to threaten us first."

"Threaten *us*?" Mark repeated incredulously. "You mean threaten *me*, don't you?" Exasperated, he shook his head.

"Listen, Mark," Dr. Paul said, seeming to change the subject, "are you at all familiar with cognitive dissonance theory? It's a social psychology term."

Still frowning, he answered, "No. I don't think I am."

"Well, in my opinion, it could explain why you're feeling so bad about yourself lately," Dr. Paul told him. "You see, it's very disturbing when we find we have two beliefs which oppose each other. Like the belief in conformity, on one hand, and the belief in truth on the other. And people who act contrary to their most important beliefs—or values, as we could call them—end up feeling bad about themselves. So sometimes, in order to be more self-consistent, we need to take stock in ourselves, prioritize our values and beliefs, and then act accordingly. I think maybe that's what you're going to have to do now."

"Is that right?" Mark said.

His obvious lack of enthusiasm wasn't lost on Dr. Paul. But, despite that, the minister persisted anyway. "What about mythology, Mark?" he asked. "Do you know much about world myths?"

"Only what I learned in school," Mark answered, shrugging.

"Well," Dr. Paul said, leaning back in his chair again, "one of the most common themes found in comparative mythology is the story of the character who goes on a quest. And, the ultimate aim of this quest is always to gain the wisdom and power needed . . . to serve others."

"I'm a teacher," Mark broke in darkly. "I've been serving others my whole life."

Ignoring the remark, Dr. Paul continued. "Anyway, on this quest the character must move out of what is safe or normal or ordinary, and then move into a place that is unknown. And by doing this, you see, the character finds a richer, more mature, condition."

Impatiently, Mark interrupted again. "Yeah, yeah, yeah," he said. "So what does all this have to do with me? Are you calling me immature now?"

Undaunted, Dr. Paul calmly went on. "Ultimately, in this motif, Mark, do you know what always happens? The character ends up giving over his or her life to something bigger than oneself. You see, according to this myth, self-sacrifice for the greater good is the key to spiritual enlightenment." Glancing up at the large framed photograph of Earth from space hanging on his wall, the minister smiled and then turned back to Mark. “Now, do you know what this universal story is called?”

Mark just stared at him.

“It’s called the hero’s journey,” Dr. Paul said, answering his own question. “And just maybe it’s about time for Mr. Edwards, science teacher, to embark on one.”

Pushing back his seat, Mark stood and started for the door. “Well, thanks for your time, Dr. Paul, but I gotta go,” he said. “I mean, I’m sorry and all that but . . . well . . . I’m sure as hell no hero.”

“I think,” Dr. Paul called after him from his chair, “there’s a young man who came in to see me the other day who just might disagree with you on that.”

Pausing in the office doorway, Mark turned back around. “Cameron?” he asked.

“You know, the problem that boy is having over his Eagle badge isn’t so dissimilar from your own,” Dr. Paul said. “And make no mistake about it, he’s watching you, Mark. Very, very closely. And I have a feeling he’s waiting so he can follow your lead.”

Mark shook his head. “Well . . . maybe he’s making a big mistake . . .”

Then he turned and walked out the door.

Chapter 23

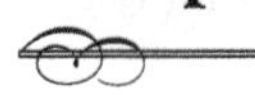

Suddenly, Cameron stared down at what little remained of the hamburger he was eating and realized that he hadn't tasted a bite of it. Still too excited, he guessed. Chuckling to himself, he shook his head.

Next to him, Mandy asked, "What's so funny?"

Turning to her, he smiled. "Well, it's just that I still can't believe it, that's all," he answered. "I still can't believe I was actually *in* the McKale Center, actually sitting *right behind* Lute Olson, actually watching the Arizona Wildcats beat USC *in person*. I mean, this has to be the best valentine I ever got, that's for sure!"

Giggling at him, Mandy stole one of the french fries off his plate, then turned her attention back to her strawberry shake.

"Well, we're really very happy you enjoyed the game so much, Cameron," Mrs. Ross said from across the restaurant booth. "We'll all have to be sure to do this again sometime."

"Really?!" Cameron exclaimed. "Oh, man. That'd be great."

Then, turning to Mandy's father, he asked, "Mr. Ross, do you always get such incredible seats?"

"Just one of the perks of being a UA alumni," the man answered, nodding.

As he prepared to finish off his burger, Cameron paused a moment, then cocked his head at the man. "So, Mr. Ross, since you're such a big fan and all, is there any chance you played for the Wildcats when you were a student at the university?"

"*Me*?" Mandy's father said, laughing. "No, son. I'm afraid not. Never was much good at basketball. Dribbled all over myself, if you know what I mean. Actually I never was much good at sports in general."

"He can't dance either," Mrs. Ross said, nudging her husband playfully.

"Oh, I'm sorry . . . ," Cameron said, chewing. Swallowing hard, he looked earnestly at the Rosses. "I didn't mean to sound—oh, what's that word?—stereotypical there. But you gotta admit, African Americans do seem to make the best basketball players."

Mr. Ross didn't answer him. The man just stared. And immediately, Cameron started to feel uncomfortable.

"Oh now, don't look so worried, son," Mandy's mom told him, smiling. "It's just that Mr. Ross doesn't like that term, that's all. He thinks it's divisive."

"What term?" Cameron asked, frowning. "You mean, stereotypi—"

"African American," Mr. Ross said, cutting him off.

Now Cameron really was confused. He glanced at Mandy for help but she just shrugged at him and continued sipping her shake. Nope, it looked like he was on his own on this one.

Finally, Mr. Ross broke the awkward silence and said, "Cameron . . . why don't you tell us about *your* extraction, son."

"My what?" Cameron asked.

"Your extraction," the man repeated. "Your . . . origin. Your ancestry."

"*Oh* . . . ," Cameron said, nodding. "You mean, where did my relatives come from? Well . . . mostly from Ireland, I guess."

"And do you consider yourself Irish-American, then?" Mr. Ross asked.

"No, not really," he answered, shaking his head. "I mean, I've never even been there. To Ireland, I mean."

"And *we've* never been to Africa," Mr. Ross said, shooting him a look. "See my point?"

Silently, Cameron nodded at him.

"Now, Bob," Mrs. Ross told her husband, patting his arm, "you're going to end up getting this young man in trouble." Turning to Cameron, she said, "Son, Mr. Ross means well, but keep in mind most blacks in America today *do* prefer to be called African Americans. You weren't wrong to use that term."

"*But*," Mandy's father said, still staring at Cameron, "you do see my point, don't you? You see, the problem with some people is they want to have their cake and eat it, too. They want to be equal but they also want to be different. They want to be the same as everybody else but, at the same time, retain their so-called cultural identity, too. And that's fine. Where the rub comes in is when they make the *different* part become more important than the ways we're all the same. When they do that, you see, it does more harm than good."

"Cameron," Mandy's mother said, making a face at her husband, "don't you take Mr. Ross here too seriously, now. He was an anthropology major in college, after all. And you know how those scientific types can be."

"You were a science major, Mr. Ross?" Cameron said, raising his eyebrows. Then, too late, he realized his comment may not have come out the way he intended it to.

"And why are you so surprised by that, son?" Mr. Ross asked him.

Glancing nervously at Mandy, Cameron sputtered, "Oh . . . uh . . . well . . ."

"Isn't it because *you* like science, too, Cameron?" Mandy asked nonchalantly, saving his hide. Then, smiling at her father, she added, "I mean, you should see Cameron in science class, Dad. He knows *everything*."

The way she said it, there was no doubt in Cameron's mind she was teasing him. Luckily though, from the looks on her parents' faces, they didn't seem to notice. Or did they?

At that moment, a waitress came by and topped off the Rosses' iced teas for them. But then when she left, Mr. Ross turned to him again. "So, Cameron," he said, "you're a science buff, too, eh? Tell me, is that science teacher of yours—Mr. Edwards, is it?—teaching you anything about ancient man this school year?"

"Not yet," Cameron answered. "But I do think he plans to. We just finished studying genetics and now we're starting to get into paleontology. I think ancient humans will come after that."

"That's good," Mr. Ross said, nodding. Then his eyes lit up. "And, you know—speaking of African Americans—I hope when you do start studying our ancient ancestors your teacher tells you all about the 'out of Africa' theory. It's fascinating."

Cameron cocked his head. "The 'out of Africa' theory?"

"Yes. Would you like me to tell you a little bit about it?" Mr. Ross asked.

"Sure," Cameron said.

"Well," Mandy's father began, leaning forward in his seat, "from what we've learned from DNA sequencing, it looks like all the world's major racial groups share a very recent common ancestor. It seems all modern humans today are descended from one *Homo erectus* woman who lived in Africa 200,000 years ago." Leaning closer still, he stared intensely at Cameron. "At that point, you see, the entire human family tree began. Now, do you realize how profound that thought is, son?"

The way Mr. Ross was looking at him, Cameron got the distinct feeling he was being tested in some way. So, considering the question for a moment, he took his best shot. "Well, Mr. Ross," he said, "I guess what that means is, we're *all* African Americans, aren't we? I mean, if you go back far enough, everybody in the world is from Africa, isn't that true?"

"*Exactly*!" Mr. Ross said, clapping his hands with obvious delight. Turning to his daughter, he grinned at her. "You know, Mandy," he said, "I think there's a very good chance I'm going to like this young man you've found."

Glancing over at Cameron, Mandy rolled her eyes. "Well, that's good, Daddy," she answered. "That's real good . . ."

Suddenly, out of nowhere, a thought struck Cameron and he must have frowned because, the next thing he knew, Mrs. Ross was asking him, "Son . . . is there something wrong? You look puzzled."

Cameron shifted nervously in his seat. He wasn't at all sure he should say anything about what was on his mind.

"Cameron?" Mrs. Ross said.

Glancing questioningly at Mandy, Cameron saw her nod, giving him the go-ahead.

Well, okay, he thought, I guess I might as well say it. Shrugging, he looked back at Mandy's mom. "Well, Mrs. Ross," he began, "it's just that I know your family is religious and all. Christian, I mean. And, well . . . I mean . . ." Finally, he just spit it out. "Well, I'm just kinda surprised that you can be religious and still believe in stuff like science, and anthropology, and *Homo erectus*, and evolution, stuff like that . . ."

"I see," Mrs. Ross answered, nodding congenially. Then, turning to her husband, she said, "Well . . . it's really not so strange that the two can go together . . . is it, Bob?"

At that instant, one of the waitresses flashed by their table. Flagging her down, Mr. Ross said, "Check please," then turned his attention back to his wife. "No, Hon, it's not strange," he told her. Then, smiling at Cameron, he said, "Think about this, son . . . I mean, we are talking about God here, aren't we? So, considering it *is* God, isn't it very possible to say He created the universe just the way all the scientists say he did—through evolution?" Looking satisfied with his explanation, Mr. Ross winked across the table at him, then sat back to sip his tea.

Silently, Cameron did think about what the man had told him. And then, he thought about it some more. And later still, as they were all leaving the restaurant together, he continued to think about it . . .

When, suddenly, he smiled.

All at once, Cameron felt very glad it seemed the Rosses were starting to like him. Because for some reason—he wasn't sure exactly why—he knew he was starting to like them, too.

Very much.

Chapter 24

"Cameron . . . it's getting late, dear. Shouldn't you be getting ready for Scouts?"

No answer.

"Cameron?" Harmony repeated a little louder.

Finally, her son raised his head off the pillow on the floor and turned to her. "Oh, Mom," he said, "do I really hafta go tonight? I'd rather stay and watch the rest of this video with you."

"Cameron, you're a patrol leader. They need you there," Harmony answered, scolding him. "Besides, when I first put this program on, I distinctly remember you telling me you thought it was boring."

"Well . . . I'm kinda into it now," he replied, staring at the TV. "I mean, this 'master of the house' guy is a real crackup. What is this show anyway?"

"Oh, come on, Cameron, you know what this is," Harmony said, reaching for the video case. "It's *Les Misérables*, one of the most popular musicals in the world. It's certainly *my* favorite."

She tossed him the case. "This is the Tenth Anniversary Gala Concert they had at the Royal Albert Hall several years ago. It's made up of all the main stars from all the play's worldwide casts. That's why it's so breathtaking." She paused and smiled. "You know, Cameron, remember how you were so excited to finally get to see the real U of A Wildcats play? Well, that's how I feel about *Les Mis*. It'd be a dream come true for me to be able to see it in person."

Studying the picture on the case, Cameron asked, "Is this supposed to be Fantine's daughter, Mom? That little girl Jean Valjean promises to look after when her mother dies?"

"Yes, Cameron. That's little Cosette," Harmony answered. "And by the end of the story, she'll be all grown up."

"Cool," he said.

"Okay, young man, enough stalling," Harmony announced finally, using the remote to stop the tape. "You can't put it off any longer. Get up right now and go put your uniform on."

"Oh, Mom . . . ," he whined.

"Listen, I'll make you a deal," she said, happy to encourage his newfound interest in the arts. "Even though it is a school night, we'll make an exception just this one time. I'll wait until you come home and then we'll watch the rest of this together. How does that sound?"

"Great, Mom," Cameron said, bouncing up. "C'mon, Barkley."

Across the room, their German shepherd got to his feet, stretched, and trotted after the boy.

"Now don't take too long, Cameron," Harmony called, watching the pair disappear down the hall. "Your dad's gonna be here any minute and you know how he gets when he's kept waiting."

"Okay, Mom," Cameron's voice called back.

Then, the phone rang.

Forcing herself off the cozy sofa, Harmony crossed the

hallway into the kitchen and picked up the receiver. "Yes, hello? . . . Well, good evening, Mrs. McGee, it's so nice to hear from you. Listen, I want to tell you how pleased we are that Ricky is going with us on our . . . what? . . . *What?* . . . Oh, no. . . . Oh no, Mrs. McGee. . . . And you say it did burst? . . . Oh, no. Well, I'm so sorry to hear that, of course. . . . Yes. . . . Yes. . . . Well, yes, Cameron will be very disappointed but the important thing is Ricky's going to be just fine. . . . Yes. . . . Yes. . . . Well, all right, Mrs. McGee, let me put him on then. . . . Okay. . . . Okay. . . . Okay, wait just a minute . . ." Covering the receiver, Harmony shouted, "Cameron . . . pick up, dear. It's Mrs. McGee. I'm afraid she has some bad news."

Listening, Harmony waited to hear Cameron get on, then hung up the phone and went back into the family room. A few minutes later, her son joined her wearing his Scout uniform.

"Oh well, Mom," he said, standing in the archway, "looks like we're one hiker short on our trip to the canyon. Appendicitis, can you believe it?"

"I know, Hon. It's just so shocking," Harmony answered, hugging a pillow. "It's like we all have this . . . this little time bomb ticking away inside of us and we just never know when it could go off."

Then, suddenly, as Cameron nodded back, the doorbell rang, startling her.

"Well . . . speaking of ticking time bombs, Mom . . . ," the boy said, sighing heavily as he headed for the front door, ". . . it looks like ours just got here."

Seconds later, Harmony smiled ironically to herself as she heard Cameron's voice say, "Well, hi. . . . Come on in, Dad."

Part 9
March

Chapter 25

The mighty canyon beckoned him.

Switching off his walkman and the cassette tape he'd been listening to, Mark Edwards stepped out onto the precipice of the gigantic black gorge and peered across its vastness toward the horizon. There, sunrise was just beginning.

Spellbound, he watched silently as one of the planet's most awesome scenes played out in front of him. Already the abyss had lightened from inky black to royal purple, then to shades of lilac and damson blue. After that, soothing blue-grays, cool greens, and angry reds gradually appeared, followed by salmon pinks, oranges, and, finally, bright shrieking yellows.

At the same time, as the canyon's colors constantly changed in the ever-growing light, so too did the astonishing shapes within it. Illuminated by sunbeams, lofty peaks and vast plateaus, flat-topped mesas and ragged ridges, high buttes and towering monoliths all became visible in the appalling depths below.

Held captive by the mind-boggling geography that could not

be, yet was, Mark started to feel overwhelmed by it all. When, suddenly, a familiar voice broke his reverie.

"What are you listening to, Mark?"

Turning, he was startled to find Cameron standing right next to him. Cocking his head, he asked, "What?"

Reaching up, Cameron moved one of the lightweight headphones away from Mark's ear. "I said, 'What are you listening to?' On your walkman there. What tape is that?"

"Oh . . . ," Mark answered, nodding. "Well, actually, I don't even have it on right now. I wanted it quiet while I was watching the sun come up. But, I *was* listening to *Les Misérables*. It's a tape your mom gave me."

"Oh, man, I love that play," Cameron exclaimed. "You think I could maybe borrow that from you later?"

"Sure," Mark said.

"So . . . was it spectacular?" Cameron asked, gazing out toward the east. "The sunrise, I mean."

Mark nodded at him. "Words just can't describe it, Cameron. I really wish you all had been here to see it with me."

"Well, everybody else is still organizing their packs," Cameron said. "I think Mom and Mandy are almost done but, Justin keeps complaining about all this stuff he forgot to bring. And boy, the *language* he's using."

Mark smiled. "Well, for every item that brother of mine left at home, I'll bet I brought something extra I don't need. My pack weighs a ton."

"Has it been a while since the two of you have been backpacking?" Cameron asked.

"A while," Mark answered, nodding.

Suddenly, Cameron raised his eyebrows and pointed down at a series of switchbacks zigzagging far below them. "Hey," he said, "is that our trail down there?"

"Yep, that's it," Mark answered. "The spectacular and exciting South Kaibab. Oh, and it's also *steep*. Thigh-pummeling steep. Even steeper coming back up, if you know what I mean. Luckily, we'll be hiking out on the Bright Angel Trail. All in all, it shouldn't be too bad."

"Do you think it's gonna be warming up soon?" Cameron asked, bouncing on his toes. "I'm a little chilly."

Mark shook his head. "Don't you worry about that, Cameron. By the time we get down to the river, you'll be complaining about the heat, not the cold."

"How far did you say it was again?"

"To the bottom?"

"Yeah."

Mark rubbed his chin. "Well, all I know for sure is, it's a little over seven miles from where we are now, on the South Rim, down to Phantom Ranch. And *that's* where we'll be eating dinner tonight."

"I know," Cameron answered, smiling. "I can't wait."

"Well now, Cameron, don't get too awful anxious," Mark said, cautioning the boy. "I mean, remember, there'll be lots of unbelievable sights between here and there. And the geology lesson you're gonna get is far better than anything I could ever give you in a classroom. You know, there'll be signs all along the way marking all the major geological formations. From the younger Kaibab Limestone, the Toroweap Formation, and the Hermit Shale on top, to the older Supai, Redwall, and Tonto Formations further down, we're gonna see 'em all. We'll even see the Tapeats Sandstone just before we get to the suspension bridge. Really, Cameron, you're just gonna love this."

"So then what are we waiting for?" the boy asked, grinning. "Let's go get the others and get goin'."

"I'm with you," Mark said, motioning for Cameron to take the lead. "After all, as John Wayne said in *The Cowboys*, 'We're burnin' daylight!'"

On the way back to Harmony's VW and Mark's pickup truck, they passed a sign that read: YAQUI POINT TRAILHEAD PARKING.

Glancing over at it, Mark suddenly felt a shiver of anticipation. A delayed response, he guessed, brought on by viewing the magnificence of the Grand Canyon firsthand. It was at that moment when he realized it had been far too long since he'd done anything like this.

"Shit, shit, *shit*!" Justin was saying as they walked up. He had his blue backpacking tent unrolled on the ground and, with his hand on his hip, he was standing over the thing shaking his head at it. "I can't believe I forgot the damn stakes," he growled through clenched teeth. "Left 'em right there in the driveway where I waterproofed the tent. And now they're still sittin' there, five hundred miles away."

"Well, don't worry about it too much, Bro," Mark told him, doing his best not to crack a smile. "We'll figure something out. Maybe we can use some of your cord and tie it to a bunch of rocks, or something."

"Yeah, except . . . ," Justin responded meekly, "I forgot the cord, too."

"No tent cord?"

"Uh . . . it's with the stakes."

Now Mark couldn't help himself and broke out in a laugh. "Justin," he said, "you are one piss-poor excuse for a one-armed outdoorsman, that's for sure." Then, shooting Cameron a look, he added, "But thankfully, you still don't have to worry because our young Scout here is always prepared and he brought plenty of cord, right Cameron?"

"That's right," the boy answered.

"Uh. . . . You think I could maybe borrow some, Cameron?" Justin asked.

"Sure thing," Cameron replied. Then, teasingly, he added, "For a price."

"Hey, what the heck's the holdup, gentlemen? Mandy and I—the *ladies*, mind you—are already ready and waiting. Come on, let's get this show on the road."

Turning at the sound of Harmony's voice, Mark watched as she and the girl walked over to them with their packs on their backs. "Sounds like a challenge to me, boys," he told the other two, grinning. "C'mon, Justin, get that tent rolled up. Let's get our packs on and get this little adventure of ours underway."

And so, that's exactly what the five of them were just about to do, and were on their way to the trailhead carrying their backpacks, when the big Suburban Silverado with an old BUCHANAN FOR PRESIDENT bumper sticker careened into the lot and parked.

As they all stood watching in stunned silence, a dark-haired man got out, unloaded a pack of his own, and hoisted it to his back. And judging from the looks on Harmony's and Cameron's faces, Mark knew immediately who it was.

John Wright.

"Cameron . . . ," Mark heard Harmony say to her son. "You didn't by any chance mention the fact that we had an extra permit, did you? After Ricky got sick, I mean?"

Looking sheepish, Cameron shrugged at her. "Well, Mom. . . . He *is* still my dad, you know."

Catching Harmony's eye as John Wright strode toward them, Mark said under his breath, "This is gonna be awkward . . ."

"John, what a surprise," Harmony called flatly, her gaze colder than the chilly mountain air.

Mimicking her tone exactly as he joined them, John Wright asked back, "Aren't you going to introduce everyone?"

In response, Harmony just continued to stare at him.

"Well . . . believe me, I'm not here to cause any of you any problems," the man said, seeming to make eye contact with everyone except Mark. "I'm just here to do a little hiking with my son, that's all. So, Cameron, are we ready to hit the trail?"

Mark saw Cameron shrug at Mandy. Obviously the boy was less than thrilled with this new turn of events. Wanting to help him out in some way, Mark started to speak but then Justin beat him to it.

"Wait," his brother said, grinning, placing his hand on John Wright's shoulder. "John—may I call you John?—my name's Justin and I'm really excited to finally get the opportunity to meet you. Maybe you and I could have a friendly conversation while we hike. About these little demonstrations of yours out in front of my hobby shop. *And* how about this theory you have that the entire Grand Canyon was formed in a matter of weeks. Hey, these things fascinate me, John. Tell me about them, won't you? . . ."

Shaking his head in amazement, Mark watched Justin usher John Wright off to the trailhead, then turned back around to face the others. The looks on their faces told him they were all just as relieved as he was. "Well, ladies," he said, motioning toward the trail, "after you." Falling in behind them then, he turned to Cameron. "Well, I guess you're gonna owe Justin a lotta tent cord for this one, aren't you?"

Nodding back, Cameron answered, "You got that right, Mark. A *whole* lotta cord."

• • •

"Isn't this just glorious!" Mark proclaimed, stretching his arms out wide toward the blue sky as he, Harmony, Cameron, and Mandy prepared to don their backpacks once again. They had just stopped for a half hour or so in the Tonto Formation to eat their lunch of crackers, salami, and squeeze cheese, and now they were about ready to resume their trek.

Mark Edwards felt great. So far, the hike down had been even more thrilling then he ever expected. Fossil ferns at Cedar Ridge, a bird's-eye view of 6,072-foot O'Neil Butte, wildlife ranging from collared lizards and Kaibab squirrels to golden eagles and bighorn sheep, and the endless variety of views and shadings in the canyon's rock layers were just some of the spectacular sights they'd seen.

And on top of that, Justin's plan to run interference for the rest of the group worked like a charm. Engaged in a heated debate over the radical Religious Right movement in America, Justin and John hadn't even been sighted for well over an hour. The pair was somewhere far ahead, past the Tipoff, already descending into the canyon's Inner Gorge. Mark just hoped, off on their own like that, the two men could somehow keep from killing each other.

As he was thinking about Justin and John, a related topic suddenly popped into Mark's mind. So, as the four hoisted their packs and started hiking again, he turned to Cameron. "Hey, Cam," he said, striding alongside the boy, "have you made any kind of a decision yet? About your Eagle badge, I mean? Have you decided yet what you're gonna tell the board?"

Shrugging beneath his pack straps, Cameron shook his head. "Not really," he answered, glancing over at Mark. "But I probably shouldn't wait too much longer. My dad says the men on my board are starting to get impatient. He says they won't wait for me forever."

"Well, I've been thinking about it, Cameron," Mark said, cocking his head, "and maybe what you're gonna need to do is go on some kind of a . . . a vision quest, or something."

"A vision quest?"

"Yeah," Mark answered, nodding. "You know, like a walkabout . . . a solitary hiking experience of some kind. The Native Americans call it a 'vision quest.' The Aborigines in Australia say 'walkabout.' An Outward Bound course I took back when I was in college used the term 'solo.' But whatever you choose to call it, going off camping for a night or two alone just might help you sort things out. It did for me. Believe it or not, my decision to become a teacher was actually made during my solo on that Outward Bound course I just mentioned. Anyway, it's something for you to think about . . ."

And, for several long minutes that followed, Cameron

seemed to be doing just that, silently pondering what Mark had told him. Finally though, sighing heavily, he looked over again and said, "Mark . . . what would *you* do? What would you do if you were in my place? Please tell me. I'd really like to know."

Now it was Mark's turn to become pensive. He knew only too well that he had a heavy responsibility here, maybe even a dangerous one. But the look in Cameron's eyes told him this meant a great, great deal and, then and there, he realized he just couldn't avoid it any longer. The boy deserved an answer. An *honest* one.

"Well?" Cameron asked.

Bolstering his resolve, Mark turned to him. "Look, Cameron," he said. "You're stuck between a rock and a hard place here. The decision these people are asking you to make isn't fair. I mean, you could very well go your entire life and never come to a final understanding about this God thing. I mean, that *is* why they call it the ultimate mystery, for crying out loud. But, on the other hand, you've worked very, very hard for your Eagle badge and it's only right that you get the damn thing."

"So . . . what are you saying, Mark?" Cameron asked, frowning. "What *would* you do if you were me?"

"I'd tell 'em what they want to hear, Cameron," Mark blurted out finally. "Just tell 'em. Just tell that bunch of stupid idiots what they frickin' want to hear."

Cameron's frown deepened.

For the next several hundred feet or so, they trudged on in silence. Then, at a switchback, they encountered a mule train. The mules had the right-of-way of course and, as Mark, Cameron, and Mandy stood to the outside of the trail to allow them to pass, Mark suddenly realized Harmony was no longer with them. Glancing quickly back up the trail, he spotted her immediately. She was standing mannequinlike with her hands on her hips.

"You kids go on ahead," Mark told Cameron and Mandy

when the mules had passed. "I'm gonna go see what's up with Harmony." Spinning around then, he hurried back toward the waiting woman. As he approached her, the look on her face told him he was in deep, deep trouble.

"Is that the kind of advice your manly hero, Captain Kirk, would have given him, Mark?" Harmony asked, glaring, when he reached her. "To lie? Would Captain Kirk have told Cameron to lie?"

"What are you talking about?" Mark said.

"I'm talking about, 'Tell them what they want to hear,' *Mark*," she answered. "I mean, is that the absolute best you could come up with? Recommending my son lie to his Eagle board? I just don't know, Mark," she said, throwing up her hands and stomping off. "Maybe you're not really the man I thought you were, after all."

"Harmony, wait—"

Suddenly, as he started after her, Mark felt himself step in something slick. Looking down, he couldn't believe it. He was standing right smack in the middle of a steaming pile of fresh mule shit.

"And I called this a *glorious* day?" he asked himself, shaking his head.

Maybe, he thought, that judgment was just a tad premature.

Chapter 26

"So . . . will we be crossing that same bridge there tomorrow when we hike back out, on our way up to Indian Gardens?" Mandy asked.

Cameron shook his head. "No, we won't be goin' across that bridge again," he told her, gazing up at the rusted, yet still impressive, structure hanging between the dark walls of the canyon's Inner Gorge. "Comin' down South Kaibab today, that old Kaibab Suspension Bridge was the quickest way to get here, to Bright Angel Campground and Phantom Ranch. But tomorrow, on our way back out, we'll be crossin' the river on that shiny new Bright Angel Bridge further down. And since there're only two bridges, it's cool that we get to use 'em both."

"I see," Mandy said. Lying back on her beach towel then, she closed her eyes, dug her toes in the sand, and smiled. "Just listen to the sound of that rushing water, Cameron. Don't you just wish we could spend the whole night here, on this very beach, right on the banks of the Colorado River?"

He barely heard her question. Earlier they'd taken a cool plunge in Bright Angel Creek to refresh themselves from their long hike, but afterward they kept their bathing suits on. And now, looking over at Mandy, at the ringlets of her hair, those dimpled lips, the curves of her body, and her chocolate skin . . . well, the Colorado River water wasn't the only thing rushing around there. All of a sudden, Cameron felt himself start to—

"Cameron?" Mandy asked, opening her almond eyes again. "Aren't you going to answer me?"

"Uh . . . yeah. I'm sorry," he said, turning quickly onto his stomach. "But, you know . . . uh, if we did—stay here all night, I mean—uh . . . we'd miss dinner." Studying her face, he wondered if she'd had time to notice his . . . situation. Thankfully, it didn't seem so.

"Speaking of dinner, what kind of food does Phantom Ranch have anyway?" she asked, rolling onto her side.

Grinning, Cameron ran his fingers through his hair. "Well, the menu isn't exactly extensive," he told her. "There are only two choices, in fact. Steak or hiker's stew. I'm goin' for the steak."

"Well then, I better get the stew," Mandy said, as she reached over and placed a hand on his butt. "That way, we can *share*!" To his surprise, she grabbed him, and grabbed him hard.

Pretending he didn't like it, Cameron cried, "*Hey*!" and started to retaliate. But before he could, he was distracted by the sound of arguing coming from where the rest of the group was sitting further down the beach.

"So, John," Justin's raised voice was saying, "just exactly what in the world did you think all those aluminum geology placards on the way down here were all about? Do you think they're part of some kind of . . . of Communist plot or something?"

"No," Cameron's father barked back, "I think it's a *Liberalist* plot."

"Well, at least it doesn't seem to be your mom and Mr. Edwards who are still fighting," Mandy said, leaning across

Cameron to get a better look. "That's good, isn't it? I mean, I'd really hate it if those two started bickering again."

"Well, I'm not sure, but I don't think their disagreement is over yet either," Cameron said, shaking his head. "But you're right. It's good it's not them who are fighting now."

Mandy started to say something else but Cameron held up his hand, silencing her.

"*Listen*, Mandy," he said, cocking his head. "Let's try to hear what's going on . . ."

"Look, John," Justin was saying, "it's not even about the hole in the ground—although, you gotta admit, it is a *big* damn hole. It's about those *thousands* of feet of strata—the three *miles* of strata—above us, all of it chock-full with a vertical record of fossils. Look around you, man. These basalt walls surrounding us are ancient beyond comprehension, the world's *oldest* exposed rock, in fact. The fossils down here are the oldest, too, with the fewest representatives of species still alive. And forget all about evolution for a minute. All this represents *time*. And two *billion* years of it—not ten thousand. And remember, it's all been confirmed by radioactive dating. I mean, compared to all this, the whole of human existence isn't even represented by so much as the thickness of a sheet of paper. Now, faced with all that, how can you possibly still say that under natural law the Grand Canyon formed quickly during a single flood, even if it were one of biblical proportions?"

"Well, you're quite the fancy speaker, aren't you, Justin?" John Wright answered, his voice thick with sarcasm. "But, you see, I'm really not all that interested in your science and natural law. Quite the contrary, I'm afraid. It's *God's* law that concerns me."

"Oh, but wait just a minute there, John," Justin said, pointing. "Weren't you the one who started this whole thing by telling us all about that cockamamy institute in San Diego, that place where you said they're supposedly reconciling science and the Bible?"

Cameron and Mandy both strained to hear but, after glancing

at one another, it seemed neither had caught John Wright's response—if indeed there had been one.

"You know what really gets me about people like you, John?" Justin went on. "You're perfectly happy *using* the technical wonders of the modern day—like that gas-guzzling Suburban of yours—yet you choose a religion that rejects the very science that gave them all to you. Why is that? Why do you do that when science has done more for the world in a hundred years than Christianity did in two thousand? What's more, with all these crazy protests you keep staging against birth control out in front of my shop, your group is no longer simply annoying, you're starting to become dangerous. No, there's no doubt about it in my mind. People like you are a threat, John. A threat to civilization itself."

In response, John Wright jumped to his feet.

"Uh-oh," Cameron told Mandy softly. "Here he goes again . . ."

"Belief in special creation is absolutely essential to salvation," his father began stridently, as if preaching. "Remember, death did not precede Adam, it was Adam's sin which caused it. Therefore, evolution *cannot be!* If evolution occurred, then there is no sin, no need for a savior. *No!* Belief in evolution is the leading cause of today's widespread decay of morality and constitutes a mutiny against God himself!"

"Well, you are right about one thing, John," they heard Justin say with a laugh. "There really is no such thing as sin. At least, not in the biblical sense anyway. And since the idea of it puts you in a . . . in a servile condition for your whole life, well, I'll take the idea of evolution by natural selection over sin any day."

It seemed John Wright had no ready response for Justin's last comment so, for the next several moments, nobody spoke. Eventually, however, it was Cameron's mother who finally broke the silence. "Mandy . . . Cameron . . . ," she called, as she got up and shook the sand from her beach towel. "I'm going up to the campsite now to start getting ready for dinner. Why don't you two come along with me?"

Bouncing up immediately, Mandy started to shake her towel off, too. Then she stopped and frowned down at Cameron. "Aren't you coming?" she asked.

"No, not just yet," he answered, sitting up. "I'm getting this funny feeling the fireworks aren't quite over yet. But you go on ahead. It'll take you two the longest to get ready anyway."

"Okay, Cameron," Mandy chirped as she turned and hurried off after his mother. "See ya later."

"Bye," he called, waving.

Turning his attention back to the three men, Cameron was surprised to see that his father was standing not over Justin now, but over Mark. What's more, he was doing it in a blatantly overbearing way.

"So, science teacher, you've been awfully quiet," he said with disdain. "Why is it that none of us have yet heard your views on evolution, or Christianity, or God? Has the cat got your tongue, or what?"

Rather than meeting John Wright's condescending gaze, Mark nodded at Justin. "Well, John," he answered, shrugging, "my brother here is almost always up for a good argument, I guess. That's who *he* is. But me? Well, I really just don't see much point to any of it, you know what I mean?"

"No, I don't know what you mean," John Wright said flatly. "And you know, if the truth were known, I suspect there's really an entirely different explanation for it. Whatever it is, I'll bet Harmony's starting to catch onto it, too, since it's obvious to everybody here that there's more than a little friction growing between you. Tell me, Mr. Edwards, isn't it just possible that the real reason you won't debate me is because you're afraid?"

For a moment, Mark simply stared at John Wright. But then, slowly and deliberately, he got to his feet, brushed off his hiking shorts, and then placed himself nose to nose with the man.

Uh-oh, Cameron thought, straightening up tensely. This did not look good.

"First," Mark said, staring directly into Cameron's father's eyes, "you wouldn't know the truth if it came along and bit you right on your arrogant ass. Second, my relationship with Harmony is none of your goddamn business, *so leave it alone*. And third, the only thing I find even remotely frightening about you is that there seem to be so many other ignoramuses out there gullible enough to swallow your line of fundamentalist crap."

"Well, well," John Wright answered, standing his ground, "it seems our science teacher here *can* talk, after all. So then tell us, science teacher, what—if anything—do you have to say on the subject of evolution, Christianity, and God?"

Mark shook his head incredulously. "Man, John, you just do not know when to quit, do you? Well, okay then. I'll humor you. *But* how 'bout if I ask *you* a question or two?"

"Go for it," John Wright said.

"All right . . . evolution. Here's a question I'd like you to answer concerning evolution," Mark began, rubbing his hands together. "If you are right, John, and evolution never occurred, then can you tell me please why, in God's name, any perfect creator in his right mind would choose to make birds with wings that can't fly?"

"Uh . . ."

"Or human males with nipples?"

"Well . . . uh . . ."

"Or people with big complex brains who, by choice, never ever use them?"

"Hey," John Wright said, frowning.

"Okay, sorry. I admit that last one was a cheap shot," Mark said, nodding. "But anyway, you get the idea. Now, about Christianity. Tell me, John, why is it that so many of your so-called Christians out there end up acting so *un*-Christian? I mean, for example, what's all this anti-Semitism all about? Granted, it must be very disturbing to all of you to be reminded of this awkward historical fact but, you must remember, *Jesus was a Jew*."

"Well, Mark, I—"

"And wait," Mark Edwards said, cutting him off, "speaking of Judaism and Christianity—and even Islam for that matter—why is it that these three greatest religions of the Western world can't ever seem to get together? I mean, they all have the exact same biblical God, don't they? So just what is it that's keeping them apart? And Christianity? God, what a joke. It's been the dominant religion in the civilized world for two thousand years now and it still hasn't been able to achieve anything even approaching a lasting peace. Obviously, John, something's wrong somewhere."

With his mouth hanging open, John Wright could only stare.

"And finally . . . God," Mark Edwards said, rolling his eyes. "You know what Einstein said about God, John? He said he couldn't imagine a God who rewards and punishes the objects of his creation, whose purposes are molded after *ours*, a God who's no more than a reflection of *our* frailties. And man, I'm with him. I mean, if God did make the world, I sure wouldn't want to be in His shoes because the misery of it all would break my heart. I mean, you just gotta ask yourself, don't you? *Why* is there suffering in the world? Is it because God is unable to prevent it and thus *not* omnipotent? Or is it because He's unwilling to prevent it and thus not merciful? Either way, you eventually have to ask yourself the question, 'Is He just?' And frankly, whether He exists or not, I'd rather believe in no God than in a petty one. Now . . . I'm finished."

With that said, Mark started to turn away. But, as Cameron watched, his father suddenly reached up and poked Mark forcibly in the shoulder. "Maybe *that's* why Harmony's starting to lose interest in you, my friend," John Wright said, sneering. "Because you're nothing but a godless little atheist."

In a flash, Mark Edwards grabbed the offending finger and

wrenched it, bringing Cameron's father instantly to his knees. "I told you, John," he said coldly, standing over the man, "*leave Harmony out of it*." Then, releasing his grip, he added, "And let's get one more thing straight—make no mistake about it, John, you and I will *never* be friends." This time, when Mark Edwards turned to leave, nobody tried to stop him.

Still, moments later, as Mark was heading up the trail toward the campsite, it seemed John Wright just couldn't resist making one more pathetic taunt. "Yeah, that's right, science teacher," Cameron's father screamed after him. "Attack me when I'm not looking and then run away like the sniveling coward you are!"

Fortunately for his dad, Cameron thought, Mark Edwards had the self-control to ignore him.

Holding his twisted finger, John Wright got back to his feet just as Justin did the same. "A friendly word of advice . . . ," the one-armed man said to him, putting his hand on Cameron's father's shoulder, "I wouldn't go pushing that brother of mine too much further if I were you, or . . . you might just find yourself regretting it."

"*Shut up!*" John Wright snapped, knocking Justin's hand away.

"Oh. . . . So you want a piece of me now, too, is that it?" Justin asked, grinning. "Well, by all means. Come on."

"Give me a break," John Wright said, curling his lips. "You're . . . *physically challenged*."

Cameron gulped. His father said the two words just exactly the same way he did when he talked about Ricky McGee being 'mentally challenged'—with contempt. Only this time, Cameron knew, the object of his father's mockery wasn't some helpless kid.

"John, you're exactly right. I am physically challenged," Justin Edwards said, shaking his head. "And since I am, I'm doing this for all of the good Planned Parenthood offices, for all of the freethinking Boy Scouts, and for all of us physically handicapped people everywhere . . ."

Without further ado, Justin Edwards delivered a punishing roundhouse karate kick directly into the center of John Wright's chest. Consequently, as Cameron watched with wide eyes, his father promptly ended up thrashing and splashing smack dab in the slimy, slippery shallows of the muddy Colorado.

"Two things, John," Justin called to him from the bank. "First, I guess those geology signs weren't the only ones you neglected to read on this trip. I mean, there's a sign right over there that says, 'Warning: *Do not* attempt to swim in this river.'" Taking a step closer, he added, "And the other thing? Well, assuming you were a bit surprised that a physically challenged person can defend himself just fine, I think you should know—my brother, Mark . . . well, he could easily kick my pansy ass on his very worst day." Winking then, Justin Edwards turned away and followed his brother on up the trail.

At last, Cameron knew, the fireworks *were* over. Getting up, he slung his towel across his shoulder and headed down the beach to where his father still floundered. Once there, shaking his head in disbelief, he extended his hand. "Come on, Dad," he said. "You have an important decision to make. But first, we'll need to get you all dried out."

Frowning quizzically as he accepted Cameron's help, John Wright asked, "A decision?"

"Yeah," Cameron answered, smiling. "Steak or hiker's stew? Dad, it's about time for you and me to get ready and then go to dinner together."

Chapter 27

Standing alone at Plateau Point, gazing down at the gorgeous views of the river and the Inner Gorge, Harmony Anderson crossed her arms in front of her to ward off the morning chill. Then, suddenly, she heard footsteps coming down the trail behind her. Glancing around, she said, "Oh . . . it's you."

Coming to stand beside her, John Wright asked simply, "So . . . are you thinking of *him*?"

Without looking up, she answered, "John, if you followed me all the way out here just so you could gloat over the problems I'm having in my relationship, then you can just turn yourself around and go back to Indian Gardens right now. Because I don't want to hear it."

"Sorry," he said.

After a few silent moments, Harmony decided to accept his apology, but then quickly proceeded to change the subject. Cocking her head, she said, "John . . . I've forgotten. What was that grueling section of trail yesterday called again? You know, all those winding hairpins and switchbacks we had to climb up to get here from Phantom Ranch? I forget the name."

"Devil's Corkscrew, I think," he answered.

"Yeah, that's it, Devil's Corkscrew," Harmony repeated, nodding to herself. Then, smiling, she turned to him. "John, you know what I kept thinking over and over again yesterday while we were struggling up that damn Devil's Corkscrew with our packs? I kept thinking how crazy it is that a bunch of so-called adults could actually fritter away an entire three-day hiking trip, in a place as magically compelling as the Grand Canyon, caught up in some silly argument over religion. Now, come on, John. Does that make any sense to you?"

He didn't answer her.

Shaking her head, Harmony turned away to gaze down into the Inner Gorge again. When suddenly, something she saw there made her grin. "You know, John," she said, her eyes still locked on the Gorge, "I think that river down there could tell us a lot about how most people feel about God. I mean, I've been watching it this whole trip and, the funny thing is, it hasn't ever looked the same to me twice. You know, depending on where the sun is throughout the day, and how many clouds there are, and the colors of the rocks around it, it just never looks the same. Always beautiful, yes, but never the same."

"And so . . . what does that have to tell us about God, Harmony?" John Wright asked.

"Well," she answered, putting her hands on her hips, "wouldn't you agree that the concept of God, the idea that our entire universe was created by *someone* for *some* purpose, is so overwhelmingly big that there's no way we should ever expect it to look just the same to everybody? I mean, grappling with the mystery of our existence is a very personal thing, isn't it? Each of us struggles with it our whole life and, as we change and grow, so do our feelings and beliefs about God. And for me, at least, that experience has been a lot like watching that river down there. Always beautiful, yet never staying exactly the same. You see?"

"Oh . . . I guess," he said, shrugging. Then he glanced at his watch and sighed. "Well, Harmony," he told her, "I think we better start heading back now. It is a mile and a half just getting back to the Gardens, after all, and then a very long *four and a half* miles on top of that to get back up to the Rim and Bright Angel Lodge. I'm sure the others will all be anxious to hit the trail by the time we get back to camp. Are you coming?"

"Just a sec, John," Harmony said, smiling a knowing smile as she continued to watch the river. "There's something I want to show you first. Come over here a minute."

"What?" he asked, obliging her.

"Well, speaking of things looking entirely different to different people," she said, pointing, "I'll bet, right here, right now, the two of us won't even be able to agree on what color that water is down there. Go ahead, take a look at it. What do you think, John? What color do *you* say that is?"

Peering down at the winding ribbon of blue-green in the bottom of the canyon, John Wright scratched his head. "Well . . . it does look familiar to me," he told her, "but, if you're asking me to *name* it, I'm not sure I can. Sea foam would be pretty close, I guess, but that's not exactly it."

Harmony raised her eyebrows at him. "You know, John," she said, "there's a reason that particular color looks familiar to you."

Puzzled, he just frowned at her as the seconds ticked by . . .

"Well, John," Harmony declared finally, shaking her head at him, "it's the color your son used on that model of his. You remember, don't you? The color you said was totally wrong. The color you said he was going to have to change. . . . Is it starting to ring any bells yet, John?"

Watching her ex-husband's expression as he nodded silently at the river, Harmony knew that *he* knew she was 100 percent right. What's more, it even looked like he might possibly have gotten the subtler point she was trying to make, too.

Now she was satisfied. Now she was ready to head back to camp. Taking his arm, she said, "Come on, John," and turned for the trail.

They had only gone a few steps when John Wright paused suddenly and asked her, "So, Harmony, tell me. Just exactly what *is* that color called anyway?"

"Well, for your information, there's a very beautiful name for that very beautiful color, John," she answered coyly.

"Yeah, so, what is it?"

She smiled. "It's called duck egg blue, John," she said, starting to walk again. "The name of that particular shade just happens to be called . . . duck egg blue."

Part 10

April

Chapter 28

Already more than a little agitated, Harmony Anderson nearly jumped out of her skin when, without warning, the phone rang, intruding on the all-too-quiet evening she was spending at home alone. Promptly she discarded the book she'd been struggling to concentrate on, then hurried into the kitchen to pick up. She answered anxiously, *"Hello?"*

"Hi, Ms. Anderson," the now familiar voice came back. "It's just me . . . Mandy."

"Oh . . . Mandy . . . good," Harmony said, a wave of relief washing over her. "How are you tonight, dear?"

"Oh, I'm fine," the girl answered, "but—" There was a long pause. "Well . . . it's just that you sound a little out of breath to me, Ms. Anderson. Is everything all right?"

Harmony smiled. "Yes, Mandy, everything's all right. It's just that I thought it might be Cameron, that's all."

"So . . . you actually went through with it then?" the girl asked. "You let him go?"

"Yes," Harmony answered. "Against my better judgment, I did. I let him go."

There was another pause, as if Mandy were thinking over the implications of what Harmony just told her. Finally, in a gentle voice, the girl said, "You know, Ms. Anderson, there aren't any phones way up there in the mountains, are there? Unless you got Cameron one of those cell phones, I mean. But you didn't do that, did you?"

"No, I'm afraid I didn't think of that before," Harmony answered, shaking her head. "And you're right, Mandy, there aren't any phones up there. No, it's just me, I know. I'm just being silly. But I can tell you one thing. After this, if I ever let that silver-tongued son of mine con me into letting him go on any more solo backpacking trips, he *will* have one of those cellular phones along. That's for sure."

"Where was it he was going again?" Mandy asked.

"To the Huachuca Mountains, over by Sierra Vista," Harmony told her. "I dropped him off early this morning at a place up in Ramsey Canyon called the Mile Hi, where the Nature Conservancy has that hummingbird sanctuary. He started hiking from there. It was so hard for me watching him go that I just had to leave. I didn't even take time to see any of the hummers. I just took off."

"Well, to be honest, Ms. Anderson," Mandy said, "I never really thought you'd let him talk you into it."

"What else could I do?" Harmony replied. "I mean, it's all the boy could talk about ever since Mark first mentioned it up at the Grand Canyon. 'Vision quest' this and 'walkabout' that, he kept saying. And then he even stooped to telling me it was the *only* thing that would make him happy for his birthday. 'Forget the big party, Mom,' he said. 'I want to go *solo*.' "

Harmony's enunciation of the word made Mandy giggle. Then the girl asked, "Well, does that mean the party you were planning is off, Ms. Anderson? Or is it still on? When Cameron gets back, I mean."

"Oh, it's still on . . . I guess," Harmony answered, sighing. Then she added quickly, "But—it'll have to be a *small* one."

"Will Mr. Edwards be there?"

Now it was Harmony's turn to pause. The girl's question had taken her completely by surprise and, thinking about Mark, she suddenly felt overcome with melancholy.

"Oh, I'm sorry, Ms. Anderson," Mandy apologized, worry in her voice. "I guess I really shouldn't ask something like that, should I?"

Rolling the phone cord back and forth between her fingers, Harmony turned and leaned pensively against the kitchen counter. "Oh . . . that's okay, Mandy, I don't mind," she said softly, reassuring the girl. "But to answer the question you asked me—no, I'm afraid I won't be inviting Mr. Edwards to come to the party."

There was another long pause. Finally, Mandy said, "Well . . . okay then, Ms. Anderson, I guess I better let you go now. But first, I want to thank you very much for talking to me tonight. You see, I guess I'm a little worried about Cameron being up there all alone, myself. And it helped me out a lot. Hearing your voice, I mean."

Her eyes tearing up at the girl's sweet remark, Harmony said, "Mandy?"

"Yes, Ms. Anderson?"

"Two things, Mandy . . ."

"Yes, Ms. Anderson?"

"First," she said, scolding the girl playfully, "stop calling me Ms. Anderson, okay? I'd really like you to call me Harmony from now on, if that's all right?"

"Okay . . . Harmony," Mandy answered with a giggle.

"And second . . ."

"Yes, Harmony?"

"And *second,*" Harmony repeated, "for your information, young lady, I'm not quite ready to let you get off the phone just yet. How 'bout you and I get comfortable and then settle in for some good old-fashioned girl talk instead? Would you be up for that? I mean, if you don't have any homework to do, that is?"

"I think I'd like that, Ms. Ander—I mean, Harmony," Mandy said. "I think I'd like that a lot."

"Well, okay then," she told the girl. "Just let me change to the other phone first, okay? It'll just take me a sec."

"Okay."

Setting the receiver on the counter, Harmony Anderson started for the hallway. But then, she stopped herself. Standing by the refrigerator, she lingered just long enough to take a deep breath, wipe away a tear, and smile.

Then she left the kitchen, hurrying down the hall to her bedroom.

Chapter 29

Sitting on an old log atop the bare summit of 9,214-foot-high Carr Peak, alone and in the dark, Cameron Wright gazed down at the city lights spread out across the valley, then up at the celestial lights twinkling in the sky. It was a breathtaking sight, that's for sure. But, so far at least, *not* a revelatory one.

Throughout his day of hiking, Cameron had mulled over all the different points of view he'd heard since last July: his father's so-called creation science and his mother's New Age metaphysics; Mark's agnosticism and Justin's atheistic certainty; Dr. Paul's comparative mythology and Mandy's 'accept God *and* science' outlook. Yet, even with all that, nothing had changed for him.

He still just didn't know.

What's more, something deep down in his being told him that, in all likelihood, he probably never would. The amazing thing about that was, it felt perfectly okay to him. Could it be? Could it actually be that, at this point in his life at least, he had no real *need* to know?

He shook his head. Getting up off the log, he stretched his trail-weary muscles, then gazed back up at the starry sky. A smile grew on his face.

"So, God," he said suddenly in a clear, loud voice, "are you out there or what?"

Only silence answered back.

Cameron shrugged. He already knew no God existed "out there." After all, the space age had shown it. What was "out there" were more and more moons and planets and comets and stars and star clusters and nebulae and galaxies and groups of galaxies and clusters of galaxies and superclusters of galaxies. But no heavenly kingdom. And no God.

So where was He hiding out anyway? In some parallel dimension maybe?

Feeling particularly bold now, Cameron looked back down at the valley and grinned. "So, Devil, are you down there?" he asked. "I mean, you're not gonna get a much better shot at a soul than at this one here. A kid, all alone, on top of a mountain in the middle of the night. Pretty easy pickings, wouldn't you say?"

Again, only silence answered back.

And once more, Cameron shrugged. He already knew there was no Devil "down there." All there was "down there," beneath the valley floor that is, were the Earth's rocky crust, its molten mantle, and its metallic core. There was no Hell there. And no Devil either.

At the same time, however, Cameron did know who the *real* devils were. Glancing over to where a set of red warning lights flashed in the sky, he could just make out the dark lines of the border surveillance blimp's black silhouette. The Drug Balloon. Its mission: to catch the drug runners, tracking them as they crossed over from Mexico into Arizona. *They* were the real devils. Them, and anyone like them, who profited from the pain and the misery and the weaknesses of others. On that score, Justin had been exactly right. There was more than enough man-made Hell right here in this world without creating an imaginary one somewhere else.

But, Cameron thought, he didn't come all the way up here, to this beautiful, peaceful place, to dwell upon gloomy thoughts. And so, taking a chestful of crisp mountain air, he blew it back out hard, expelling every trace of negativity along with the discharged breath. "That's the ticket," he told himself then. "I feel much better now."

Looking back up at the blazing stars, he listened as a sudden gust of wind whooshed through the Douglas fir needles and aspen leaves that blanketed the steep slopes below. Nature's breath commingling with his own, he mused.

Then he smiled and hugged himself. No, he thought, shaking his head, there wasn't anything supernatural out here, or anywhere else in the universe for that matter. No need for it. There was simply no need for some interested, omnipotent being to be behind it all. Because, as Cameron knew so well from his years of hiking and camping, nature was plenty miraculous enough all by itself.

So then, he thought with a shrug, just exactly where did that leave Cameron Wright, Eagle Scout candidate? Clearly he still really wanted his badge. He *deserved* it. But he also knew that, if he was totally honest with the board, there was no way they would ever award it to him.

He cocked his head, deliberating. *Tell 'em what they want to hear*, Mark Edwards had said. Would taking that advice really be so wrong? After all, it was the kind of lie where nobody would get hurt. Wasn't it? Off hand, he couldn't think of anyone. So then why was this uneasy feeling still nagging at him?

Cameron sighed heavily. At that moment, it seemed he might never know what to do. "Vision quest, schmision quest," he said in frustration, snatching up his flashlight. And flicking it on, he headed back down the short peak spur trail toward his campsite.

Miraculously, he'd gone just about halfway when, out of the

blue, something seemed to click. And it was then and there that, at long last, Cameron Wright finally came to his decision.

At least, he thought he had.

Chapter 30

"Yeah, but what about what the Bible has to say about all this? You know, Adam and Eve and all that? Go ahead, tell us, how does all that fit in here?"

Mark Edwards cringed. He knew without turning around that it was that little blonde creationist, Kelly Brown, who had asked the question.

He'd suspected something like this might happen as soon as he got a look at the T-shirt she was wearing today—and not by accident, either, if he knew Miss Brown. It had pictures of an amoeba, a chimpanzee, and Man, with arrows pointing from one to the next in that order. Above them, a caption read: OVER BILLIONS OF YEARS SINGLE-CELLED ORGANISMS EVOLVED INTO MAN. . . . But then, below them, it said, *NOT!* and had a quotation from Genesis. It was obvious. Today his young Christian nemesis was loaded for bear.

Stopping in the middle of his notes on "Early Humans," which he'd been putting on the chalkboard, Mark took a deep breath and slowly turned to face the class. Then, in his most tactful teacher's voice, he answered, "Well, of course, Kelly, the Bible *is* a unique library of religious books, and an important one. But we must also keep in mind, it's only one among many. Depending on your religion, there are also books like the Talmud and the Koran, for example. And remember, most of the people in the world—and even a few of us right here in this room, I'd suspect—don't consider the Bible to be absolute truth."

Looking around at his students, he continued. "Now, all that aside, what it really gets down to is, *this* is a science class. The *Bible* is religion. And since science is objective, concerned only with what is observable, then it must be totally free to ask, to doubt, to seek, and to correct. Therefore, any religious book, including the Bible, really has no place here." He started to turn back to the board. "Now, to return to our discussion of ancient hu—"

"But what about Jesus, and God?" Kelly blurted out, cutting him off.

Mark frowned. He really was in no mood for this. Ever since Harmony had told him she couldn't see him anymore, his entire outlook on life had darkened abysmally. So had his temper. And, in this type of situation, he knew there was a very real possibility he just might explode.

"Well?" Kelly said impatiently.

Silently, Mark counted to ten. Then, forcing a smile, he turned back to the girl. "Kelly," he answered, measuring his words carefully, "Jesus was, of course, a great teacher and religious leader. One of many, actually, like Buddha or Muhammad. But, if I'm reading you right, I would imagine *you* consider him much more than that. However, we must remember again, not everyone believes the same things about Jesus. Many believe he was simply a human being like ourselves, and I don't think I'd be going out on much of a limb to say that's exactly how most scientists feel."

She rolled her eyes.

"Now, the problem with 'God' is," Mark went on, "it's just too ambiguous . . . too subjective, a term. For example, Christians may define God one way, but then other religions in other parts of the world might define it much differently. And as far as science is concerned, I'm afraid . . . well, since the God hypothesis is inherently untestable, science must remain mute on the subject."

"Jeez, what religion *are* you, man?" Kelly barked, sneering. "You know, my dad's a Promise Keeper, are *you*? Have you ever even *heard* of 'em before? And, hey, why aren't we using *this* book in this class?" She held up *Of Pandas and People*. "I mean, it's a lot better than these stupid textbooks you've been making us read all year."

Mark Edwards could feel it. He had almost reached his limit. Struggling to remain calm, he said, "Frankly, Miss Brown, as a public school teacher, it would be inappropriate for me to discuss my personal religious beliefs here at school—and *you* shouldn't, either. The Constitution's separation of church and state forbids that kind of thing, I'm afraid. And as to that book of yours, I've seen it. It isn't science and shouldn't be taught as such. Now, we've probably said way too much on this subject already so, if you'll allow me, I'd like to get back to the evolution of modern man—"

"*Evolution is nothing but a lie!*"

Immediately, all eyes in the room focused on Kelly Brown, who, in turn, glared directly at Mark. Following her lead then, everybody else turned to look at him, waiting with baited breath to see what would happen next.

All right, that's it, Mark thought. Stepping back up to the chalkboard, he took an eraser and wiped away a large portion of the notes he'd written there. Then, underlining twice, in big capital letters, followed by three exclamation points, he wrote: EVOLUTION IS A FACT!!!

The gasp Kelly let out in response was audible clear across the room. Mark ignored it.

Pointing at the board, he told the class emphatically, "And not only is evolution a fact, people, it is also the *central organizing principle of all biology!*"

A hand went up then. For the first time that period, another student had mustered the courage to jump into the fray. Not surprisingly, it was Cameron Wright.

"Yes, Cameron?" Mark said.

"Well . . . it's just that you always hear it called the *theory* of evolution, that's all," the boy replied. "Is it a theory? Or is it just like you said? A fact?"

"It's a fact, Cameron," he answered, without hesitation. "It's just the details about the *how* of evolution, the *process* of natural selection, that are still theoretical. *However*, there is absolutely no doubt whatsoever that evolution did occur in the past, and that it's still occurring today. I mean, come on, you guys," he said, raising his chalk again, "you've all already seen the evidence. And there's a great, great deal of it from many, many scientific disciplines."

Feverishly, he wrote: #1—THE FOSSIL RECORD.

Stepping over to where Cameron's Grand Canyon model was prominently displayed in the front corner of the room, Mark gestured to it. "Remember, there's nature's own history book, the geological strata we've accurately dated through radioactive decay. And that's just our *first* category of evidence."

Quickly, he crossed back to the board and added: #2—COMPARATIVE ANATOMY.

"Homologous structures, our *second* category of evidence," he told the class. "The fact that so many *different* creatures in this world share so many *similar* anatomical structures, leading us to one unavoidable conclusion: a *common* origin. And *third*—"

He listed: #3—DNA.

"—probably the most irrefutable evidence of all," he said,

dropping the chalk and spinning around, "the *genetic code*. The fact that the same biochemistry is shared by *all* life on Earth. And it's not just that it's similar, it's the *degree* of similarity that's most important. It's the fact that, for example, our amino acid sequence differs from a tuna's by twenty-one, but then it's virtually identical to a chimpanzee's, showing a remarkable *99 percent* similarity."

He paused for a breath. Some of his students were beginning to nod at him, looking agreeable—but not enough of them. He decided to press further.

"And also," he said, starting to walk around the room, "don't forget that we can actually *see* evolution happening all around us every day. Bacteria becoming immune to the latest antibiotic, for example. Insects impervious to new insecticides. Hey, it's evolution, folks, plain and simple."

He stopped walking, and put his hands on his hips. "Nope. There's no doubt about it. The evidence from geology and paleontology and anatomy and biogeography and embryology and biochemistry and molecular biology is just too conclusive, ladies and gentlemen. The fact that life changes on Earth is as well-documented as anything can be in this uncertain world. Evolution *is* a fact. And you can take that to the bank."

"Well, why should we take your word for it?" Kelly asked, leering. "I mean, after all, you are *just* a teacher."

"Then don't, Kelly," Mark answered flatly. "Don't take my word for it. But, if I were you, I *would* listen to guys like Robert Bakker and Jack Horner and Stephen Jay Gould, all those paleontologists whose work we learned about in this class. And what about the other scientists, like Jacques Cousteau and Carl Sagan, who we saw in our science videos? Or, hey, how 'bout Walter Cronkite? He was once considered the most trusted man in America, did you know that? Do you think he ever would've hosted those two science documentaries we saw, on dinosaurs and ancient humans, if *he* thought evolution was a lie? Or

Michael Crichton and Steven Spielberg. Do you think *Jurassic Park* ever would've come to be if *they* thought it was a lie?"

Suddenly, he had a devilish thought. Smiling slyly, he said, "Newt Gingrich! Hey, I saw Newt Gingrich guest-hosting for Larry King the other night and Jack Hanna was on with all his zoo animals. And Newt was saying to Jack, 'fossils' this, and 'after millions of years of evolution' that. . . . *He* must even believe in evolution—and *he's* as conservative as you can get!"

"Who *is* Newt Gingrich, Mr. Edwards?" somebody asked.

Mark frowned. Then, thinking about it, he raised his eyebrows. "Yeah, I guess you're right," he said, nodding. "There really isn't any reason you guys should know who he is *these* days, is there?"

Suddenly, the bell rang, and his students started getting out of their seats.

"Wait, everybody," he called, holding up a hand. "Before you go, there's something else I want to say. About those questions Kelly was asking a little while ago. They're very important to her, and to some of the rest of you, I'm sure. That's because they speak to the . . . well, to the ultimate meaning of life here on Earth. And I must apologize to you because there's a good chance you won't find all the answers to *that* question in this modest high school science class. But, if there's one thing I, as your teacher, could encourage you to do this year, it would be to make the search for yourself. I mean, nobody really knows for absolute certain, do they? But we all have to be free to search. Be tolerant of one another. *Learn* from one another. And *make the search*. . . . Now, see you guys tomorrow."

As the students filed out of the classroom, Mark glanced over at Kelly Brown. He hoped his parting words might've mollified her to some degree, but they hadn't. She left in an obvious huff. Then Mark noticed Cameron standing next to him.

"Mark?"

"Yeah, what is it, Cameron?"

"Well," the boy answered, "you know how I told you the other day that I met with my Eagle board again and I was finally gonna get my badge?"

"Yeah."

"Well, the thing is, now I'm having second thoughts about it. I mean. . . ." Cameron frowned at Mark. "Well, it's just that, watching you just then, you sure didn't tell Kelly Brown what *she* wanted to hear, did you?"

Mark smiled ironically. "No, Cameron, I don't think I did," he admitted. "*And* it was probably a big, fat mistake on my part, too."

"A mistake?"

"Yeah, a mistake," Mark repeated. He paused a moment, then shook his head. "Cameron?"

"Yeah, Mark?"

"Let me give you some *good* advice for a change."

"Okay."

Looking intently at the boy, he said, "From now on, Cameron, don't listen to a single damn word I have to say, all right? I'm sure, in the long run, you'll be much better off that way."

For a long moment, Cameron just stared at Mark. It was obvious that the poor kid didn't have any idea what to say. Finally, he just shrugged, and headed for the door.

"Cameron?" Mark said.

The boy turned around.

"How did your birthday party go?"

Cameron shrugged again. "Oh, you know, it was okay, *but* . . ." The boy looked imploringly at him.

"It's okay, you don't have to say it," Mark said, feeling positively awful. "I mean, I already know. And, Cameron . . . more than anything, *I* really wish I'd been there, too."

Silently, the boy nodded at him, then continued out the door.

Part 12
May

Chapter 31

"Mark, I am sorry to have to tell you this," Claude Caruthers said, scratching his potbelly, "but we've been getting more and more calls from parents lately complaining about your science class. And not just at this office either. The curriculum director, the superintendent, and the school board president have all been receiving them. And when *they* do, you know who hears from each of them, don't you?"

Mark Edwards stared up at the Mexican fast-food bag sitting on top of the principal's file cabinet. Obviously, he thought, the red stuff in Caruthers's moustache today must be hot or mild sauce. Then, he realized Caruthers had asked him a question.

"Oh . . . well, *you*, Claude," he answered with a shrug. "I would imagine they call you."

"That's right, Mark," Caruthers said, frowning, "they call me. And when that happens, it puts me in a very difficult position." He rubbed his pockmarked face with his fleshy hand. "Now, before we get into this any further, I want you to know that, in all honesty—"

The insincerity in the man's voice was palpable and immediately Mark's BS-o-meter redlined.

"—*I* would be inclined to side with you on this one," the principal continued. "But at this point in time, I'm afraid, it's already been taken out of my hands. So, that said, about this 'evolution is a fact' business."

"Evolution *is* a fact," Mark replied flatly.

Almost as if controlled by a switch, the principal's put-on congeniality evaporated, turning now to heavy-handed authoritarianism. The response didn't surprise Mark and, staring back into Caruthers's glaring face, he braced himself for what was sure to come.

"Don't misunderstand me, Mr. Edwards," Caruthers said darkly. "I didn't call you over here to *discuss* it. Now, I'm gonna tell you what you *will* do, and I'm gonna tell you what you *won't*. So, listen up."

Mark straightened in his seat, his heart pounding.

"First," Caruthers said, "you *will* have your students paste disclaimers in their science textbooks making it clear evolution is a controversial theory. Second, you *will* incorporate the books *Darwin on Trial* and *Of Pandas and People* into your curriculum as supplemental resources. Third, you *will* start teaching evolution as only *one* of a variety of theories on the origin of life, to include both creation science and the intelligent-design theory as other possibilities."

Mark gulped. This was worse than he expected.

"And fourth," Caruthers said with even more intensity, "you absolutely *will not* ever again tell your students, in any way, shape, or form, that evolution is a fact. Now, do I make myself perfectly clear on all of this, Mr. Edwards?"

Mark shifted in his seat. "Is this a directive . . . sir?" he asked.

Caruthers smiled, but not happily. "Well, Mr. Edwards," he answered, wiping a hand over his bald head, "it hasn't been put into writing just yet, but yeah, you can surely consider it a directive. *And*, I might add, one I would highly recommend you don't ignore."

Mark started to get up. "Is that all, sir?"

"Yeah," Caruthers said. "Oh—except for this, that is." He tossed Mark a document across the desk. "It's your teaching contract for next year. It's due back to me in a month." He smiled again, adding, "You might want to give it some real serious thought, though, before actually returning it to me."

"Yeah, thanks, Claude . . . ," Mark said coldly as he opened the door and exited the office. "I'll make sure I do that."

Chapter 32

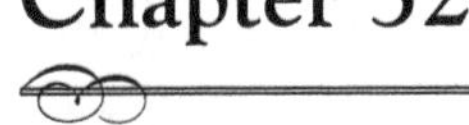

Cameron's big night had finally arrived, his Eagle Scout court of honor.

But something was wrong.

Standing there, in his dress uniform, in front of all those people seated in the church sanctuary, a very uneasy feeling started to come over him. For some reason, things just didn't feel right.

In the seconds that passed as he waited for Scoutmaster Smith to take the coveted Eagle badge out of its box, he glanced nervously at the faces in the audience. Practically everybody he knew was there.

Dr. Paul had brought his wife. That was nice. But there was a look in the minister's eyes Cameron just couldn't put his finger on. A look that bothered him. And earlier, before the ceremony, the man had seemed unusually reserved. Sad almost. Oh well, Cameron thought, he was probably just having a bad day.

Then he spotted Mark and Justin. The brothers were seated on the right side of the church, the *opposite* side from where his mother had been sitting a few moments earlier. Awkward, very awkward, he thought, shaking his head. Plus, he still hadn't figured out *why* his mom had been so upset with what Mark said at the Grand Canyon. Heck, maybe he'd never understand it. Frowning, he decided to look for a happier face.

Like Mrs. Morales, surrounded by her ever-growing brood of exuberant children. When she spoke to Cameron coming into the church, she thanked him for what must have been the millionth time for the red-tile roof he gave her family for his Eagle project. What's more, the woman had called him an *ángel*. But, Cameron wondered, did he really deserve such a compliment?

Glancing down in front of him, he suddenly noticed Randall LaRue and Ricky McGee in the first pew. They were sitting together, of course, next to Ricky's mom. As it turned out, they were best friends now. Cameron smiled at the thought of it. It was true, *anything* was possible.

And Mrs. McGee. What a nice lady. Like most of the people there, she'd given him a greeting card to congratulate him. But hers was more meaningful than most of the cards he got. The front had a picture of a desert tortoise and inside she'd written, "Thank you so much, Cameron, for your kindness and patience with my son and for teaching him that sometimes slow and steady *can* win the race. You're a true role model, Cameron, and we're all so very proud of you."

Obviously the glowing words made him feel very proud—at the time. But now, as Cameron's nagging uneasiness continued to grow, he just had to stop and ask himself: Was he really worthy of being a role model for anyone? Shaking his head again, he looked back out into the crowd.

And then he saw Mandy.

She was seated between her parents, gazing up at him with those amazing, gentle almond eyes of hers. But tonight, just like Dr. Paul, she wasn't smiling at him. All by itself, that was enough to give Cameron pause.

Before, in the vestibule, she'd slipped him a note. In it, she copied down all the lyrics to a Whitney Houston song she liked, a song called *Greatest Love of All*. Cameron knew the song and now, while he waited, he recalled the passage the girl had underlined for him. It was all about not walking in other people's shadows, always doing what you believe in, and living with dignity, no matter what. In other words, practicing the greatest love of all.

But just exactly what *was* the greatest love of all anyway? As it so happened, Mandy underlined that for him, too. Learning how to love yourself, *that* was the greatest love of all. But beyond that message, Cameron wondered, just what was it Mandy was trying to tell him?

Without warning, somebody in the audience suddenly took a picture and the flash reflected brightly off something to his right. The stained glass window, pride and joy of his Scout troop and of the entire congregation at Mesquite Evangelical Lutheran. The words TO DO MY DUTY TO GOD stood out prominently from the rest, but they weren't the ones Cameron noticed then. Instead, TO KEEP MYSELF MORALLY STRAIGHT was the passage that jumped out at *him*.

And then something else happened. As he stood there, contemplating the words written in the glass, he started to hear music. It made him frown. The music wasn't coming from the church. *It was inside his head*. And from *Les Misérables* of all things.

"Cameron?"

The voice startled him even more than the music had. It was Mr. Smith. He was holding up the red, white, and blue Eagle award. Finally the moment had come.

"Ms. Anderson," the Scoutmaster said, "would you be good enough to pin this on your son's left pocket flap for me, please?"

Cameron shot a glance over his shoulder at his mother and father who were standing proudly behind him. At Mr. Smith's request, his mom started to step forward.

And then, suddenly, everything became clear.

"*Wait!*" Cameron said, holding up his hand. "I'm sorry. But I just can't go through with this."

Glancing quickly at the Scoutmaster and then at each other, his parents both knitted their brows at him, their eyes full of questions. Reaching over, he took their hands.

"Mom, Dad . . . Mr. Smith," he suggested quietly, "why don't you guys go and have a seat?"

For a few long moments, the three of them just stood there, paralyzed by the shock of it. But then, much to Cameron's relief, they nodded silently at him and obliged. *Now*, he knew, he had some mighty tall explaining to do.

Taking a deep breath then, he turned to face the expectant congregation. And when he spoke to them, his voice was the only sound.

"Way back in July," he began, "my Eagle board asked me a very personal question. It doesn't really matter what the question was. What matters is, I answered it as honestly as I possibly could. But for that, unfortunately, I ended up failing my review."

A few hushed gasps echoed through the church.

Cameron smiled then, but not out of pleasure. "At the time," he went on, "I remember telling my dad that it made me feel like Galileo. You guys remember him, don't you? He was one of those old scientists who the Inquisition imprisoned for saying the Earth wasn't the center of the universe. Anyway, that's how it made me feel. It seemed wrong to me then, and it still does."

Taking another breath, he shrugged and shook his head. "But—after thinking about it for this whole school year, thinking about how bad I wanted my Eagle badge and about how telling one little white lie probably wouldn't really hurt anyone, I finally decided to give in and get back together with my board. So that's what I did. And in the end, I ended up giving them the answer I knew they wanted to hear even though I didn't believe it myself. . . . And, I'm afraid," he added, feeling ashamed, "that's the story explaining how all of you came to be sitting here in this church tonight."

In response, no one uttered a sound.

"Now, are you guys ready to hear the really weird part?" Cameron asked, smiling again. "Just a few minutes ago, pretty much out of the blue, I started to hear music playing in my head, from this musical my mom likes called *Les Misérables*. In that play, this guy Jean Valjean has to decide whether or not to let another man go to prison for a crime he himself committed. Anyway, he makes the right choice, of course, but before he does he says to himself, 'If I speak, I am condemned. . . . If I stay silent, I am damned!' And, I guess," Cameron said, cocking his head, "that pretty much says it all for me, too."

Thinking he was finished at last, he started down the aisle. But then, suddenly, he stopped himself. There was still one last thing he definitely needed to say.

"You know, everybody," he said, doing his best to make eye contact with all of them, "the saddest thing about all this *isn't* that I don't get my Eagle badge." He paused, fighting a lump in his throat. "The saddest thing about it," he added finally, "is that, after tonight, there's just no way I can ever consider myself a Boy Scout again."

That did it. At that point, Cameron would have been hard pressed to find a single dry eye in the house. And so, feeling bad because he'd made everybody else feel bad, he continued down the aisle toward the door.

He was almost there when, behind him, somebody shouted, "Eagle or no Eagle, Scout or no Scout, it doesn't matter to us, *hijo*. We all still love you just as much."

Turning, he saw it was Mrs. Morales. She was standing up. And she was clapping.

Cameron's jaw dropped. Before he knew it, everyone else was clapping, too. What's more, Mandy and Dr. Paul were both *smiling* at him now, despite the tears running down their cheeks.

And then, all of a sudden, it seemed the whole place was *standing* and clapping. *Everybody was giving him an ovation.*

Everybody, that is, except John Wright.

But then, their eyes met. And as Cameron looked imploringly at this father, he saw the familiar dark expression soften just a little as his dad nodded at him.

And to Cameron, that one small nod of acceptance was far more meaningful than all the standing ovations in all the world.

Chapter 33

Making her way through the groups of people standing and chatting in the church sanctuary after the court of honor, Harmony suddenly heard someone call to her. "Oh, Ms. Anderson," the voice said.

Spinning, she saw it was her minister. "Yes, Dr. Paul?"

"You see, Harmony?" the man said, winking at her. "Remember that day in your plant nursery? I told you you have a little hero there."

She smiled back at him. "Well, have you seen that little hero of mine, recently, Dr. Paul? I'm trying to find him."

He pointed to the vestibule. "I think I saw him go through there."

"Thanks," she said.

Hurrying into the crowded vestibule, she looked and looked but had no luck. Finally she decided to check outside. Pushing through the front doors, she started down the steps to the sidewalk—then froze.

She saw him. But he was talking to *Mark*.

Taking a few steps back, she positioned herself strategically behind a thick oleander hedge, and she listened.

"So . . . what two things?" she heard Cameron say.

"Well, first," Mark replied, "ever since your mom gave me that *Les Misérables* tape last November, I've been racking my brains trying to figure out just exactly why I like it so much. But I've never been able to. Then tonight, when you were up there in front of all of us and you repeated those two simple lines . . . well, now I understand. And I wanted to say thanks."

There was a long pause.

Then Cameron said, "And the second thing?"

Another pause.

Finally, she heard Mark answer, "Well, Cameron . . . I'm sure you recall that somewhat *controversial* advice I gave you up at the Grand Canyon, don't you?"

"Tell 'em what they want to hear?" Cameron said.

"That was it."

"Yeah, what about it?" the boy asked.

Peeking out from behind the hedge, Harmony watched as Mark extended his hand to her son.

"Well . . . I just wanted you to know," the man said as he and Cameron shook on it, "I was wrong."

Well, it's about time, Harmony thought. And, taking a quick moment to compose herself, she continued down the steps to the sidewalk.

She joined them then. And when she did, the smile that passed between her and the man she loved said it all.

Part 12
June

Chapter 34

Sitting in the cozy cab of the '64 Chevy pickup on the way out of town, Mark on one side of her and Cameron on the other, Harmony Anderson sighed with contentment. Try as she might, she just couldn't remember a happier moment.

Cameron leaned forward and said, "So, Mark, enough with the big secrets, already. Just where is it that we're goin' on this mystery vacation of yours anyway?"

Drumming cheerfully on the steering wheel as he drove, Mark glanced over. "Well . . . how does New York City sound to you, Cameron? I mean, how would you guys like to catch a *live* performance of *Les Mis* this month? If we can hunt one down, that is?"

Harmony gasped in surprise as Cameron simply answered, "Cool."

Then Mark added, "But first, we're headed up Sedona way. As it just so happens, there's a very important question I need to ask your maternal grandparents before we can leave on our trip."

Harmony eyed her son as he glanced at her, shock on his face. "Well, just what exactly are you saying, Mark?" the boy asked. "I mean . . . those aren't *wedding bells* I'm hearing, are they?"

Before either of them could answer, Mark suddenly downshifted the Chevy and turned off the street they were on—into the mostly vacant parking lot of Mesquite High School.

"*Oh, man*," Cameron exclaimed, frowning. "What in the world are we doin' *here*? I mean, Mark, haven't you heard? *School's out*."

Pulling into a space, Mark cut the engine and opened his door. Then, grabbing some kind of document off the dashboard, he jumped out.

"This won't take but a sec," he said, winking at Harmony. "I've just gotta drop this off."

Closing the door behind him then, he jogged off in the direction of the school office.

Chapter 35

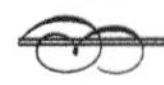

Claude Caruthers was just popping a sugar-glazed donut hole in his mouth when Mark Edwards blew through the principal's door without so much as a knock and dropped his signed teaching contract on the desk. Then he simply waited for a response.

Finally, his mouth full of donut, Caruthers looked up at him and said, "Well, I must admit, Mark, you had me going for a little while there. Today *is* the deadline, you know. I was beginning to think there was a chance you might not be back with us next year."

"No, Claude," he answered flatly, shaking his head. "That would have been the easy way out."

"What do you mean?" Caruthers asked, frowning.

"I'll tell you what I mean," Mark said, starting to relish the moment. "The other night, I watched a student of mine do one of the bravest things I've ever seen anyone do. You see, in order to be totally true to himself, this young man made the choice to take a stand on something very, very difficult. And when he did that, the moment was an inspiration to me. And, well, if standing up was good enough for a high school freshman—"

Now Caruthers was scowling. "Just what are you saying, Mr. Edwards?" the principal asked.

"Well," Mark replied, just the hint of a smile playing on his face, "first, I'm gonna tell you what I *won't* do. And then, I'm gonna tell you what I *will*. What I absolutely *won't* do is have anything whatsoever to do with text disclaimers, cheesy supplemental books, and half-baked alternative origin-of-life theories. But, on the other hand, what I *will* do, Claude, is simply always tell the truth to my students. Now, evolution *is* a fact, and that's just exactly what this ex-milksop school teacher is gonna be teaching from now on."

Caruthers started to speak but Mark cut him off.

"And Claude, this time, before you try and browbeat me into seeing it your way, I think you should know. I've been a very busy boy the last couple of days. The teachers union, the ACLU, the National Center for Science Education, and the National Academy of Sciences were all very intrigued by the little story I had to tell them. And consequently, Claude, the upcoming school year should prove to be a very interesting one for all of us."

At that point, Caruthers could only stare.

"So, Claude," Mark said finally, rubbing his hands together as he started out of the office, "enjoy your break, won't you? And, hey, we'll see you in the fall."

He stopped in the doorway. "Oh, yeah, one more thing," he said, glancing back around. "That *teacher*-sponsored Christian club of ours? It's definitely against the law. I'm afraid we're going to have to do something about that, too."

Then, smiling, Mark waved good-bye to all the office secretaries and continued back out into the Arizona sun.

Chapter 36

Cameron Wright watched as Mark climbed back into the cab.

"So, Mr. Edwards," his mother asked as he started the truck, "just what was it you were doing in there anyway?"

Turning to her, he answered, "Well, Harmony, it's really pretty funny when you think about it. I mean, you know how you're always telling me that praying is 'honest work,' and 'taking stock,' and 'following your bliss' stuff like that? Well . . . I *guess* what I was just doing in there was something I told old Caruthers back in August I'd never, ever do."

"And what's that?" Cameron asked.

"Practicing school prayer, Cameron," the man answered, grinning widely. "Amazingly, Mark Edwards, science teacher, has just been practicing a little school prayer."

Mark laughed then.

And his laugh was infectious.

And before they knew it, they were all laughing as, together, they left the empty school buildings behind them and drove off happily into the summer.

About the Author

An Eagle Scout and veteran science teacher, Derrick Neill was born in Tucson in 1958 but considers Sierra Vista, Arizona, his hometown. He has a B.S. from Northern Arizona University in Flagstaff and an M.A. from United States International University in San Diego. From playing the lead in dinner theater comedy and leading a month-long wilderness backpacking expedition for the National Outdoor Leadership School, to studying wild killer whales in the Puget Sound and scaling the heights of California's Mt. Whitney, he enjoys a wide variety of pastimes. A SAMLA Middle Level Educator of the Year and NAU Distinguished Education Alumni Award winner, he still makes Sierra Vista his home base where he and his wife, Martha, teach in a public middle school. His first novel, *Adventures in Spacetime,* was published by Dan River Press in 1996. *Duck Egg Blue* is his second.

www.ingramcontent.com/pod-product-compliance
Lightning Source LLC
Chambersburg PA
CBHW020526310726
48979CB00014B/2224/J

* 9 7 8 1 5 7 3 9 2 6 8 5 0 *